Open Your 中英互譯邏輯腦

跟著8大翻譯要點，
快速提升80% Up翻譯＋寫作能力

連緯晏 Wendy Lien
Matthew Gunton ◎著

翻譯老手傳授多年
對於中英互譯領悟後的技巧
由淺入深引領讀者先從【英譯中】著手
再推進至【中譯英】練習！

拋開翻譯理論的包袱，多看、多讀、多寫、多思考，
跟著本書的方法練就一身「**翻譯＋寫作**」語感好功夫！

深根中英互譯＋英文寫作能力的「**雙效**」學習步驟看這邊：

Step 1 吸收**關鍵翻譯要點＋熟悉主題文章**
Step 2 掌握**重點字彙＋試著翻**
Step 3 詳讀**中／英文譯文＋討論同時**
√先確認文章脈絡、理解是否正確 → 最重要！
√再探索中英語態、語句與思維邏輯差異 → 打好翻譯基礎能力！
√三思考語句是否通順、用字是否精準、優美，更要符合中／英語句邏輯順序 → 精還要更精！

) be taped in full

trols a three-fourths
113-seat Legislative

rticle 71 of the pro-
vould be amended.
consultations, which
r months according
ould come to an end

ogressive Party leg-
consider the
posed amendment
too far."
e agreed the inter-
ions have to be
ction on bills would
ayed if the amend-
ade the way the

Kuomintang wants," said a DPP heavyweight, who refused to be named.

For one thing, government officials asked to testify before the consulting lawmakers may not tell the truth, if they know what they say would be fully made public.

"You know," the lawmaker said, "only those controversial bills need inter-party consultation. Officials dare not say what they really think is right, if the TV camera is on them."

As the period of consultation is shortened, the DPP legislator said, "more lawmakers will demand more inter-party consultations, jamming the Legislative Yuan agenda."

genes found related to
ıson's in Han Chinese

onal cooperative pro-
spotted a
ated gene mutation
ops in Han Chinese.
ry this mutation are
likely to develop
ease.
n, known as R1628P
gene LRRK2, which
rotein Leucine-rich
2, according to a
d from the project,
d by the cabinet-level
ce Council and pub-
ience journal, Annals

disease, also known
yndrome, is a degen-
ler of the central
n that often impairs
speech and move-

experts from Taiwan,
pan and the United
ready reported other
ated mutations
2, and has found cor-
een different ethnic
ndividual mutations.
he experts found that
S is a common cause
among Berber Arabs
Jews.
group reported that
385R in LRRK2, was
kinson's in Asians,
Chinese. Individuals

carrying the mutation were more than twice more likely to develop the disease than non-carriers, it was reported. The LRRK2-G2385R mutation does not appear to play a role in Parkinson's disease within other racial groups, according to the research results published in 2005.

Their analysis concluded that the G2385R mutation occurred approximately 4,800 years ago, corresponding with the rise of Chinese civilization.

The study of LRRK2-G2385R was mainly conducted by subgroups of the project based in National Taiwan University Hospital (NTUH) in Taipei and the Mayo Clinic in Jacksonville, Florida.

On the newly found R1628P, Wu Ruey-meei, director of NTUH's Center for Parkinson's and Movement Disorder, and a participant in the study, noted that LRRK2-R1628P mutation could also double the risk of Han Chinese developing Parkinson's syndrome. Japanese, who were also a target group in the research of 2007-2008, showed no indication for such a mutation, he said.

The incidence rate of R1628P mutation is estimated to be three in 100 among Han Chinese, Wu said, adding that this mutation might be have been passed down some 2,500 years ago.

from others, as candidacy registration will not close until tomorrow. If no other "suitable" candidates come forward, he said he will throw his hat into the ring.

He named former DPP Chairman Lin Yi-hsiung and former Presidential Secretary General Chen Shih-meng as two "suitable" candidates for leading the DPP out of the doldrums. He said the new chairman must have a strong sense of "Taiwanese" and impartiality, an open mind and vision, and the ability to consolidate the party and introduce sweeping reforms.

"The future party chairman is very important, because the DPP has reached its nadir. And if it fails to diagnose its sickness and give it the right medication, it is not impossible that it will never rise again," said You.

DPP Chairman Frank Hsieh tendered his resignation after his crushing defeat to Kuomintang rival Ma Ying-jeou in the March 22 presidential election, but has agreed to stay on until a successor is elected in May. Hsieh's defeat, plus the DPP's dismal showing in the January legislative elections, has left the party struggling for a revival. There have been calls from the young Turks, such as former Legislator Luo Wen-jia, for the elders to step aside and let the younger generations take charge.

A group of young DPP reformers said yesterday that the party must give top priority to "integrity" and "incorruptibility," as its eight years of rule were tainted by various corruption

race, but he said he has yet to d
whether or not to run.

accusations. Anyone wil
devote him or herself to th
has the right to run for th
manship, but the new ch
must be able to "refuse t
his or her soul with the de
group said.

Chou Yu-hsiu, who repr
group who call themsel
"Taiwan Youth Den
Alliance," said the bigges
that the new chairman mus
is to get rid of the "dummy
bers. The dummy memb
employed to boost the sup
DPP candidates in the
internal elections. The allia
not specify which generati
believe the new chairman
come from. Vice President
Lu warned that the lea
transition should not mean
between different generatio

While different factio
generations are stepping
race for the top party p
said he is not represent
specific side. He is also be
tious in expressing his int
the post by naming Lin a
as two ideal candidates
job. But Lin and Chen n
qualify for the chairmansh
tion.

Lin has already announ
break with the party, whi
has stopped playing an act
in the party, with his mem
fees long overdue. You sa
"technicalities" could be ov
if the pair wished to run
election.

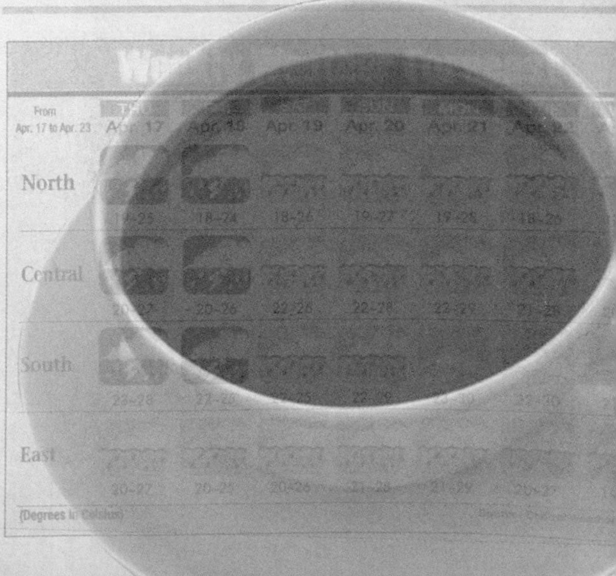

作者序

首先要謝謝你的支持，沒錯，就是你。購買或翻閱這本書的你！恭喜，你的翻譯與寫作功力即將有所進展。再來要不免俗地感謝我的家人，我那兩個分別為 8 歲、6 歲活力充沛創造力十足，卻在寫作期間令我充滿驚奇的兒子（異常地體諒懂事），以及與我一同協力完成本書的先生。還有要特別感謝貴社美君編輯和出版團隊的專業引導，本書才得以順利出版，提供想精進翻譯寫作能力，以及有志從事翻譯或練習寫作的學習者多一個選擇。

多年在兩種不同語言之間練體操，摔搗、扭傷的次數不勝枚舉，思緒也不時就會來個前空翻，唯有不斷練習並虛心汲取各方經驗與意見，才能將每個動作調整至一氣呵成的優美演出，最後再以震憾全場的劈腿來作為每場精湛演出的完美句點。

不同語言代表的不只是文字上的相異，語言涵括了文化背景，譯文的呈現方式並無絕對，但力求正確與通暢。

希望你能以無預設立場的欣賞角度來消化書中每篇文章（否則可能會發現自己在跟「文字」拌嘴），翻譯的不可違教條即是忠於原文，不加諸個人情緒、意見。

翻譯要譯得興緻盎然，才能讓人讀（看）得賞心悅目。

Wendy Lien

編者序

中英翻譯首重在文章脈絡理解是否正確，再求字句優美、通順，精通翻譯沒有捷徑，就是多看、多想、多練習；多看即多看不同類型的文章、多想則是想想為什麼要那樣翻，多練習就是自己動筆。而翻譯也和寫作關聯緊密，本書不僅提供英翻中的訣竅，更希望能藉由中文的概念翻轉成英文的學習方式，讓讀者體會並理解真正用英文思維構成的文章，幫助提升英文寫作能力。

編輯部

目 次

PART 1
商業篇 Business

PART 2
財經篇 Finaces & Economics

PART 3

教育篇 Education

PART 4

文化篇 Culture

PART 5

科普篇 Popular Science

PART 6

醫療保健篇 Medical Health Care

PART 7

資訊科技篇 IT

PART 8

新聞篇 News

Unit 1

1.1 中英筆譯互譯要點【英譯中】

Tips 英譯中要點提示

1. 常見的國家名、人名、城市名、著作名、公司組織名，以及專有名詞皆需譯出，否則保留原文即可。

2. 專業術語字詞的意思需查證，同樣的字詞在不同專業領域表達的意涵不同。

3. 百分比寫法以阿拉伯數字及%表達，如 10%、55%等。查證常見的國家專有名詞譯法。

4. 留意俚語或動詞片語的中文意思。rule of thumb 是「經驗法則」的意思。double 是「加倍、多一倍」的意思。the States 是「美國」的意思。

As anyone who has visited the States knows, tipping is an important part of the service culture. It's customary for a gratuity to be given to waiters and bartenders in restaurants and bars, as well as taxi drivers, parking valets and hotel porters. It is important to realize that many workers in these industries in the US are paid at or even below the minimum wage, and therefore tips are a vital source of income for them.

While the size of tips is not fixed and varies greatly according to the establishment, a good rule of thumb that many use in restaurants is to double the tax on their check, and around 15 to 20 percent is expected in bars and taxis.

While it might not be illegal to tip in Singapore, it is most definitely frowned upon by the government. Not surprisingly in places like airports, it is strictly prohibited to tip staff, but also many restaurants already charge a 10 percent service charge and so actively discourage any further tipping, further underlining the fact that tipping is neither required nor expected.

---

* tipping n. 給小費　　* gratuity n. 小費
* parking valets 代客停車的服務人員

中文譯文對照
Chinese Translation

去過美國的人都知道，在美國給小費是服務業文化的一個重要部分。在餐廳和酒吧給服務生和酒保小費是一種慣例，另外也會給計程車司機、泊車服務員以及飯店行李員小費。重要的是要了解許多美國服務業從業人員的薪資屬最低或甚至低於最低工資，因此小費是彌補他們收入很重要的一部分。

而給小費的金額多寡亦不盡相同，視場所而定，以一般在餐廳給小費的經驗法則來説，是以該餐帳單稅額的加倍金額做為小費，而在酒吧和計程車則是以帳單約 15% 至 20% 的金額給予小費。

然而在新加坡（Singapore）給小費也許並非違法，但是政府完全不贊同。不意外地，在新加坡像機場這種地方就禁止給予工作人員小費，許多餐廳已經收取 10% 服務費，因此積極地不鼓勵給小費，且進一步強調既不需要，也不預期顧客給小費。

D 英譯中譯文討論
iscussions

1. 原　文「As anyone who has visited the States knows, tipping is an important part of the service culture.」，譯文需符合中文語法，時間、地點需先交待清楚再接續敘述，由第一句知道在敘述的地點為「美國」，譯為「去過美國的人都知道，在美國給小費是服務業文化的一個重要部分。」。

2. 「the size of the tips」不可直譯為「小費的大小」，不符合中文語法，譯文以「小費金額的多寡」才通順。

3. 英文常用到的代名詞，以及在敘述某個地方、時間、背景時，通常只會提到一次便繼續加以敘述，如本文原文「Not surprisingly in places like airports, it is strictly prohibited to tip staff」，句中「airport」指的是新加坡的機場，所以譯文在這裡應該加入「新加坡」有助讀者了解，譯為「不意外地，在新加坡像機場這種地方就禁止給予工作人員小費」。

Unit 1

1.2 中英筆譯互譯要點【中譯英】

Tips 中譯英要點提示

1. 要符合英語文法，不可直譯。
2. 百分比數值僅以阿拉伯數字譯出即可，百分比可譯出或以符號表示皆可。
3. 英文只要語法通順且正確，常會有很多的寫法可表達相同中文意思。譯文的寫法並沒有正確解答，但傳達的意思必須正確無誤。
4. 「以一般在餐廳給小費的經驗法則來說」，本句關鍵是必須將「經驗法則」即 rule of thumb 譯出。

主題短文 Article

去過美國的人都知道，在美國給小費是服務業文化的一個重要部分。在餐廳和酒吧給服務生和酒保小費是一種慣例，另外也會給計程車司機、泊車服務員以及飯店行李員小費。重要的是要了解許多美國服務業從業人員的薪資屬最低或甚至低於最低工資，因此小費是彌補他們收入很重要的一部分。

而給小費的金額多寡亦不盡相同，視場所而定，以一般在餐廳給小費的經驗法則來說，是以該餐帳單稅額的加倍金額做為小費，而在酒吧和計程車則是以帳單約 15% 至 20% 的金額給予小費。

然而在新加坡（Singapore）給小費也許並非違法，但是政府完全不贊同。不意外地，在新加坡像機場這種地方就禁止給予工作人員小費，許多餐廳已經收取 10% 服務費，因此積極地不鼓勵給小費，且進一步強調既不需要，也不預期顧客給小費。

■ 請試著翻劃底線的部分。

E 英文譯文對照 English Translation

As anyone who has visited the States knows, tipping is an important part of the service culture. It's customary for a gratuity to be given to waiters and bartenders in restaurants and bars, as well as taxi drivers, parking valets and hotel porters.（詳見下頁討論 1 與 2） It is important to realize that many workers in these industries in the US are paid at or even below the minimum wage（詳見下頁討論 3）, and therefore tips are a vital source of income for them.

While the size of tips is not fixed（詳見下頁討論 4）, and varies greatly according to the establishment, a good rule of thumb that many use in restaurants is to double the tax on their check, and around 15 to 20 percent is expected in bars and taxis.

While it might not be illegal to tip in Singapore, it is most definitely frowned upon by the government.（詳見下頁討論 5） Not surprisingly in places like airports, it is strictly prohibited to tip staff, but also many restaurants already charge a 10 percent service charge and so actively discourage any further tipping, further underlining the fact that tipping is neither required nor expected.

D 中譯英譯文討論
Discussions

1. 英語語法有時態，中翻英時必須看完整個句子、段落，了解其意思之後再譯出，每個句子皆需選擇文法與時態。

2. 原文「在餐廳和酒吧給服務生和酒保小費是一種慣例」，亦可譯作「It is a custom to tip bartenders and waiters in bars and restaurants」。

3. 原文「許多美國服務業從業人員的薪資屬最低或甚至低於最低工資」，這一句可譯作被動語態「many US servers are paid at or less than the country's minimum wage,」，亦可譯作「many US servers have salaries around the minimum wage」。

4. 原文「小費的金額多寡」亦可譯作「The amount people tip」。

5. 然而在新加坡（Singapore），給小費並非違法，連接詞「while」亦可譯為「**Although** it might not be illegal to tip in Singapore,」。

Unit 2

2.1 中英筆譯互譯要點【英譯中】

Tips 英譯中要點提示

1. 中文語法無被動語態，要避免直譯。
2. 留意前後譯文的連貫性與流暢度，一些主詞／代名詞可在隨後接續的譯文中省略。
3. 英語語法與中文語法不同，不可用直譯方式逐字翻譯，需看完整個句子、整個段落，了解意思後再譯出。不可省略或誤譯重點文字、數值，更不可更改原意。

A 主題短文 Article

Technology is changing faster than ever before. The old is being replaced and the new speedily established in everyday life more rapidly than at any time before. Consumer electronics have developed drastically, changing the way we communicate and collect information. This push to innovate has extended into other, more understated parts of our lives, even to the bathroom where improvements from chamber pots and outhouses to flushing toilets are now being supplemented with the rise of bathroom technologies. This recent innovation has transformed the act of visiting the bathroom from a routine task to even an enjoyable experience. The hotel industry has been the most notable in quickly taking advantage of these new found luxuries.

We all feel comfortable with our regular routines, and changing lifelong habits to make room for the new is never an easy task. However, including the new into our daily life is what keeps our lives fresh and exciting, expanding our horizons to endue greater possibilities and experiences.

＊ consumer electronics n. 家用電子產品
＊ drastically adv. 大大地；徹底地
＊ understated adj. 淡化的；不那麼在意的
＊ chamber pot n. 尿壺；夜壺
＊ outhouse n. 戶外廁所
＊ supplement v. 增補；補充
＊ routines n. 例行公事
＊ endue v. 賦予

中文譯文對照
Chinese Translation

科技正以前所未有的速度汰舊換新。舊有科技迅速被取代，而新的科技比以往更迅速地建立於我們的日常生活中。家用電子產品急速發展，改變了我們溝通和收集資訊的方式。這使得革新擴大至其他領域，甚至擴大至生活中較被淡化的浴廁領域，發展沿革從夜壺到戶外廁所，再到沖水馬桶，興盛的浴廁科技增配了許多設備。這個近期的創新，轉變了人們去浴廁的行為，把它從原本單調的例行公事變成一種令人愉悅的體驗。最受惠於這些浴廁奢華新享受的產業，就屬飯店業了。

我們慣於日常的例行公事，而且要我們改變生活習慣來接納新的事物可是一點也不容易。無論如何，在日常生活中加入新事物，就是讓生活保有新鮮和刺激感的方式，這開拓了我們的眼界，賦予更大的可能性和體驗。

D 英譯中譯文討論 iscussions

1. 翻譯時，為了流暢度並讓讀者充分了解文章要表達的意思，可在不更改原意的前提下，適時加入譯出文。避免錯字、異體字。

2. 「Technology is changing faster than ever before.」，不把「changing」直譯為「改變」，而是視文章內容譯其意，譯作「科技正以前所未有的速度汰舊換新。」更為貼切。

3. 「The old is being replaced and the new is speedily established in everyday life more rapidly than at any time before.」，其「the old」指的是「old technology」;「the new」指的是「new technology」，譯作「舊有科技迅速被取代，而新的科技比以往更迅速地建立於我們的日常生活中。」。

4. 「This recent innovation has transformed the act of visiting the bathroom from a routine task to even an enjoyable experience.」，在譯文中加入「單調的」，才能跟後文「**an enjoyable experience**」「令人愉悅的體驗」相呼應，光是只譯出「例行公事」，無法表達出與「令人愉悅的體驗」之間的對比，譯作「這個近期的創新，轉變了人們去浴廁的行為，把它從原本單調的例行公事變成一種令人愉悅的體驗。」。

Unit 2

2.2 中英筆譯互譯要點【中譯英】

Tips 中譯英要點提示

1. 英語語法有**時態**、**詞性**變化，中翻英時必須看完整個句子、段落，了解其意思之後再譯出，每個句子皆需選擇文法與時態。

2. 翻譯時，為了流暢度並讓讀者充分了解文章要表達的意思，可在不更改原意的前提下，適時加入譯出文。避免錯字、異體字。

3. 譯文前後的連貫性與流暢度需符合英語語法，主詞在隨後接續的敘述中盡量皆以代名詞／指示代名詞表示，不要一直重複名詞主詞。

4. 敘述事件或物品時常出現英語語法中的被動語態。

5. 重點的關鍵字彙以及前後關係與對比須清楚譯出。
   如：「前所未有的速度」是「faster than ever before」。
   「例行公事」是「a routine task」;「 day-to-day routines」。
   「夜壺」是「chamber pot」。

科技正以前所未有的速度汰舊換新。舊有科技迅速被取代，而新的科技比以往更迅速地建立於我們的日常生活中。家用電子產品急速發展，改變了我們溝通和收集資訊的方式。這使得革新擴大至其他領域，甚至擴大至生活中較被淡化的浴廁領域，發展沿革從夜壺到戶外廁所，再到沖水馬桶，興盛的浴廁科技增配了許多設備。這個近期的創新，轉變了人們去浴廁的行為，把它從原本單調的例行公事變成一種令人愉悅的體驗。最受惠於這些浴廁奢華新享受的產業，就屬飯店業了。

我們慣於日常的例行公事，而且要我們改變生活習慣來接納新的事物可是一點也不容易。無論如何，在日常生活中加入新事物，就是讓生活保有新鮮和刺激感的方式，這開拓了我們的眼界，賦予更大的可能性和體驗。

■ 請試著翻劃底線的部分。

Technology is changing faster than ever before. The old is being replaced and the new is speedily established in everyday life more rapidly than at any time before.（詳見下頁討論 1）Consumer electronics has developed drastically, changing the way we communicate and collect information. This push to innovate has extended into other, more understated parts of our lives, even to the bathroom where improvements from chamber pots to outhouses to flushing toilets are now being supplemented with the rise of bathroom technologies. This recent innovation has transformed the act of visiting the bathroom from a routine task to even an enjoyable experience. The hotel industry has been the most notable in quickly taking advantage of these new found luxuries.（詳見下頁討論 2）

We all feel comfortable with our regular routines,（詳見下頁討論 3） and changing lifelong habits to make room for the new is never an easy task. However, including the new into our daily life is what keeps our lives fresh and exciting, expanding our horizons to endue greater possibilities and experiences.（詳見下頁討論 4）

D 中譯英譯文討論
iscussions

1. 「舊有科技迅速被取代，而新的科技比以往更迅速的建立於我們的日常生活中。」，英語有被動語態，在這裡皆為現在式被動語態（主詞＋現在式 be 動詞＋過去分詞），亦可譯作「Technology is changing faster than ever before. The old is being replaced by the new, and is speedily established in our everyday life more than at any time before.」。

2. 「最受惠於這些浴廁奢華新享受的產業，就屬飯店業了。」亦可以關係代名詞帶領的形容詞子句詮釋這段譯文，關係代名詞 which/that 皆可用來代表在它之前的事 / 物（名詞），譯作「The industry that（也可譯為 which） takes most advantage of these newly developed luxuries is the hotel industry」。

3. 「我們慣於日常的例行公事」，亦可譯為「We are used to our day-to-day routines」。

4. 「無論如何，在日常生活中加入新事物，就是讓生活保有新鮮和刺激感的方式，開拓了我們的眼界，賦予更大的可能性和體驗。」，亦可譯作「However, expanding our horizons to add new possibilities and experiences into our daily life will keep our lives fresh and exciting.」。

Unit 3

3.1 中英筆譯互譯要點【英譯中】

Tips 英譯中要點提示

1. 英語語法中，敘述人常放在敘述內容之後，但中文語法慣用先表明說話者為何。

2. 專有名詞、國家名若有固定譯名皆需譯出，若是十分普遍常見的譯名，可不需再加註原文，否則第一次出現於文中時需以圓括號引註原文，其後則以譯名表示即可。

3. 專業術語／名詞之字詞譯名需查證。

4. 數值及小數點符號的譯文皆以阿拉伯數字與符號表示即可。

5. 翻譯時，為了流暢度並讓讀者充分了解文章要表達的意思，可在不更改原意的前提下，適時加入譯出文。

主題短文 Article

Consumer confidence was up again last month for the fourth consecutive month hitting a 14-year high. The wealth effect was boosted by stock market rallies and end-of-year bonuses, a National Central University survey showed yesterday.

The monthly poll showed a rise in the Consumer Confidence Index to 89.44 last month, up 1.21 points from January with five of the six component measures seeing positive movements.

Following the Lunar New Year holiday the TAIEX showed the biggest increase rallying past 9,600 and pushing the stock investment sub-index up five points to 97.3, the survey said.

Most companies reported a material earnings improvement last year, mainly due to the recovering US economy and slumping crude oil prices, economists said.

＊ wealth effect 財富效果
＊ stock market rallies 股市止跌回升
＊ end-of-year bonuses 年終獎金
＊ Consumer Confidence Index 消費者信心指數
＊ TAIEX 加權股價指數
＊ stock n. 股票；股票（若是出現於零售業，則表示「存貨」）
＊ sub-index 分指數
＊ crude oil 原油

中文譯文對照 Chinese Translation

由上個月的消費者信心再次回升，已接連4個月持續升高達14年新高。國立中央大學（National Central University）進行的總體研究昨日顯示，年終獎金和股市止跌回升強化了財富效果（wealth effect）。

每月進行的民意調查顯示消費者信心指數（Consumer Confidence Index）上個月升至89.44，自一月至今上升了1.21個百分點，在以6個部分進行的測量中，其中5個部分皆能看到樂觀的動向。

總體研究表示在農曆新年假期過後，加權股價指數（TAIEX）表現出最大幅的止跌回升，突破9,600點大關並讓股市投資前景分指數（sub-index）上揚了5個百分點，來到97.3。

經濟學家表示，多數公司公佈上一年度的實質收益增加，這主要是由於美國經濟復甦，以及原油價格鋭減的結果。

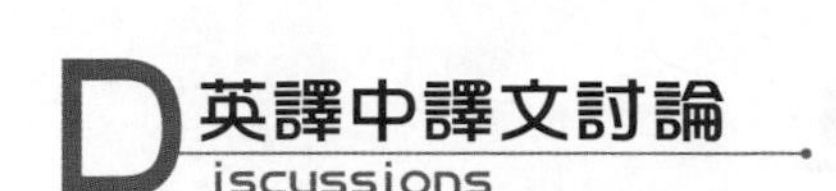

英譯中譯文討論 Discussions

1. 英語語法中，敘述人常放在敘述內容之後，但中文語法慣用先表明説話者為何，譯文需通順並有助譯者了解。

2. 原　文「Consumer confidence was up again last month for the fourth consecutive month hitting a 14-year high. The wealth effect was boosted by stock market rallies and end-of-year bonuses, a National Central University survey showed yesterday.」翻譯時，應先看完一段，再消化其中的前因後果、相對應關係，譯文需符合中文語法。**亦可譯作「由國立中央大學（National Central University）進行的總體研究昨日顯示，因年終獎金和股市止跌回升強化了財富效果（wealth effect），上個月的消費者信心再次回升，接連 4 個月持續升高，達 14 年新高。」**。

3. 原文「Following the Lunar New Year holiday the TAIEX showed the biggest increase rallying past 9,600 and pushing the stock investment sub-index up five points to 97.3, the survey said.」，亦可譯作「**隨著農曆新年假期過後，總體研究顯示加權股價指數（TAIEX）呈現最大幅的止跌回升，突破 9,600 點大關並將股市投資前景分指數（sub-index）上漲 5 個百分點，來到 97.3。**」。

4. 原　文「Most companies reported a material earnings improvement last year, mainly due to the recovering US economy and slumping crude oil prices, economists said.」，其「last year」譯作「上一年度」才符合專業術語，亦可譯作「**經濟學家表示，多數公司公佈上一年度的實質收益增加，主要是因為美國經濟復甦與及原油價格銳減。**」。

Unit 3

3.2 中英筆譯互譯要點【中譯英】

Tips 中譯英要點提示

1. 數值僅以阿拉伯數字譯出即可，小數點以符號表示。
2. 本身為英文名的專有名詞直接譯回原文，不需再附上中文譯文。
3. 英語語法有時態、詞性變化，中翻英時必須看完整個句子、段落，了解其意思之後再譯出，每個句子皆需選擇文法與時態。特別留意中文不易在文字中看出英語語法的時態，翻譯時需符合英語語法。
4. 英語語法中，敘述人常放在敘述內容之後。
5. 專業術語／名詞之字詞譯名需查證，同樣的字詞在不同專業領域表達的意涵不同。
6. 其它：
   - a 年終獎金是「year-end bonuses」、「end-of-year bonuses」。
   - b 總體研究是「survey」。
   - c 股市止跌回升是「stock market rally」。
   - d 股市投資是「stock investment」。
   - e 美國經濟復甦是「the recovering US economy」，「the recovering economy in the US」。
   - f 價格銳減是「slump」。

Part 1

主題短文 Article

由上個月的消費者信心再次回升，已接連 4 個月持續升高達 14 年新高。國立中央大學（National Central University）進行的總體研究昨日顯示，年終獎金和股市止跌回升強化了財富效果（wealth effect）。

每月進行的民意調查顯示消費者信心指數（Consumer Confidence Index）上個月升至 89.44，自一月至今上升了 1.21 個百分點，在以 6 個部分進行的測量中，其中 5 個部分皆能看到樂觀的動向。

總體研究表示在農曆新年假期過後，加權股價指數（TAIEX）表現出最大幅的止跌回升，突破 9,600 點大關並讓股市投資前景分指數（sub-index）上揚了 5 個百分點，來到 97.3。

經濟學家表示，多數公司公佈上一年度的實質收益增加，這主要是由於美國經濟復甦，以及原油價格銳減的結果。

■ 請試著翻劃底線的部分。

英文譯文對照 English Translation

Consumer confidence was up again last month for the fourth consecutive month hitting a 14-year high. The wealth effect was boosted by stock market rallies and end-of-year bonuses, a National Central University survey showed yesterday.（詳見下頁討論 1）

The monthly poll showed a rise in the Consumer Confidence Index to 89.44 last month, up 1.21 points from January with five of the six component measures seeing positive movements.

Following the Lunar New Year holiday the TAIEX showed the biggest increase rallying past 9,600 and pushing the stock investment sub-index up five points to 97.3, the survey said.（詳見下頁討論 2）

Most companies reported a material earnings improvement last year, mainly due to the recovering US economy and slumping crude oil prices, economists said.（詳見下頁討論 3）

1. 敘述已發生事件時通常為過去式、完成式。原文「國立中央大學（National Central University）進行的總體研究昨日顯示，年終獎金和股市止跌回升強化了財富效果（wealth effect）。」亦可譯作「A survey, conducted by National Central University, showed that year-end bonuses and stock rallies have boosted the wealth effect.」。

2. 原文「總體研究表示在農曆新年假期過後，加權股價指數（TAIEX）表現出最大幅的止跌回升，突破 9,600 點大關並讓股市投資前景分指數（sub-index）上揚了 5 個百分點，來到 97.3。」，亦可譯作「**The survey reported that after the Lunar New Year holiday, the TAIEX rallied past 9,600, and the sub-index on stock investment had the biggest increase up five points to 97.3.**」。

3. 原文「經濟學家表示，多數公司公佈上一年度的實質收益增加，這主要是由於美國經濟復甦，以及原油價格銳減的結果。」，亦可譯作「**Economists said that most companies reported a material earnings improvement last year because they were aided mainly by the recovering economy in the US, and also falling crude oil prices.**」。

Unit 4

4.1 中英筆譯互譯要點【英譯中】

Tips 英譯中要點提示

1. 地名、公司組織名，以及專有名詞若有固定譯名皆需譯出，若是十分普遍常見的譯名，可不需再加註原文，否則第一次出現於文中時需以圓括號引註原文，其後則以譯名表示即可。在無固有譯名的情況下，直接以原文譯出。

2. 譯文以白話文為主，以正常速度唸文章時，該停頓換氣時，原則上就是需要下逗號的位置，但仍視原文而定。

3. 專業術語／名詞之字詞譯名需查證，同樣的字詞在不同專業領域表達的意涵不同。

4. 數字以阿拉伯數字表示，百分比以符號代替即可。

Qualcomm Inc, the largest maker of semiconductors for mobile devices, has developed a new chip design that it says will help sustain its dominant position in smartphones.

The company's new line of chips based on the Kryo processor design will begin testing in the second half of the year, the San Diego, California-based company said yesterday.

Qualcomm's advanced chips have propelled it to become the key supplier of technology to the smartphone industry. According to researcher IDC, last year more than 80 percent of phones connected to the fastest 4G networks were based on Qualcomm's products.

Competition is increasing; however, as the likes of Samsung Electronics Co, MediaTek Inc and Intel Corp add features to their products.

---

* Qualcomm 高通通訊公司
* mobile device n. 手機
* IDC 國際數據資訊
* Intel Corp 英特爾
* semiconductor n. 半導體
* San Diego 聖地牙哥
* MediaTek Inc 聯發科

C 中文譯文對照
Chinese Translation

手機最大半導體製造商高通通訊公司（Qualcomm Inc）研發了一項新晶片設計，表示這將有助保有該公司在智慧型手機的領先地位。

高通通訊公司基於 Kryo 處理器所設計的新晶片輪廓，將於下半年開始進行測試，這間位於美國加州聖地牙哥（San Diego）的公司昨天表示。

高通通訊公司的先進晶片使得該公司成為智慧型手機產業的主要技術供應商。根據國際數據資訊研究公司（IDC），去年超過 80% 連結至速度最快的 4G 網路手機，皆為高通通訊公司的產品。

競爭愈來愈多，不過像三星電子（Samsung Electronics Co）、聯發科（MediaTek Inc），以及英特爾（Intel Corp）這類公司，皆仍在自家產品注入特色。

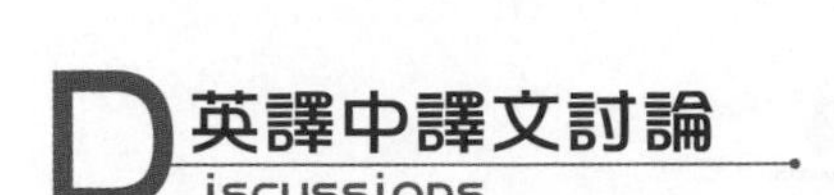

1. 英文單字在不同領域有不同意思，原文「Qualcomm Inc, the largest maker of semiconductors for mobile devices, has developed a new chip design that it says will help sustain its dominant position in smartphones.」，這裡的「**chips**」在科技業中為「晶片」而不是「洋芋片」。

2. 原文「has introduced a new chip design」，其所有格代名詞「its」表示「Qualcomm's」，亦可譯作「手機最大半導體製造商高通通訊公司（Qualcomm Inc），研發了一項認為有助於維持該公司在智慧型手機領先地位的新晶片設計。」。

3. 原　文「The company's new line of chips based on the Kryo processor design will begin testing in the second half of the year, the San Diego, California-based company said yesterday.」，其「The company」，所指的就是「Qualcomm Inc」，譯出完整主詞會比只譯出「該公司」更好，**亦可譯作「位於美國加州聖地牙哥（San Diego）的高通通訊公司昨天表示，該公司基於 Kryo 處理器所設計的新晶片輪廓，將於下半年開始進行測試。」**。

4. 原文「Competition is increasing; however, as the likes of Samsung Electronics Co, MediaTek Inc and Intel Corp add features to their products.」，亦可譯作「競爭者愈來愈多，然而像是三星電子（Samsung Electronics Co）、聯發科（MediaTek Inc），以及英特爾（Intel Corp）這類公司，皆在產品中注入特色。」。

Unit 4

4.2 中英筆譯互譯要點【中譯英】

Tips 中譯英要點提示

1. 數值僅以阿拉伯數字譯出即可，百分比可譯出或以符號表示皆可。
2. 本身為英文名的專有名詞直接譯回原文，不需再附上中文譯文。公司構構名稱，需先查證固有譯名。
3. 英語語法有時態、詞性變化，中翻英時必須看完整個句子、段落，了解其意思之後再譯出，每個句子皆需選擇文法與時態。
4. 譯文前後的連貫性與流暢度需符合英語語法，主詞在隨後接續的敘述中盡量皆以代名詞／指示代名詞／其他名詞表示。
5. 其它：

   a 半導體是「semiconductor」。

   b 晶片是「chip」。

   c 領先地位是「dominant position」。

手機最大半導體製造商高通通訊公司（Qualcomm Inc）研發了一項新晶片設計，表示這將有助保有該公司在智慧型手機的領先地位。

高通通訊公司基於 Kryo 處理器所設計的新晶片輪廓，將於下半年開始進行測試，這間位於美國加州聖地牙哥（San Diego）的公司昨天表示。

高通通訊公司的先進晶片使得該公司成為智慧型手機產業的主要技術供應商。根據國際數據資訊研究公司（IDC），去年超過 80% 連結至速度最快的 4G 網路手機，皆為高通通訊公司的產品。

競爭愈來愈多，不過像三星電子（Samsung Electronics Co）、聯發科（MediaTek Inc），以及英特爾（Intel Corp）這類公司，皆仍在自家產品注入特色。

■ 請試著翻劃底線的部分。

Qualcomm Inc, the largest maker of semiconductors for mobile devices, has developed a new chip design that it says will help sustain its dominant position in smartphones.（詳見下頁討論 1）

The company's new line of chips based on the Kryo processor design will begin testing in the second half of the year, the San Diego, California-based company said yesterday.（詳見下頁討論 2）

Qualcomm's advanced chips have propelled it to become the key supplier of technology to the smartphone industry. According to researcher IDC, last year more than 80 percent of phones connected to the fastest 4G networks were based on Qualcomm's products.（詳見下頁討論 3）

Competition is increasing, however, as the likes of Samsung Electronics Co, MediaTek Inc（聯發科）and Intel Corp add features to their products.

中譯英譯文討論 Discussions

1. 原文「手機最大半導體製造商高通通訊公司（Qualcomm Inc）研發了一項新晶片設計，表示這將有助保有該公司在智慧型手機的領先地位。」，亦可譯作「**The largest maker of semiconductors for the mobile device industry, Qualcomm Inc, has developed a new chip design that it says will help maintain its dominance in smartphones.**」。

2. 原文「高通通訊公司基於 Kryo 處理器所設計的新晶片輪廓，將於下半年開始進行測試，這間位於美國加州聖地牙哥（San Diego）的公司昨天表示。」，亦可譯作「**The company will begin testing its new line of chips which are based on the Kryo processor design in the second half of the year, the San Diego, California-based company said yesterday.**」。

3. 原文「高通通訊公司的先進晶片使得該公司成為智慧型手機產業的主要技術供應商。根據國際數據資訊研究公司（IDC），去年超過 80% 連結至速度最快的 4G 網路手機，皆為高通通訊公司的產品。」，亦可譯作「**Qualcomm's advanced chips have made it the main supplier of technology to the smartphone industry. According to researcher IDC, last year more than 80% of phones which connected to the fastest 4G networks were Qualcomm's.**」。

4. 由於「MediaTek Inc」是台灣的公司，其中文名較為台灣讀者所知，故在譯文中加註「（聯發科）」，有利讀者了解。

Unit 5

5.1 中英筆譯互譯要點【英譯中】

Tips 英譯中要點提示

1. 不要執著在每個英語單字的意思，在不同內容下，會有不同的詮釋方式，要譯其意。不可省略或誤譯重點文字、數值，更不可更改原意。

2. 專業術語／名詞之字詞譯名需查證。

3. 日期若合併年、月、日，可以阿拉伯數字譯出，若是單只出現月份則儘量以中文字譯出。

4. **翻譯時，為了流暢度並讓讀者充分了解文章要表達的意思，可在不更改原意的前提下，適時加入譯出文。**

5. 國家名、公司組織名，以及專有名詞若有固定譯名皆需譯出，若是十分普遍常見的譯名，可不需再加註原文，否則第一次出現於文中時需以圓括號引註原文，其後則以譯名表示即可。在無固有譯名的情況下，直接以原文譯出。

6. 數值皆以阿拉伯數字表示即可。

China's manufacturing activity improved more than originally thought last month, but falling foreign demand and declining prices signaled that the world's No. 2 economy still faces multiple headwinds, HSBC said yesterday.

The British Bank released its final purchasing managers' index（PMI） for the month at 50.7 up from a preliminary 50.1 and the highest since 51.7 in July last year.

PMI readings above 50 point to expansion, while anything below suggests contraction.

This closely followed index which tracks activity in China's factories and workshops and is a good indicator of the health of the Asian economic giant was compiled by Markit, an information service provider.

---

* foreign demand 外國需求
* No. 2 第二
* headwind n. 逆風
* HSBC 匯豐銀行
* British Bank 不列顛銀行
* PMI（Purchasing Managers' Index）採購經理人指數
* reading 讀數
* contraction 收縮

中文譯文對照 Chinese Translation

匯豐銀行（HSBC）昨天表示，中國大陸上個月的製造業活動比起初認為的進步更多，但是外國需求減弱且價格下降，表示這個世界第二大經濟體仍面臨多重困難。

不列顛銀行（British Bank）公開了該銀行當月的最終採購經理人指數（purchasing managers' index；PMI）從一開始的 50.1 上升至 50.7，是自去年七月達 51.7 以來的最高點。

PMI 讀數超過 50 點就代表膨脹，而只要低於這個讀數即代表收縮。

這個追蹤中國大陸工廠與工作室商業活動的指數，由資訊服務提供者 Markit 公司編彙，是個詳盡觀察這個亞洲經濟巨人健全狀態的指標。

D 英譯中譯文討論 iscussions

1. 英語語法中，敘述人常放在敘述內容之後，但中文語法慣用先表明說話者為何。原文「China's manufacturing activity improved more than originally thought last month, but falling foreign demand and declining prices signaled that the world's No. 2 economy still faces multiple headwinds, HSBC said yesterday.」， 其「**headwinds**」單字片面的意思為「逆風」，文中意指「難以順利前進發展」的意思，譯文應先說明提述者，再集中敘述內容有助讀者理解，譯作「匯豐銀行（HSBC）昨天表示，中國大陸上個月的製造業活動比起初認為的進步更多，但是外國需求減弱且價格下降，表示這個世界第二大經濟體仍面臨多重困難。」。

2. 原 文「PMI readings above 50 point to expansion, while anything below suggests contraction.」，在商業金融領域，「**expansion**」和「**contraction**」分別為相互對比的「膨脹」和「收縮」，譯作「PMI 讀數超過 50 點就代表膨脹，而只要低於這個讀數即代表收縮。」。

3. 原 文「This closely followed index which tracks activity in China's factories and workshops and is a good indicator of the health of the Asian economic giant was compiled by Markit, an information service provider.」，其「**the index**」表示「**PMI**」，在「**activity**」的譯文加入「商業」兩字，可讓譯文更順暢，亦可譯作「這個追蹤中國大陸工廠與工作室商業活動的指數，是由資訊服務提供者 Markit 公司編彙的詳盡觀察亞洲經濟巨人健全狀態的指標。」。

Unit 5

5.2 中英筆譯互譯要點【中譯英】

Tips 中譯英要點提示

1. 英語語法中，敘述人常放在敘述內容後。
2. 譯文前後的連貫性與流暢度需符合英語語法，**主詞在隨後接續的敘述中盡量皆以代名詞／指示代名詞／其他名詞表示**，不要一直重複名詞主詞。
3. 月份的譯文必須以英文字表示，不可以阿拉伯數字代替。
4. 數值僅以阿拉伯數字譯出即可。
5. 中文不易在文字中看出英語語法的時態與被動語態、倒裝句（除了「場所副詞」放在句首，需使用倒裝句外；當強調動作／事情發生的時間、主詞的狀態或當句中的主詞帶有一長串的修飾語，也常常將「時間副詞」或「形容詞」放在句首，形成倒裝句），翻譯時需符合英語語法。
6. 本身為英文名的專有名詞直接譯回原文，不需再附上中文譯文。有縮寫形式的英文名專有名詞，在第一次翻譯時須在括號內附上英文原文，其後僅以縮寫原文表示即可。
7. 其它：

   a 膨脹是「expansion」。

   b 收縮是「contraction」。

Part 1

匯豐銀行（HSBC）昨天表示，中國大陸上個月的製造業活動比起初認為的進步更多，但是外國需求減弱且價格下降，表示這個世界第二大經濟體仍面臨多重困難。

不列顛銀行（British bank）公開了該銀行當月的最終採購經理人指數（purchasing managers' index；PMI）從一開始的 50.1 上升至 50.7，是自去年七月達 51.7 以來的最高點。

PMI 讀數超過 50 點就代表膨脹，而只要低於這個讀數即代表收縮。

這個追蹤中國大陸工廠與工作室商業活動的指數，由資訊服務提供者 Markit 公司編彙，是個詳盡觀察這個亞洲經濟巨人健全狀態的指標。

■ 請試著翻劃底線的部分。

China's manufacturing activity improved more than originally thought last month, but falling foreign demand and declining prices signaled that the world's No. 2 economy still faces multiple headwinds, HSBC said yesterday.（詳見下頁討論 1）

The British Bank released its final purchasing managers' index（PMI） for the month at 50.7 up from a preliminary 50.1 and the highest since 51.7 in July last year.（詳見下頁討論 2）

PMI readings above 50 point to expansion, while anything below suggests contraction.

This closely followed index which tracks activity in China's factories and workshops and is a good indicator of the health of the Asian economic giant was compiled by Markit, an information service provider.（詳見下頁討論 3）

Part 1

D 中譯英譯文討論 Discussions

1. 原文「匯豐銀行（HSBC）昨天表示，中國大陸上個月的製造業活動比起初認為的進步更多，但是外國需求減弱且價格下降，表示這個世界第二大經濟體仍面臨多重困難。」，亦可譯作倒裝句「Last month, China's manufacturing activity increased more than initially thought, but weakening foreign demand and declining prices signaled that the world's No. 2 economy still faces multiple challenges, HSBC said yesterday.」。

2. 原文「不列顛銀行（British Bank）公開了該銀行當月的最終採購經理人指數（purchasing managers' index；PMI）從一開始的 50.1 上升至 50.7，是自去年七月達 51.7 以來的最高點。」，亦可譯作「The British Bank said in a statement that its final purchasing managers' index（PMI） for the month came in at 50.7, up from its preliminary reading of 50.1. This is the highest reading since 51.7 last July.」。

3. 原文「這個追蹤中國大陸工廠與工作室商業活動的指數，由資訊服務提供者 Markit 公司編彙，是個詳盡觀察這個亞洲經濟巨人健全狀態的指標。」整篇文章敘述商業，英語譯文可省略重複敘述「商業」字彙。**英語文法是現在式被動語態**，亦可譯作「The PMI was compiled by Markit which is an information services provider that tracks activity in China's factories and workshops; it's also a closely watched indicator of the health of the Asian economic giant.」。

Unit 6

6.1 中英筆譯互譯要點【英譯中】

Tips 英譯中要點提示

1. 財經商業文章最常出現也最重要的就是數值、年分，以及專有名詞國家名、人名、公司機構名稱，需查證固有譯名，需要時可在括號內加註原文，若無慣用譯名則以原文譯出。
2. 英語人名的譯文要在姓氏與名字之間以音界號「·」分隔，且採直譯的方式，不可將姓氏與名字的順序調換，英語人名的寫法為名字在前，姓氏在後。
3. 百分比的譯法皆以阿拉伯數字加百分比符號表示。
4. 西元年分以阿拉伯數字寫法表達，不譯為中文字。

Part 2

The International Monetary Fund has predicted global growth of 3.8% in 2015. This represents a steady if unspectacular advance after the financial crisis seven years ago. However, a major theme remains the divergence of the world economies, with the US and UK well ahead of other advanced nations.

The MSCI World Index for developed nations was up 2.9% last year（compared with 14.1% in 2013）; in contrast, difficulties among some developing nations meant that the MSCI index of emerging markets fell 4.6% in 2014. Emerging market specialist William Hardy of Stockport Holdings notes that although some developing nations have implemented reforms which have increased domestic demand, the strong dollar remains the primary challenge for emerging markets.

The slowdown in China will also continue to affect the world's commodity producing nations, despite its near 7% growth remaining impressive by most standards.

---

* International Monetary Fund 國際貨幣基金會，簡稱 IMF
* divergence n. 嚴重的意見分歧
* MSCI World Index 全球（股市）指數
* emerging market 新興市場
* implement v. 貫徹；執行
* domestic demand 國內需求
* reform v./n. 改革；改進
* commodity n. 商品

C 中文譯文對照
Chinese Translation

國際貨幣基金會（International Monetary Fund）預估 2015 年全球成長 3.8%。自 7 年前的金融危機後，這呈現出一個雖不輝煌但算是個平穩的進步。然而，主要的議題仍是全世界在經濟上的嚴重分歧，包括比其他國家更進步的英、美兩國。

已開發國家的 MSCI 全球指數（MSCI World Index）去年成長了 2.9%（相較於 2013 年的 24.1%）；跟一些開發中國家的經濟困境形成顯著對比，表示 2014 年新興市場的 MSCI 指數下滑 4.6%。Stockport Holdings 的新興市場專家威廉．哈帝（William Hardy）下了一個註解，他認為即使一些開發中國家已執行改革，增加了國內需求，影響力大的美元仍是新興市場的首要挑戰。

中國大陸經濟成長趨緩的現象，也會持續影響全球的商品生產，僅管如此，以多數的標準來看，這個低於 7% 的成長率仍十分出色。

D 英譯中譯文討論
iscussions

1. 英文語法在敘述事情時，不會一直重述主詞，常以代名詞或接續內容敘述，但在中文譯文裡，必須適時加入主詞或有助於讀者了解的代名詞。原文「However a major theme remains the divergence of the world economies, with the US and UK well ahead of other advanced nations.」，其「with」是「和；有；伴隨」的意思，表示在全世界經濟上的嚴重分歧也有英、美兩國，稍加潤飾譯文譯作「然而，主要的議題仍是全世界在經濟上的嚴重分歧，包括比其他國家更進步的英、美兩國。」

2. 原　文「Emerging market specialist William Hardy of Stockport Holdings notes that although some developing nations have implemented reforms which have increased domestic demand, the strong dollar remains the primary challenge for emerging markets.」，其整段敘述皆為 William Hardy 的想法，故在譯文中多加入「他認為」使譯文更加通暢，亦可譯作「**Stockport Holdings** 的新興市場專家威廉・哈帝（**William Hardy**）下了一個註解，他認為即使一些開發中國家已執行改革並增加國內需求，新興市場的首要挑戰仍是影響力大的美元。」

3. 原　文「The slowdown in China will also continue to affect the world's commodity producing nations, despite its near 7% growth remaining impressive by most standards.」，其「near 7%」表示「接近 7%，但還不到 7%」，亦可譯作「中國大陸經濟成長趨緩的現象，也會持續影響全球的商品生產，僅管如此，以多數的標準來看，這個不到 7% 的成長率仍十分出色。」。

Unit 6

6.2 中英筆譯互譯要點【中譯英】

Tips 中譯英要點提示

1. 年分、數字、數值僅以阿拉伯數字譯出即可，百分比可譯出或以符號表示皆可。

2. 數值與專有名詞國家名、人名、公司機構名稱若有附上原文，只接以原文譯出，若有出現專業術語，需查證是否有慣用的固定名稱。

3. 英語語法有時態、詞性變化，中翻英時必須看完整個句子、段落，了解其意思之後再譯出，每個句子皆需選擇文法與時態。

4. 英語中的分號用於連接獨立的子句，比起句號更能顯示出兩個子句之間的相關性。

國際貨幣基金會（International Monetary Fund）預估 2015 年全球成長 3.8%。自 7 年前的金融危機後，這呈現出一個雖不輝煌但算是個平穩的進步。然而，主要的議題仍是全世界在經濟上的嚴重分歧，包括比其他國家更進步的英、美兩國。

已開發國家的 MSCI 全球指數（MSCI World Index）去年成長了 2.9%（相較於 2013 年的 24.1%）；跟一些開發中國家的經濟困境形成顯著對比，表示 2014 年新興市場的 MSCI 指數下滑 4.6%。Stockport Holdings 的新興市場專家威廉．哈帝（William Hardy）下了一個註解，他認為即使一些開發中國家已執行改革，增加了國內需求，影響力大的美元仍是新興市場的首要挑戰。

中國大陸經濟成長趨緩的現象，也會持續影響全球的商品生產，僅管如此，以多數的標準來看，這個低於 7% 的成長率仍十分出色。

■ 請試著翻劃底線的部分。

The International Monetary Fund has predicted global growth of 3.8% in 2015. This represents a steady if unspectacular advance after the financial crisis seven years ago.（詳見下頁討論 1） However, a major theme remains the divergence of the world economies, with the US and UK well ahead of other advanced nations.（詳見下頁討論 2）

The MSCI World Index for developed nations was up 2.9% last year（compared with 14.1% in 2013）; in contrast, difficulties among some developing nations meant that the MSCI index of emerging markets fell 4.6% in 2014.（詳見下頁討論 3） Emerging market specialist William Hardy of Stockport Holdings notes that although some developing nations have implemented reforms which have increased domestic demand, the strong dollar remains the primary challenge for emerging markets.

The slowdown in China will also continue to affect the world's commodity producing nations, despite its near 7% growth remaining impressive by most standards.（詳見下頁討論 4）

D 中譯英譯文討論 iscussions

1. 原文「這代表跟自金融危機後7年的平淡表現相比較之下，雖不輝煌但算是個平穩的進步。」，亦可譯作「Seven years since the financial crisis, this marks a stable but underwhelming recovery.」。

2. 原文「然而，主要的議題仍是全世界在經濟上的嚴重分歧，包括比其他國家更進步的英、美兩國。」，亦可譯為「However, the main issue remains the divergence of the world economies, including the US and UK which are well ahead of other advanced nations.」。

3. 原文「跟一些開發中國家的經濟困境形成顯著對比，表示2014年新興市場的MSCI指數下滑4.6%。」，其「下滑」可譯為「dropped; slid」，亦可譯作「in contrast, the MSCI index of emerging markets slid 4.6% in 2014 due to problems in some developing nations.」。

4. 原文「不過，以大多數的標準來看，這個低於7%的成長率仍十分出色。」，亦可譯作「although sub-7% growth remains impressive by most standards.」。

Unit 7

7.1 中英筆譯互譯要點【英譯中】

Tips 英譯中要點提示

1. 譯文以白話文為主，以正常速度唸文章時，該停頓換氣時，原則上就是需要下逗號的位置，但仍視原文而定。
2. **英語人名的譯文要在姓氏與名字之間以音界號「・」分隔，且採直譯的方式，不可將姓氏與名字的順序調換，英語人名的寫法為名字在前，姓氏在後。**
3. 專有名詞國家名、人名、公司機構名稱需查證並使用固有的譯名，若無固有譯名就直譯原文即可。
4. 專業術語字詞的意思需查證，同樣的字詞在不同專業領域表達的意涵不同。英語的破折號用於介紹某種說法，加入強調語氣、定義，或是解釋。也用於隔開兩個子句。

For global investors, London is still a destination of choice. It is the lure of capital that has helped buoy Britain's commercial property market – and as Richard Lockhart of Hardines notes it is the stable income yield offered by this sector that attracts a significant amount of this capital. Belief in the UK as a safe haven has also further strengthened the pound. Looking from the Middle East or the countries of the former Soviet Union, the UK and its property market would seem like an oasis of stability. But there are political pitfalls on the horizon. Markets do not like uncertainty and the risk of a hung parliament following the upcoming general election, the unresolved details of devolution following the Scottish referendum, and the future of the UK within the European Union are all unknowns. This, as fund manager Carl Hatford notes, is already a source of market uncertainty.

Meanwhile, with low inflation, falling unemployment, lower food and petrol prices, and signs of long-awaited wage increases, there is plenty of good news for UK households.

---

* Middle East 中東
* pitfall n 隱患
* devolution 權力下放
* European Union 歐盟
* buoy v 鼓舞
* former Soviet Union 前蘇聯
* hung parliament 懸峙國會
* referendum 全民公投
* inflation 通膨

C 中文譯文對照
Chinese Translation

對全球投資人來說，倫敦仍是最終的選擇。倫敦為英國首都的誘因，有助鼓舞英國的商業性不動產市場——Hardines公司的理查·朗克赫特（Richard Lockhart）指出，是這個區塊所提供的穩定所得收益，吸引了鉅額資金。深信英國猶如一個安全的避難所，也更進一步地使英鎊走強。從中東（Middle East）或以前蘇聯（Soviet Union）國家的觀點來看，英國與本身的不動產市場，就像是一塊穩定性的樂土。但是有放眼可及的政治隱患。商業性不動產市場不喜歡不確定性，而即將舉行的大選可能產生無多數黨的議會，以及伴隨蘇格蘭舉行全民公投的權力下放細節尚未解決，還有英國在歐盟（European Union）的未來動向也仍是未知數。基金經理人卡爾·海特福特（Carl Hatford）指出，這些事態已經是市場不確定性的一個來源。

在這同時，低通貨膨脹、失業率下降、食物及汽油降價，還有期盼已久的薪資調漲跡象，對英國住戶來說，仍有夠多的好消息。

Part 2

D 英譯中譯文討論 Discussions

1. 翻譯時，為了流暢度並讓讀者充分了解文章要表達的意思，可在不更改原意的前提下，適時加入譯出文。避免錯字、異體字。

2. 原文「It is the lure of of the capital that has helped buoy Britain's commercial property market」，在譯文中若直譯為「首都的誘因」，不夠清楚讓讀者理解，因此加入國家名來更清楚的表達，譯為「倫敦為英國首都的誘因，有助鼓舞英國的商業性不動產市場。」。

3. 原　文「Markets do not like uncertainty and the risk of a hung parliament following the upcoming general election, the unresolved details of devolution following the Scottish referendum, and the future of the UK within the European Union are all unknowns.」，其「**market**」指的是「**commercial property market**」，在「大選」後加入「可能」兩字，在「英國在歐盟的未來」後加入了「動向」兩字，讓整句譯文更加通順，譯作「商業性不動產市場不喜歡不確定性，而即將舉行的大選可能產生無多數黨的議會，以及伴隨蘇格蘭舉行全民公投的權力下放細節尚未解決，還有英國在歐盟的未來動向也仍是未知數。」。

Unit 7

7.2 中英筆譯互譯要點【中譯英】

Tips 中譯英要點提示

1. 譯文前後的連貫性與流暢度需符合英語語法，**主詞在隨後接續的敘述中盡量皆以代名詞／指示代名詞／其他名詞表示，不要一直重複名詞主詞。**

2. 英語語法有時態、詞性變化，中翻英時必須看完整個句子、段落，了解其意思之後再譯出，每個句子皆需選擇文法與時態。

3. 本身為英文名的專有名詞直接譯回原文，不需再附上中文譯文。

4. 專業術語字詞的意思需查證。

Part 2

對全球投資人來說，倫敦仍是最終的選擇。倫敦為英國首都的誘因，有助鼓舞英國的商業性不動產市場 —— Hardines 公司的理查・朗克赫特（Richard Lockhart）指出，是這個區塊所提供的穩定所得收益，吸引了鉅額資金。深信英國猶如一個安全的避難所，也更進一步地使英鎊走強。從中東（Middle East）或以前蘇聯（Soviet Union）國家的觀點來看，英國與本身的不動產市場，就像是一塊穩定性的樂土。但是有放眼可及的政治隱患。商業性不動產市場不喜歡不確定性，而即將舉行的大選可能產生無多數黨的議會，以及伴隨蘇格蘭舉行全民公投的權力下放細節尚未解決，還有英國在歐盟（European Union）的未來動向也仍是未知數。基金經理人卡爾・海特福特（Carl Hatford）指出，這些事態已經是市場不確定性的一個來源。

在這同時，低通貨膨脹、失業率下降、食物及汽油降價，還有期盼已久的薪資調漲跡象，對英國住戶來說，仍有夠多的好消息。

■ 請試著翻劃底線的部分。

E 英文譯文對照 English Translation

For the global investors, London is still a destination of choice. It is the lure of the capital has helped buoy Britain's commercial property market – and as Richard Lockhart of Hardines notes it is the stable income yield offered by this sector that attracts a significant amount of this capital. Belief in the UK as a safe haven has also further strengthened the pound.（詳見下頁討論 1） Looking from the Middle East or the countries of the former Soviet Union, the UK and its property market would seem like an oasis of stability.（詳見下頁討論 2） But there are political pitfalls on the horizon.（詳見下頁討論 3） Markets do not like uncertainty and the risk of a hung parliament following the upcoming general election, the unresolved details of devolution following the Scottish referendum, and the future of the UK within the European Union are all unknowns.（詳見下頁討論 4） This, as fund manager Carl Hatford notes, is already a source of market uncertainty.

Meanwhile, with low inflation, falling unemployment, lower food and petrol prices, and signs of long awaited wage increases, there is plenty of good news for UK households.（詳見下頁討論 5）

D 中譯英譯文討論 iscussions

1. 原文「深信英國猶如一個安全的避難所，也更進一步地使英鎊走強。」，亦可譯作「This faith in the UK as a safe haven has also strengthened the pound.」。

2. 原文「從中東（Middle East）或以前蘇聯（Soviet Union）國家的觀點來看，英國與本身的不動產市場，就像是一塊穩定性的樂土。」，亦可譯作「From those in the Middle East or the former Soviet Union, the UK and its property market must appear an oasis of stability.」。

3. 原文「但是有放眼可及的政治隱患。」，亦可譯作「But there are political risks on the horizon.」。

4. 原文「商業性不動產市場不喜歡不確定性，而即將舉行的大選可能產生無多數黨的議會，以及伴隨蘇格蘭舉行全民公投的權力下放細節尚未解決，還有英國在歐盟的未來動向也仍是未知數。」，亦可譯作「Commercial property markets do not like uncertainty. The upcoming general election could bring a hung parliament, the details of a devolved UK following the Scottish referendum have yet to be agreed, and the UK's future within the European Union is still undecided.」。

5. 原文「在這同時，低通貨膨脹、失業率下降、食物及汽油降價，還有期盼已久的薪資調漲跡象，對英國住戶來說，仍有夠多的好消息。」，亦可譯作「Meanwhile, with inflation low, unemployment falling, food and petrol prices down and signs of elusive wage increases, there is still plenty of good news for UK residents.」。汽油亦可譯為「gasoline」。

Unit 8

8.1 中英筆譯互譯要點【英譯中】

Tips 英譯中要點提示

1. 專有名詞國家名、人名、貨幣單位譯名皆需查證。僅以貨幣單位符號表示適用於較廣為熟悉的貨幣，否則應以譯文文字說明。
2. 各國貨幣符號盡量譯出譯名，不要只用符號表示，若是常用且辨識率高的貨幣，只以符號譯出亦可。
3. 數字、日期以阿拉伯數字表示，百分比以符號表示。
4. 英文人名的譯文要在姓氏與名字之間以音界號「·」分隔，且採直譯的方式。
5. 英語的引號用於引述人物言語；中文譯文以單引號表示引述人物言語。

主題短文 Article

Turkmen Bank head fired

In the wake of economic troubles that have brought the country's currency down 18.5% so far this year, the Turkmen President, Gurbanguly Berdimuhamedov has dismissed both the head of the country's central bank and his counterpart at its natural gas company.

The authoritarian leader said, "Difficult financial and economic circumstances in certain countries directly affect Turkmenistan." He appears to be referring to Russia. The fall of oil prices and Western sanctions have pushed the ruble down around 45%. On Jan 1st, Turkmenistan devalued its own currency, the Turkmen new manat, from 2.85 to 3.5 to the US dollar.

---

* Turkmen adj./n. 土庫曼的；土庫曼語
* Gurbanguly Berdimuhamedov 是土庫曼總統「庫爾班古力．別爾德穆哈梅多夫」
* in the wake of 隨～之後而來
* Turkmenistan 土庫曼（國家名）
* ruble n. 盧布（俄羅斯貨幣單位）
* Western sanctions 西方國家制裁
* devalue v. 使…貶值
* manat 馬納特（土庫曼的新貨幣）

土庫曼銀行首長遭解職

隨著今年目前為止的經濟問題讓幣值大跌 18.5% 之後，土庫曼（Turkmen）總統庫爾班古力．別爾德穆哈梅多夫（Gurbanguly Berdimuhamedov）開除了該國中央銀行首長的職務，以及其兼任天然氣公司首長一職。

這位專制的領導者說，「某些國家正遭遇的經濟和財務困境，對土庫曼（Turkmenistan）有直接的影響。」他似乎是在說有關俄羅斯的遭遇，在石油價格下跌，以及西方國家制裁的壓力下，俄羅斯的貨幣盧布（ruble）已下跌約 45%。在元月 1 日，土庫曼自己的貨幣貶值，貨幣新馬納特（manat）從 2.85 馬納特對 1 美元來到 3.5 馬納特對 1 美元。

1. 翻譯時，為了流暢度並讓讀者充分了解文章要表達的意思，可在不更改原意的前提下，適時加入譯出文。

2. 原文「Turkmen bank head fired」，為了譯文的流暢，不直譯為「土庫曼的銀行首長遭解職」，該譯文後伴隨著名詞，故在中文語法中可清楚了解其意思，應省去贅字「的」，譯作「土庫曼銀行首長遭解職」。

3. 原文「the Turkmen President, Gurbanguly Berdimuhamedov has dismissed both the head of the country's central bank and his counterpart at its natural gas company.」，不直譯為「土庫曼的總統」，省去贅字「的」，其「his」指的是「the head of the country's central bank」的這個人的另一同等職務，也就是「天然氣公司首長」，其「its」指的是「the country's」，譯作「土庫曼（Terkmen）總統庫爾班古力．別爾德穆哈梅多夫（Gurbanguly Berdimuhamedov）開除了該國中央銀行首長的職務，以及其兼任天然氣公司首長一職。」

4. 原文「He appears to be referring to Russia.」，為了使譯文通暢所以在譯文加入「遭遇」，譯作「他似乎是在說有關俄羅斯的遭遇」。

5. 原文「the Turkmen new manta, from 2.85 to 3.5 to the US dollar.」，亦可譯作「土庫曼的貨幣新馬納特（manat）從 2.85 對 1 美元來到 3.5 對 1 美元。」

Unit 8

8.2 中英筆譯互譯要點【中譯英】

Tips 中譯英要點提示

1. 中文的單引號用於引述人物言語，英語以引號引述人物言語。
2. 譯文前後的連貫性與流暢度需符合英語語法，主詞在隨後接續的敘述中盡量皆以代名詞／指示代名詞／其他名詞表示，不要一直重複名詞主詞。
3. 常見且辨識率高的各國貨幣符號僅以符號表示，或譯出譯文皆可。
4. 英語語法有時態、詞性變化，中翻英時必須看完整個句子、段落，了解其意思之後再譯出，每個句子皆需選擇文法與時態。
5. 本身為英文名的專有名詞直接譯回原文，不需再附上中文譯文。
6. 數值的譯法僅以阿拉伯數字譯出即可，百分比可以符號表示或譯出英文字皆可。

土庫曼銀行首長遭解職

隨著今年目前為止的經濟問題讓幣值大跌 18.5% 之後，土庫曼（Turkmen）總統庫爾班古力．別爾德穆哈梅多夫（Gurbanguly Berdimuhamedov）開除了該國中央銀行首長的職務，以及其兼任天然氣公司首長一職。

這位專制的領導者說，「某些國家正遭遇的經濟和財務困境，對土庫曼（Turkmenistan）有直接的影響。」他似乎是在說有關俄羅斯的遭遇，在石油價格下跌，以及西方國家制裁的壓力下，俄羅斯的貨幣盧布（ruble）已下跌約 45%。在元月 1 日，土庫曼自己的貨幣貶值，貨幣新馬納特（manat）從 2.85 馬納特對 1 美元來到 3.5 馬納特對 1 美元。

■ 請試著翻劃底線的部分。

英文譯文對照 English Translation

Turkmen bank head fired（詳看下頁討論 1）

In the wake of economic troubles that have brought the country's currency down 18.5% so far this year,（詳看下頁討論 2） the Turkmen President, Gurbanguly Berdimuhamedov has dismissed both the head of the country's central bank and his counterpart at its natural gas company.

The authoritarian leader said, "Difficult financial and economic circumstances in certain countries directly affect Turkmenistan." He appears to be referring to Russia. The fall of oil prices and Western sanctions have pushed the ruble down around 45%. On Jan 1st, Turkmenistan devalued its own currency, the Turkmen new manat, from 2.85 to 3.5 to the US dollar.（詳看下頁討論 3）

D 中譯英譯文討論
Discussions

1. 原文「土庫曼銀行首長遭解職」，亦可譯為「The head of Turkmenistan's Central Bank has been fired」。

2. 原文「隨著今年目前為止的經濟問題讓幣值大跌 18.5% 之後」，「隨著～之後」而來的用法為「in the wake of」，亦可譯作「following economic troubles that have weakened the country's currency by18.5 percent so far this year」。

3. 原文「他似乎是在説有關俄羅斯的遭遇，在石油價格下跌，以及西方國家制裁的壓力下，俄羅斯的貨幣盧布（ruble）已下跌約 45%。在元月 1 日，土庫曼自己的貨幣貶值，新貨幣馬納特（manat）從 2.85 馬納特對 1 美元來到 3.5 馬納特對 1 美元。」，亦可譯作「He appears to be referring to Russia, where the ruble has lost about 45 percent of its value under pressure from falling oil prices and Western sanctions. On the 1st of January, Turkmenistan devalued its currency, the Turkmen new manat, from 2.85 to 3.5 to the US dollar.」。日期的寫法，元月 1 日可亦可譯為「the 1st of January」。

Unit 9

9.1 中英筆譯互譯要點【英譯中】

Tips 英譯中要點提示

1. 英語語法與中文語法不同，不可用直譯方式逐字翻譯，需看完整個句子、整個段落，了解意思後再譯出。不要執著在每個英語單字的意思，在不同內容下，會有不同的詮釋方式，要譯其意。不可省略或誤譯重點文字、數值，更不可更改原意。

2. 譯文以白話文為主，以正常速度唸文章時，該停頓換氣時，原則上就是需要下逗號的位置，但仍視原文而定。

3. 英語以引號表示強調內容，也用於指明意涵和單字有不尋常含糊不清意涵的狀態。中文的單引號用於強調內容。

4. 專有名詞、國家名、地名、公司名稱皆需查證固有譯名，若無固有譯名，則以原文譯出，若是十分普遍常見的譯名，可不需再加註原文，否則第一次出現於文中時需以圓括號引註原文，其後則以譯名表示即可。

5. 數值、日期、百分比，以阿拉伯數字、百分比符號表示即可。

A 主題短文 Article

Toys "R" Us Inc on Friday announced the third straight year of declining holiday sales. Same-store sales for the nine weeks through Jan 4 fell 2.7 percent. Fewer promotions were used in order to protect profitability, the Wayne, New Jersey-based company said in a statement. Revenue in the US, where it generates around 60 percent of its sales, declined by 5 percent. The world's largest toy chain has struggled to boost sales amid more competition from Amazon.com and a sluggish toy industry that is losing kids to electronics earlier than ever.

---

* Toys "R" Us 玩具反斗城　　* promotion n. 促銷
* Amazon.com 亞馬遜（一家網路購物平台的名稱）
* sluggish adj. 蕭條的

C 中文譯文對照
Chinese Translation

玩具反斗城（Toys "R" Us），在週五宣佈連續第 3 年的假期特賣營業額衰退。特賣為期 9 週，至隔年元月 4 日的同門市營業額減少了 2.7%。這間總部設於紐澤西州韋恩鎮（Wayne, New Jersey）的公司在聲明稿中表示，他們以較少的促銷來保護獲利。玩具反斗城在美國的收益佔營業額約 60%，減少了 5%。這間全球最大的玩具連鎖店面對更具競爭力的 Amazon.com 線上購物網站，掙扎地奮力增進營業額，而蕭條的玩具產業正以前所未有的速度被電子產品搶走小孩客群。

D 英譯中譯文討論 Discussions

1. 原文「Toys “R” Us Inc」，譯文未將「Inc」表示的「公司」譯出，並不影響譯文的正確性，大家也都知道「玩具反斗城」是間公司。

2. 原文「Same-store sales for the nine weeks through Jan 4 fell 2.7 percent.」，從原文可以知道拍賣是從 1 月 4 日往前推 9 個禮拜開始，大概是 11 月初左右，為求語意通順，在譯文中加入「特賣」和「隔年」，譯為「特賣為期 9 週，至隔年元月 4 日的同門市營業額減少了 2.7%。」。

3. 原 文「Revenue in the US, where it generates around 60 percent of its sales, declined by 5 percent.」，在譯文加入「數值」，其「its」表示「玩具反斗城的營業額」，譯作「玩具反斗城在美國的收益佔營業額約 60%，減少了 5%。」。

4. 原文「Amazon.com」，並未表明是為哪種性質的網站，為求讀者了解，在譯文加註該網站的性質，譯作「Amazon.com 線上購物網站」。

5. 原 文「losing kids to electronics earlier than ever」 中，「小孩」（kids） 是玩具業的主要客群，譯作「小孩客群」而不是直譯為「小孩」。」，亦可譯作「在電子產品的競爭下，蕭條的玩具產業正以前所未有的速度流失小孩客群」。

Unit 9

9.2 中英筆譯互譯要點【中譯英】

Tips 中譯英要點提示

1. 留意前後譯文的連貫性與流暢度，主詞在隨後接續的敘述中皆以代名詞表示，不要一直重複名詞主詞。

2. 日期月份需譯出英文字，不可以阿拉伯數字取代，日的部分則皆可。

3. 專業術語／名詞之字詞譯名需查證，同樣的字詞在不同專業領域表達的意涵不同。

4. 百分比譯法可以阿拉伯數字加百分比符號譯出，亦可譯出英文字。

5. 本身為英文名的專有名詞直接譯回原文，不需再附上中文譯文。

6. 其它：

   a 衰退用「decline」或「drop」皆可。

   b 營業額是「sale」。

   c 收益是「revenue」。

   d 總部設立地點的寫法是「地名 +based」。

玩具反斗城（Toys "R" Us），在週五宣佈連續第 3 年的假期特賣營業額衰退。特賣為期 9 週，至隔年元月 4 日的同門市營業額減少了 2.7%。這間總部設於紐澤西州韋恩鎮（Wayne, New Jersey）的公司在聲明稿中表示，他們以較少的促銷來保護獲利。玩具反斗城在美國的收益佔營業額約 60%，減少了 5%。這間全球最大的玩具連鎖店面對更具競爭力的 Amazon.com 線上購物網站，掙扎地奮力增進營業額，而蕭條的玩具產業正以前所未有的速度被電子產品搶走小孩客群。

■ 請試著翻劃底線的部分。

英文譯文對照 English Translation

Toys "R" Us Inc on Friday announced the third straight year of declining holiday sales.（詳看下頁討論 1） Same-store sales for the nine weeks through Jan 4 fell 2.7 percent.（詳看下頁討論 2） Fewer promotions were used in order to protect profitability, the Wayne, New Jersey-based company said in a statement. Revenue in the US, where it generates around 60 percent of its sales, declined by 5 percent.（詳看下頁討論 3） The world's largest toy chain has struggled to boost sales amid more competition from Amazon.com and a sluggish toy industry that is losing kids to electronics earlier than ever.（詳看下頁討論 4）

中譯英譯文討論 Discussions

1. 原文「玩具反斗城（Toys "R" Us），在週五宣佈連續第 3 年的假期特賣營業額衰退。」，亦可譯作「Toys "R" Us posted a decline in holiday sales for the third year in a row on Friday.」。

2. 原文「特賣為期 9 週，至隔年元月 4 日的同門市營業額減少了 2.7%。」，亦可譯作「Same-store sales for the nine weeks through the 4th of Jan fell 2.7%.」。

3. 原文「玩具反斗城在美國的收益佔營業額約 60%，減少了 5%。」，亦可譯作「Revenue has declined by 5% in the market where it generates around 60% of its sales.」。

4. 原文「這間全球最大的玩具連鎖店面對更具競爭力的 Amazon.com 線上購物網站，掙扎地奮力增進營業額，而蕭條的玩具產業正以前所未有的速度被電子產品搶走小孩客群。」，亦可譯作「The world's largest toy chain has fought hard to increase sales amid more competition from Amazon.com and a sluggish toy industry that is losing kids to electronics earlier than ever.」。

Unit 10

10.1 中英筆譯互譯要點【英譯中】

Tips 英譯中要點提示

1. 英語常用代名詞／指示代名詞連貫敘述，需適時在不容易了解該代名詞指向何者時，在譯文中把代名詞換成名詞。
2. 數值的譯文皆以阿拉伯數字表示。
3. 為了流暢度並讓讀者充分了解文章要表達的意思，可在不更改原意的前提下，適時加入譯出文。
4. 專業術語字詞的意思需查證，同樣的字詞在不同專業領域表達的意涵不同。
5. 國家名、城市名，以及專有名詞若有固定譯名皆需譯出，若是十分普遍常見的譯名，可不需再加註原文，否則第一次出現於文中時需以圓括號引註原文，其後則以譯名表示即可。

For the world's central banks slow, steady and predicable decision making is aim. So when interest rates are increased by a massive 6.5 percent by bankers meeting in the dead of night, it suggests there is something wrong.

With the arrival of the much feared Russian currency crisis and the mood in Moscow close to panic, Russians are right to be worried. The economy is heading for a lethal combination of deep recession and runaway inflation.

The majority of Russia's difficulties start overseas with high dependence on its oil-and-gas companies. Hydrocarbons dominate the economy accounting for over half the federal budget and two-thirds of exports. The links between the government and industry go deep with the state holding large stakes in both energy firms and the state- sponsored bank that fund them.

---

* the dead of night 夜深人靜
* runaway inflation 惡性通貨膨脹
* hydrocarbon [ˏhaɪdrəˋkarbən] n. 碳氫化合物
* recession [rɪˋsɛʃən] n. 經濟衰退

中文譯文對照
Chinese Translation

全世界的中央銀行業務目標是以緩慢、穩定、可預測的方式做決策。所以當銀行家們在夜深人靜時分聚首，又大舉將匯率提高 6.5 個百分點時，就暗示情況非常不妙。

過於懼怕俄羅斯貨幣危機（Russian currency crisis）真實上演，而首都莫斯科（Moscow）的氣氛也接近恐慌。俄羅斯人是該擔憂。經濟正朝極度衰退和惡性通貨膨脹的致命組合邁進。

俄羅斯的大多數災難從國外開始，因為俄羅斯極度依賴自己的石油與天然氣公司。光是碳氫化合物（hydrocarbons）就主導超過一半的聯邦經費，且佔總出口的三分之二。俄羅斯政府和工業有很深的關係，與許多能源公司和資助他們的國有銀行皆有重大利害關係。

D 英譯中譯文討論
iscussions

1. 適時在不容易了解該代名詞指向何者時，在譯文中把代名詞換成名詞。從前文可以知道原文「The majority of Russia's difficulties start overseas with high dependence on its oil-and-gas companies.」，其「its」是指「俄羅斯的」，所以在中文譯文中不譯為「俄羅斯的大多數災難從國外開始，因為極度依賴它的石油與天然氣公司。」，而是明確表達主詞「俄羅斯極度依賴自己的石油與天然氣公司」有助譯文流暢易懂。

2. 原文「The links between the government and industry go deep with the state holding large stakes in both energy firms and the state-sponsored bank that fund them.」，其「the state」指的是「國家」，也就是「俄羅斯」。

3. 「Moscow」是俄羅斯首都，譯文中加入「首都」兩字加深「莫斯科」與俄羅斯的關聯性。

4. 原文「deep recession」在譯文中加入「經濟」兩字，有助了解是什麼性質的「極度衰退」，譯為「經濟極度衰退」。

5. 原文「The majority of Russia's difficulties start overseas with high dependence on its oil-and-gas companies.」，亦可譯作「因為高度依賴自己的石油與天然氣公司，俄羅斯的大多數災難是從國外開始。」。

Unit 10

10.2 中英筆譯互譯要點【中譯英】

Tips 中譯英要點提示

1. 譯文前後的連貫性與流暢度需符合英語語法，主詞在隨後接續的敘述中盡量皆以其他名詞／代名詞／指示代名詞表示，不要一直重複名詞主詞。
2. 數字僅以阿拉伯數字譯出。
3. 英文名的專有名詞直接譯出，不需再附上中文譯文。
4. 看完整個句子、段落，了解其意思之後再譯出，每個句子皆需選擇文法與時態。
5. 翻譯時，為了流暢度並讓讀者充分了解文章要表達的意思，可在不更改原意的前提下，適時加入譯出文。避免錯字、異體字。

全世界的中央銀行業務目標是以緩慢、穩定、可預測的方式做決策。所以當銀行家們在夜深人靜時分聚首，又大舉將匯率提高 6.5 個百分點時，就暗示情況非常不妙。

過於懼怕俄羅斯貨幣危機 (Russian currency crisis) 真實上演，而首都莫斯科 (Moscow) 的氣氛也接近恐慌。俄羅斯人是該擔憂。經濟正朝極度衰退和惡性通貨膨脹的致命組合邁進。

俄羅斯的大多數災難從國外開始，因為俄羅斯極度依賴自己的石油與天然氣公司。光是碳氫化合物 (hydrocarbons) 就主導超過一半的聯邦經費，且佔總出口的三分之二。俄羅斯政府和工業有很深的關係，與許多能源公司和資助他們的國有銀行皆有重大利害關係。

■ 請試著翻劃底線的部分。

E 英文譯文對照
English Translation

For the world's central banks slow, steady and predicable decision making is aim.（詳看下頁討論 1）So when interest rates are increased by a massive 6.5 percent by bankers meeting in the dead of night, it suggests there is something wrong.

With the arrival of the much feared Russian currency crisis and the mood in Moscow close to panic, Russians are right to be worried.（詳看下頁討論 2）The economy is heading for a lethal combination of deep recession and runaway inflation.

The majority of Russia's difficulties start overseas with high dependence on its oil-and-gas companies.（詳看下頁討論 3）Hydrocarbons dominate the economy accounting for over half the federal budget and two-thirds of exports. The links between the government and industry go deep with the state holding large stakes in both energy firms and the state- sponsored bank that fund them.

D 中譯英譯文討論
iscussions

1. 本文主體為陳述常態與未來會發生的事，大多以現在式與未來式文法表達。原文「全世界的中央銀行業務目標是以緩慢、穩定、可預測的方式做決策」，亦可譯為「The aim of the world's central banks is to make decisions in a slow, steady and predictable way」。

2. 首都莫斯科可直接譯為「Moscow」，不需再加上「capital」，因為不會影響莫斯科是俄羅斯首都的事實，譯出「capital」僅有助於讀者理解。原文「過於懼怕俄羅斯貨幣危機（Russian currency crisis）真實上演，而首都莫斯科（Moscow）的氣氛也接近恐慌。俄羅斯人是該擔憂。」，亦可譯作「Russians are right to be worried. The mood in Moscow is close to panic as the much feared currency crisis becomes a reality.」

3. 原文「俄羅斯的大多數災難從國外開始，因為俄羅斯極度依賴自己的石油與天然氣公司。」，亦可譯作「The problems for Russia stem from being highly dependent on the international market for its oil-and-gas companies.」。

4. 譯文前後的連貫性與流暢度需符合英語語法，前文已提過「Russia」，本段隨後接續的敘述在「俄羅斯」的部分就應以其他名詞「the country、the state」代替。

Unit 11

11.1 中英筆譯互譯要點【英譯中】

Tips 英譯中要點提示

1. 英語常用代名詞／指示代名詞／名詞連貫敘述，這裡使用的 we 和 our，指的是「我們（國家）的」，翻譯時視文章可理解度與通順與否來斟酌是否譯出「國家」。
2. 年代以阿拉伯數字表示即可，20th century、21st century 可譯為「20 世紀」、「21 世紀」或是「二十世紀」、「二十一世紀」皆可。二十世紀指的是西元 1900 年 ~1999 年。二十一世紀指的是西元 2000 年 ~2099 年。
3. 要特別留意英語語法中的時態、被動語態、倒裝句，譯文需符合中文語法，不可直譯。

A new national education debate is needed to build on the extraordinary gains that have been made since 1976. However, our schools and universities are still geared towards the needs of the last century, with students simply assessed on regurgitating facts, but often incapable or unwilling to think independently.

Part 3

Universities are often far from impressed with school leavers, and even go as far as to set their own exams to separate the gifted from the merely well drilled. Employers are equally critical of the lack of skills exhibited by those they are looking to employ. Meanwhile, young people themselves show little sign of being happier or more satisfied with their lives, with increasing incidence of stress and depression.

The competitive world that the 21st century has become needs young people who have the ability to think creatively, work-cooperatively, and have highly developed personal and social skills.

---

* building on 在…的基礎上發展　　* geared towards 適合於
* regurgitate v. 在文章中是「照本宣科」的意思。
* school leaver 高中應屆畢業生　　* critical of 挑剔

中文譯文對照
Chinese Translation

我們需要一個新的全國性教育辯論會，並以自 1976 年達成的許多卓越進展基礎上發展。然而我們的學校和大學仍僅適合上個世紀的需求，學生以照本宣科的論據做測驗，但是常沒有能力或不願意獨立思考。

大學常對高中應屆畢業生的表現非常不滿意，甚至不滿意到得制定自己的測驗，要從僅是會讀書的人之中，篩選出有才智天賦的人。雇主也同樣挑剔那些他們正在尋找雇用的員工缺乏技能展現。同時，年輕人並沒有顯得更快樂或更滿意自己的生活，還有越來越多伴隨而來的壓力和沮喪。

二十一世紀已經成為競爭性強的世界，需要年輕人有創造力地思考，分工合作，並且擁有高度發展的個人與社交技能。

D 英譯中譯文討論
Discussions

1. 原文「A new national education debate is needed to build on the extraordinary gains that have been made since 1976.」，為符合中文語法與譯文通順，了解前後文關聯性後，在譯文加入「我們」，譯為「我們需要一個新的全國性教育辯論會，並以自 1976 年達成的許多卓越進展基礎上發展。」。

2. Our schools and universities，指的是「我們國家的學校和大學」，整篇文章以 we「我們」做為第一人稱貫穿敘述，除非文章一開始即譯為「我們國家」，否則以代名詞「我們」譯出已可清楚明白譯文所指之意。原文「Universities are often far from impressed with school leavers」，英語語法中的被動語態，這句直譯為「大學幾乎不對高中應屆畢業生的表現感到佩服」，但是這樣的譯文並不通順，故取其表達的意思，譯為「大學常對高中應屆畢業生的表現非常不滿意」。

3. and even go as far as to set their own exams to separate the gifted from the merely well drilled，為了譯文完整性，加入「甚至不滿意到」，解釋了為何要制定自己的測驗的原故，譯作「甚至不滿意到得制定自己的測驗，要從僅是會讀書的人之中，篩選出有才智天賦的人。」

Unit 11

11.2 中英筆譯互譯要點【中譯英】

Tips 中譯英要點提示

1. 譯文前後的連貫性與流暢度需符合英語語法，主詞在隨後接續的敘述中盡量皆以代名詞／指示代名詞／其他名詞表示，不要一直重複名詞主詞。
2. 英語語法有時態、調性變化，中翻英時必須看完整個句子、段落，了解其意思之後再譯出，每個句子、子句皆需選擇文法與時態。
3. 特別留意中文不易在文字中看出英語語法的時態與被動語態、形容詞子句等，翻譯時需符合英語語法。
4. 年分、數字僅以阿拉伯數字譯出即可。

主題短文 Article

我們需要一個新的全國性教育辯論會，並以自 1976 年達成的許多卓越進展基礎上發展。然而我們的學校和大學仍僅適合上個世紀的需求，學生以照本宣科的論據做測驗，但是常沒有能力或不願意獨立思考。

大學常對高中應屆畢業生的表現非常不滿意，甚至不滿意到得制定自己的測驗，要從僅是會讀書的人之中，篩選出有才智天賦的人。雇主也同樣挑剔那些他們正在尋找雇用的員工缺乏技能展現。同時，年輕人並沒有顯得更快樂或更滿意自己的生活，還有越來越多伴隨而來的壓力和沮喪。

二十一世紀已經成為競爭性強的世界，需要年輕人有創造力地思考，分工合作，並且擁有高度發展的個人與社交技能。

■ 請試著翻劃底線的部分。

A new national education debate is needed to build on the extraordinary gains that have been made since 1976.（詳看下頁討論 1）However, our schools and universities are still geared towards the needs of the last century（詳看下頁討論 2）, with students simply assessed on regurgitating facts, but often incapable or unwilling to think independently.

Universities are often far from impressed with school leavers, and even go as far as to set their own exams（詳看下頁討論 3）to separate the gifted from the merely well drilled. Employers are equally critical of the lack of skills exhibited by those they are looking to employ. Meanwhile young people themselves show little sign of being happier or more satisfied with their lives, with increasing incidence of stress, and depression.（詳看下頁討論 4）

The competitive world that the 21st century has become needs young people who have the ability to think creatively, work-cooperatively, and have highly developed personal and social skills.（詳看下頁討論 5）

D 中譯英譯文討論 Discussions

1. 「我們需要一個新的全國性教育辯論會，並以自 1976 年達成的許多卓越進展基礎上發展。」，亦可譯為「In order to build on the many exceptional gains made since 1976, we need a new national education debate.」。

2. 「然而我們的學校和大學仍僅適合上個世紀的需求」，亦可譯為「But our schools and universities are still fit for the requirements of the last century」。

3. 「大學常對高中應屆畢業生的表現非常不滿意，甚至不滿意到得制定自己的測驗」，亦可譯為「Universities are often not impressed by school leavers at all; they even set their own exams to sort the gifted from the well-trained.」。

4. 「同時，年輕人並沒有顯得更快樂或更滿意自己的生活，還有越來越多伴隨而來的壓力和沮喪。」，亦可譯作「Meanwhile, with increasing levels of stress and depression, young people do not appear to be happier or more satisfied with their lives.」。

5. 「二十一世紀已經成為競爭性強的世界，需要年輕人有創造力地思考，分工合作，並且擁有高度發展的個人與社交技能。」，亦可譯作「The 21st century has become a competitive world, and it requires young people to think creatively, work co-operatively, and have highly developed personal and social skills」。

Unit 12

12.1 中英筆譯互譯要點【英譯中】

Tips 英譯中要點提示

1. 翻譯時要留意譯文前後的連貫性與流暢度，一些主詞／代名詞／指示代名詞可在隨後接續的譯文中省略。

2. 不可用直譯方式逐字翻譯，需看完整個句子、整個段落，了解意思後再譯出。不要執著在每個英語單字的意思，在不同內容下，會有不同的詮釋方式，要譯其意。

3. 譯文以白話文為主，以正常速度唸文章時，該停頓換氣時，原則上就是需要下逗號的位置，但仍視原文而定。

4. 百分比以符號代替即可。

The world we now find ourselves in has become an interconnected marketplace, and we need to prepare our kids for it.

That preparation must include such skills as speaking outstanding English. English has maintained its position as the key language in global business, science, and technology, so it is imperative that we address the alarmingly low levels of English proficiency that we see in many of our students. According to recent state test data, only 30% of US students are proficient English-language readers.

Our kids need to be prepared to navigate a global economy in which a key advantage in attaining higher-paying jobs will be knowledge of languages and cultures other than our own.

It is inevitable that China will be a major economic, political, and cultural force in our children's future. It is time to start preparing them, so that they are able to engage, collaborate, and compete with their Chinese peers.

∗ interconnect v. 相互聯繫
∗ address v. 設法解決
∗ navigate v. 操縱；航行於
∗ collaborate v. 合作
∗ imperative adj. 迫切的；急需處理的
∗ attain v. 獲得；達到
∗ peer n. 同儕

Part 3

C 中文譯文對照
Chinese Translation

我們現在身處在一個已成為相互聯繫的市場裡，我們需要讓孩子準備好來應付這一切。

準備工作必須包括像是擁有說一口流利英語的技能。英語在全球商業、科學、科技領域中，仍屬最重要的語言，所以設法解決在國內許多學生身上看到的那令人擔憂的低英語精熟度，是十分迫切的。根據最近期的州考試資料，美國的學生僅 30% 可精熟閱讀英語。

我們的孩子必須準備好縱橫於全球經濟中，擁有其他語言和文化的知識，是獲得高薪工作的關鍵優勢。

無可避免地，在我們孩子的未來，中國大陸必然是主要的經濟、政治和文化勢力。是時候開始讓我們的孩子準備好，他們才能進擊、合作，並與中國大陸的同儕競爭。

1. 原文「The world we now find ourselves in has become an interconnected marketplace and we need to prepare our kids for it.」，其代名詞「we」，貫穿整篇文章，在本文內容裡指的是「我們」，以及代表「美國的父母們」。**代名詞出現的次數與譯文譯出的次數沒有一定關係，為了譯文通順，在語意明確的情況下，需省略不譯**，譯為「我們現在身處在一個已成為相互聯繫的市場裡，我們需要讓孩子準備好來應付這一切。」。

2. 原　文「English has maintained its position as the key language in global business, science and technology, so it is imperative that we address the alarmingly low levels of English proficiency that we see in many of our students.」，加入「領域」兩字使譯文更為通順，譯為「英語在全球商業、科學、科技領域中，仍屬最重要的語言，所以設法解決在國內許多學生身上看到的那令人擔憂的低英語精熟度，是十分迫切的。」。

3. 原文「Our kids need to be prepared to navigate a global economy in which a key advantage in attaining higher-paying jobs will be knowledge of languages and cultures other than our own.」，其「our kids」是泛指所有美國父母的小孩們，譯作「我們的孩子必須準備好縱橫於全球經濟中，擁有其他語言和文化的知識，是獲得高薪工作的關鍵優勢。」。

4. 原　文「It is time to start preparing them, so that they are able to engage, collaborate and compete with their Chinese peers.」，其代名詞受詞「them」，指的是「我們的小孩們」，譯作「是時候開始讓我們的孩子準備好，他們才能進擊、合作，並與中國大陸的同儕競爭。」

Unit 12

12.2 中英筆譯互譯要點【中譯英】

Tips 中譯英要點提示

1. 譯文前後的連貫性與流暢度需符合英語語法，主詞在隨後接續的敘述中盡量皆以代名詞／指示代名詞／其他名詞表示，不要一直重複名詞主詞。

2. 國家名若是十分普遍常見的譯名，可不需再加註原文。

3. 數值僅以阿拉伯數字譯出即可，百分比可譯出或以符號表示皆可。

4. 要特別留意中文語法中不易看出的英語語法時態、被動語態、倒裝句。

我們現在身處在一個已成為相互聯繫的市場裡，我們需要讓孩子準備好來應付這一切。

準備工作必須包括像是擁有說一口流利英語的技能。英語在全球商業、科學、科技領域中，仍屬最重要的語言，所以設法解決在國內許多學生身上看到的那令人擔憂的低英語精熟度，是十分迫切的。根據最近期的州考試資料，美國的學生僅30%可精熟閱讀英語。

我們的孩子必須準備好縱橫於全球經濟中，擁有其他語言和文化的知識，是獲得高薪工作的關鍵優勢。

無可避免地，在我們孩子的未來，中國大陸必然是主要的經濟、政治和文化勢力。是時候開始讓我們的孩子準備好，他們才能進擊、合作，並與中國大陸的同儕競爭。

■ 請試著翻劃底線的部分。

英文譯文對照
English Translation

The world we now find ourselves in has become an interconnected marketplace and we need to prepare our kids for it.（詳看下頁討論 1）

That preparation must include such skills as speaking outstanding English. English has maintained its position as the key language in global business, science and technology, so it is imperative that we address the alarmingly low levels of English proficiency that we see in many of our students.（詳看下頁討論 2） According to recent state test data only 30% of US students are proficient English-language readers.（詳看下頁討論 3）

Our kids need to be prepared to navigate a global economy in which a key advantage in attaining higher-paying jobs will be knowledge of languages and cultures other than our own.（詳看下頁討論 4）

It is inevitable that China will be a major economic, political and cultural force in our children's future.（詳看下頁討論 5） It is time to start preparing them, so that they are able to engage, collaborate and compete with their Chinese peers.

D 中譯英譯文討論 Discussions

1. 原文「我們現在身處在一個已成為相互聯繫的市場裡，我們需要讓孩子準備好來應付這一切。」，亦可譯為「We are now living in a global interconnected economy, so it's necessary to prepare our kids for it.」，其代名詞「it」即表示「a global interconnected economy」。

2. 原文「準備工作必須包括像是擁有說一口流利英語的技能。英語在全球商業、科學、科技領域中，仍屬最重要的語言，所以設法解決在國內許多學生身上看到的那令人擔憂的低英語精確度，是十分迫切的。」，亦可譯為「Since English remains a key language in global business, science, and technology, the preparation must include such skills as speaking fluent English, so addressing the alarmingly low levels of English proficiency that we see in many of our students is urgent.」。

3. 原文「根據最近期的州考試資料，美國的學生僅30%可精熟閱讀英語。」，亦可譯作「According to the latest U.S. state test data, only 30 percent of students are proficient English readers.」。

4. 原文「我們的孩子必須準備好縱橫於全球經濟中，擁有其他語言和文化的知識，是獲得高薪工作的關鍵優勢。」，亦可譯作「We also need to prepare our kids to navigate a global workplace in which knowledge of languages and cultures other than our own is vital.」。

5. 原文「無可避免地，在我們孩子的未來，中國大陸必然是主要的經濟、政治和文化勢力。」，亦可譯為「In our children's future, China will have an inevitable economic, political and cultural impact.」。

Unit 13

13.1 中英筆譯互譯要點【英譯中】

Tips 英譯中要點提示

1. 英語常用代名詞／指示代名詞／名詞連貫敘述，需適時在不容易了解該代名詞指向何者時，在譯文中把「你（的）／我／他（她）／其／那些／這／那」…等代名詞／其他名詞換成主詞名詞。

2. 專有名詞國家名若有固定譯名皆需譯出，若是十分普遍常見的譯名，可不需再加註原文，否則第一次出現於文中時需以圓括號引註原文，其後則以譯名表示即可。

3. 翻譯時，為了流暢度並讓讀者充分了解文章要表達的意思，可在不更改原意的前提下，適時加入譯出文。避免錯字、異體字。

The current trend of pushing Mandarin teaching in schools and colleges only provides added incentives for U.S. companies to continue supporting irresponsible policies.

Instead of teaching Mandarin, why don't we invest in teaching science, engineering, and mathematics in the hope of sparking innovation? Let's bring the focus back on returning production to the U.S. and lowering the unemployment rate. If China wants to continue with its open access to our markets, let's demand that it employs stricter labor and environmental regulations. We should also educate our children about all these issues. Failure to do so will not only cause further harm to our economy, but also do a great disservice to future generations.

Part 3

---

* incentive n. 激勵
* access to 機會；權利
* disservice n. 幫倒忙；傷害
* in the hope of 懷著…的希望
* employ v. 採取

中文譯文對照
Chinese Translation

推動在大學和學院的普通話（Mandarin）教學，只是更加激勵美國企業繼續支持不負責任的政策。

懷著燃起創新的希望，與其教授普通話，我們何不投入於教授科學、工程學，以及數學呢？讓我們把焦點回到把生產端移回美國並降低失業率。如果中國大陸想繼續暢通進入我國市場，那就讓我們要求它採取更嚴格的勞工與環境規章。我們也應該教育小孩有關所有這些憂慮。若不這麼做，不只對我們的經濟造成更多傷害，也會造成未來世代的經濟損害。

1. 原　文「The current trend of pushing Mandarin teaching in schools and colleges only provides added incentives for U.S. companies to continue supporting irresponsible policies.」，從「schools and colleges」可以知道其「schools」指的是「大學；系所」，而不是泛指所有學校，亦可譯作「在大學和學院推動教授普通話（Mandarin），只是更加激勵美國企業繼續支持不負責任的政策。」。

2. 原文「Instead of teaching Mandarin, why don't we invest in teaching science, engineering and mathematics in the hope of sparking innovation?」，需看完整段內容，再以符合中文語法的譯文譯出，亦可譯作「與其教授普通話，我們何不投入於教授科學、工程學和數學，並期望從中激起創新呢？」。

3. 原　文「If China wants to continue with its open access to our markets, let's demand that it employs stricter labor and environmental regulations.」，其代名詞主詞「it」指的是「China」，其「our markets」指的是「U.S. markets」，亦可譯作「如果中國大陸想繼續暢通進入美國市場，那我們就強烈要求中國大陸採取更嚴格的勞工與環境規章。」。

4. 原 文「Failure to do so will not only cause further harm to our economy, but also do a great disservice to future generations.」，其「not only... but also」為譯出文的重點字「不只…也」，譯作「若不這麼做，不只對我們的經濟造成更多傷害，也會造成未來世代的經濟損害。」。

Unit 13

13.2 中英筆譯互譯要點【中譯英】

Tips 中譯英要點提示

1. 譯文前後的連貫性與流暢度需符合英語語法，主詞在隨後接續的敘述中盡量皆以代名詞／指示代名詞／其他名詞表示，不要一直重複名詞主詞。

2. 國家名、專有名詞若有固定譯名皆需查證。

3. 本文為敘述現況的文章，主體以現在式為主，但翻譯時需符合句子敘述所需使用的時態。

4. 其他：

   a 科學是「science」。
   b 工程學是「engineering」。
   c 數學是「mathematics」。

推動在大學和學院的普通話（Mandarin）教學，只是更加激勵美國企業繼續支持不負責任的政策。

懷著燃起創新的希望，與其教授普通話，我們何不投入於教授科學、工程學，以及數學呢？讓我們把焦點回到把生產端移回美國並降低失業率。如果中國大陸想繼續暢通進入我國市場，那就讓我們要求它採取更嚴格的勞工與環境規章。我們也應該教育小孩有關所有這些憂慮。若不這麼做，不只對我們的經濟造成更多傷害，也會造成未來世代的經濟損害。

Part 3

■ 請試著翻譯底線的部分。

E 英文譯文對照 English Translation

The current trend of pushing Mandarin teaching in schools and colleges only provides added incentives for U.S. companies to continue supporting irresponsible policies.

Instead of teaching Mandarin, why don't we invest in teaching science, engineering and mathematics in the hope of sparking innovation?（詳看下頁討論 1）Let's bring the focus back on returning production to the U.S. and lowering the unemployment rate.（詳看下頁討論 2）If China wants to continue with its open access to our markets, let's demand that it employs stricter labor and environmental regulations. We should also educate our children about all these issues.（詳看下頁討論 3）Failure to do so will not only cause further harm to our economy, but also do a great disservice to future generations.（詳看下頁討論 4）

D 中譯英譯文討論
iscussions

1. 原文「懷著燃起創新的希望，與其教授普通話，我們何不投入於教授科學、工程學，以及數學呢？」，亦可譯作「Instead of teaching Mandarin, let's invest in teaching science, engineering, and mathematics in the hope of inspiring innovation.」。

2. 原文「讓我們把焦點回到把生產端移回美國並降低失業率。」，在這裡可用所有格代名詞「our」來表示前文已提及的「the U.S.」，亦可譯作「Let's focus on bringing production back to the U.S. and lowering our unemployment rate」。

3. 原文「我們也應該教育小孩有關所有這些憂慮。」，亦可譯作「We should also educate our children about all these worries.」。

4. 原文「若不這麼做，不只對我們的經濟造成更多傷害，也會造成未來世代的經濟損害。」，亦可譯作「If we fail to do so, we will not only cause our economy further damage, but also do a great disservice to later generations.」。

Unit 14

14.1 中英筆譯互譯要點【英譯中】

Tips 英譯中要點提示

1. 英語的破折號用於介紹某種説法，加入強調語氣；可用於下定義，或是解釋。也用於隔開兩個子句。**中文譯文可譯出破折號或以逗號取代皆可。**

2. 英語語法與中文語法不同，不可用直譯方式逐字翻譯，需看完整個句子、整個段落，了解意思後再譯出。

3. 專業術語／名詞之字詞譯名需查證，同樣的字詞在不同專業領域表達的意涵不同。

4. 數值以阿拉伯數字表示即可。

5. 破折號用於介紹某種説法，加入強調語氣、定義，或是解釋。也用於隔開兩個子句。

主題短文 Article

Thirty years after its introduction, bilingual education is still the subject of controversy.

Bilingual education has, in recent years, sparked as much controversy as any other education issue.

It is agreed by both educators and parents that the main goals in educating students with a native language other than English are mastery of English and content in academic areas. But the best way to achieve these goals and how important it is to preserve children's original language in the process has resulted in a heated academic and political battle.

Teachers use several methods to instruct students whose English is limited – including immersion, transitional bilingual education, and development or maintenance bilingual education.

Part 3

∗ bilingual adj. 雙語的
∗ content 在這裡是「具體內容」的意思，不是「滿足」的意思。
∗ immersion n. 沉浸式　　∗ transitional adj. 過渡期的

中文譯文對照
Chinese Translation

在推行了 30 年後，雙語教育至今仍是個爭議話題。

近年來，雙語教育所點燃的爭議，就跟任何其他教育議題的爭議一樣多。

教育工作者跟家長一致認同，教育英語非母語的學生，主要目標是要讓學生精通英語並充分了解學業領域的具體內容。但是學界激烈的討論與政治上的論戰，仍在如何以最好的方式達成這些目標，以及過程中保有學生精通原始母語的重要性上爭論不休。

教師用一些方法來指導英語能力有限的學生—包括沉浸式（immersion）、過渡期（transitional）的雙語教育，以及發展期（developmental）或維持期（maintenance）的雙語教育。

D 英譯中譯文討論
Discussions

1. 原　文「Thirty years after its introduction, bilingual education is still the subject of controversy.」，句中的代名詞所有格「its」表示「bilingual education」，在譯文加入「至今」來跟「**30 年後**」呼應，亦可譯作「雙語教育在推行了 **30** 年後，至今仍是個爭議話題。」。

2. 原文「with a native language other than English」，意思是「母語為英文以外的語言」，譯作「英語非母語」。

3. 原文「It is agreed by both educators and parents that the main goals in educating students with a native language other than English are mastery of English and content in academic areas.」，其「mastery」用在「content」時，譯作「充分了解具體內容」而非「精通」。從前後文可以知道整個段落在說明以英語與學生本身母語的雙語教育狀況，亦可譯作「老師與家長皆有共識，以英語來教育英語非母語的學生，主要目標是要讓學生精通英語並能充分了解學業領域的具體內容。」。

Unit 14

14.2 中英筆譯互譯要點【中譯英】

Tips 中譯英要點提示

1. 數值通常以阿拉伯數字表示即可，但若是置於句首用於表示數量的量詞，通常在譯出文為英語時會以英文字譯出。
2. 英語的破折號用於介紹某種說法，加入強調語氣；可用於下定義或是解釋。也用於隔開兩個子句。
3. 隨後接續的敘述中盡量皆以代名詞／指示代名詞／其他名詞表示，不要一直重複名詞主詞。
4. 英語語法有時態、詞性變化，中翻英時必須看完整個句子、段落，了解其意思之後再譯出，每個句子皆需選擇文法與時態。
5. 其它：

   a 雙語教育是「bilingual education」。

   b 母　語　是「mother tongue」、「native language」、「original language」。

在推行了 30 年後，雙語教育至今仍是個爭議話題。

近年來，雙語教育所點燃的爭議，就跟任何其他教育議題的爭議一樣多。

教育工作者跟家長一致認同，教育英語非母語的學生，主要目標是要讓學生精通英語並充分了解學業領域的具體內容。但是學界激烈的討論與政治上的論戰，仍在如何以最好的方式達成這些目標，以及過程中保有學生精通原始母語的重要性上爭論不休。

教師用一些方法來指導英語能力有限的學生一包括沉浸式（immersion）、過渡期（transitional）的雙語教育，以及發展期（developmental）或維持期（maintenance）的雙語教育。

■ 請試著翻劃底線的部分。

英文譯文對照 English Translation

Thirty years after its introduction, bilingual education is still the subject of controversy.（詳見下頁討論 1）

Bilingual education has, in recent years, sparked as much controversy as any other education issue.

It is agreed by both educators and parents that the main goals in educating students with a native language other than English are mastery of English and content in academic areas.（詳見下頁討論 2） But the best way to achieve these goals and how important it is to preserve children's original language in the process has resulted in a heated academic and political battle.（詳見下頁討論 3）

Teachers use several methods to instruct students whose English is limited – including immersion, transitional bilingual education, and development or maintenance bilingual education.

中譯英譯文討論
Discussions

1. 原文「在推行了30年後，雙語教育至今仍是個爭議話題。」，亦可以過去式被動語態譯作「**Thirty years after bilingual education was introduced, it is still generating controversy.**」，或是「**Thirty years after bilingual education was introduced, controversy is still being generated.**」。

2. 原文「教育工作者跟家長一致認同，教育英語非母語的學生，主要目標是要讓學生精通英語並充分了解學業領域的具體內容。」，其「讓」亦可譯作「有助；協助」的意思，「Educators and parents agree that when educating students who are non native speakers, the main goals are helping them master English and content in academic areas.」。

3. 原文「但是學界激烈的討論與政治上的論戰，仍在如何以最好的方式達成這些目標，以及過程中保有學生精通原始母語的重要性上爭論不休。」，亦可譯作「**But an acrimonious academic and political debate continues over what the best way to reach these goals is and the importance of preserving students' mother tongue in the process.**」。

Part 3

Unit 15

15.1 中英筆譯互譯要點【英譯中】

Tips 英譯中要點提示

1. 國家名、城市名、公司組織名，以及專有名詞若有固定譯名皆需譯出，如果是十分普遍常見的譯名，可不需再加註原文，否則第一次出現於文中時需以圓括號引註原文，其後則以譯名表示即可。

2. 譯文以白話文為主，以正常速度唸文章時，該停頓換氣時，原則上就是需要下逗號的位置，但仍視原文而定。

3. 英語語法與中文語法不同，不可用直譯方式逐字翻譯，需看完整個句子、整個段落，了解意思後再譯出。

4. 不要執著在每個英語單字的意思，要譯其意。

5. 在英語原文中有以引號「“ ”」標註的文字，在譯文加上單引號強調譯文，再以圓括弧加註原文。

The government's counter-terrorism strategy has been fiercely criticized by teachers for stifling classroom discussions on sensitive issue with children afraid that they will be reported to the police, and teachers uneasy with their obligation to do so.

The "Prevent Strategy" to tackle radicalization has turned teachers into "spies", resulting in teachers who are unwilling to discuss current affairs for fear that children will express controversial views, a teaching union has claimed.

Children require space to raise and debate difficult topics, a series of delegates told the National Union of Teachers' conference in Harrogate.

The new duty to actively promote British values to counter extremist views has also angered delegates. They claim that all it has done is stigmatize and alienate young Muslims.

---

* prevent strategy 預防策略
* radicalization [ˏrædɪkḷaɪˋzeʃən] n. 激進
* National Union of Teachers 全國教師工會
* Harrogate 哈洛蓋特市
* stigmatize [ˋstɪgməˏtaɪz] n. 帶來恥辱
* Muslim n. 穆斯林教徒

中文譯文對照
Chinese Translation

教師因課堂裡討論敏感議題的窒息氛圍，嚴厲批評政府的反恐策略，因為學童擔憂自己會被舉報警方處理，而教師們更是對這個舉報的義務憂慮不安。

教師工會主張這個要逮到激進分子的「預防策略」（Prevent strategy），儼然把教師變成了「間諜」，導致教師因害怕學童會表達出有爭議的觀點，而不願意討論時事。

一連串的與會代表在哈洛蓋特市（Harrogate）舉行的全國教師工會（National Union of Teachers）研討會中説明，學童需要空間來引起並辯論棘手的話題。

積極發揚英國價值以反對極端主義者觀點的新義務也激怒了與會代表們。這些代表主張這些做法全是在汙名化並疏離年輕穆斯林（Muslims）。

D 英譯中譯文討論
iscussions

1. 原文「The “Prevent Stragegy” to tackle radicalization has turned teachers into “spies”, resulting in teachers who are unwilling to discuss current affairs for fear that children will express controversial views, a teaching union has claimed.」，英語語法中，敘述人常放在敘述內容之後，但中文語法慣用先表明說話者為何，在譯文中先說明發表言論者有助譯文脈絡清楚，譯文置於引號內以強調內容，亦可譯作「教師工會主張，這個目的逮到激進分子的「預防策略」(Prevent strategy)，儼然把教師變成了「間諜」。」。

2. 原文「Children require space to raise and debate difficult topics, a series of delegates told the National Union of Teachers’ conference in Harrogate.」，英語語法中，敘述人常放在敘述內容之後，但中文語法慣用先表明說話者為何，在譯文中先說明發表言論者有助譯文脈絡清楚，儘量不把敘述人放在句尾。

3. 原文「The new duty to actively promote British values to counter extremist views has also angered delegates. They claim that all it has done is stigmatize and alienate young Muslims.」，一般常見的譯法是將 Islam、Muslim 皆譯為「回教徒」，但這是個十分籠統的譯法，較為慎重的譯法應將 Islam 譯為「伊斯蘭教」；Muslim 譯為「穆斯林」並附上原文。

Unit 15

15.2 中英筆譯互譯要點【中譯英】

Tips 中譯英要點提示

1. 譯文前後的連貫性與流暢度需符合英語語法，主詞在隨後接續的敘述中盡量皆以代名詞／指示代名詞／其他名詞表示，不要一直重複名詞主詞。
2. 英文引號用於強調內容。
3. 本身為英文名的專有名詞直接譯回原文，不需再附上中文譯文。
4. 其他：

   a 批評可寫成「criticise」英式、「criticize」美式。

   b 汙名化可寫成「stigmatise」英式、「stigmatize」美式。

   c 逮到是「tackle」。

   d 反恐策略是「counter-terrorism strategy」。

   e 英國價值是「British values」。

主題短文 Article

教師因課堂裡討論敏感議題的窒息氛圍，嚴厲批評政府的反恐策略，因為學童擔憂自己會被舉報警方處理，而教師們更是對這個舉報的義務憂慮不安。

教師工會主張這個要逮到激進分子的「預防策略」（Prevent strategy），儼然把教師變成了「間諜」，導致教師因害怕學童會表達出有爭議的觀點，而不願意討論時事。

一連串的與會代表在哈洛蓋特市（Harrogate）舉行的全國教師工會（National Union of Teachers）研討會中說明，學童需要空間來引起並辯論棘手的話題。

積極發揚英國價值以反對極端主義者觀點的新義務也激怒了與會代表們。這些代表主張這些做法全這是在汙名化並疏離年輕穆斯林（Muslims）。

■ 請試著翻劃底線的部分。

Part 3

E 英文譯文對照 English Translation

The government's counter-terrorism strategy has been fiercely criticised by teachers for stifling classroom discussions on sensitive issue with children afaid that they will be reported to the police, and teachers uneasy with their obligation to do so.

The "Prevent Strategy" to tackle radicalization has turned teachers into "spies", resulting in teachers who are unwilling to discuss current affairs for fear that children will express controversial views, a teaching union has claimed. （詳看下頁討論 1）

Children require space to raise and debate difficult topics, a series of delegates told the National Union of Teachers' conference in Harrogate. （詳看下頁討論 2）

The new duty to actively promote British values to counter extremist views has also angered delegates. They claim that all it has done is stigmatize and alienate young Muslims. （詳看下頁討論 3）

D 中譯英譯文討論
Discussions

1. 原文「教師工會主張這個要逮到激進分子的「預防策略」(Prevent strategy)，儼然把教師變成了「間諜」，導致教師因害怕學童會表達出有爭議的觀點，而不願意討論時事。」，亦可譯作「A teaching union has raised fears that teachers are being turned into spies by the Prevent strategy on tackling radicalization. Many teachers are unwilling to allow pupils to discuss current affairs for fear of children expressing controversial views.」。

2. 原文「一連串的與會代表在哈洛蓋特市 (Harrogate) 舉行的全國教師工會 (National Union of Teachers) 研討會中說明，學童需要空間來引起並辯論棘手的話題。」，亦可譯作「A series of speakers at the National Union of Teachers' conference in Harrogate disputed the policy, arguing that children needed space in order to feel free to discuss difficult topics.」。

3. 原文「積極發揚英國價值以反對極端主義者觀點的新義務也激怒了與會代表們。這些代表主張這些做法全這是在汙名化並疏離年輕穆斯林 (Muslims)。」，亦可譯作「The policy of promoting British values in schools was also criticized by delegates, saying the effect was to stigmatize and alienate young Muslims..」。

Unit 16

16.1 中英筆譯互譯要點【英譯中】

Tips 英譯中要點提示

1. 金額以阿拉伯數字合併金額單位表示，如 3 million 譯為 300 萬。
2. 國家名、城市名，以及專有名詞若有固定譯名皆需譯出，若是十分普遍常見的譯名，可不需再加註原文，否則第一次出現於文中時需以圓括號引註原文，其後則以譯名表示即可。
3. 英文標點符號分號「；」，用於連接獨立的子句。顯示出兩個子句之間的相關性。
4. 不可用直譯方式逐字翻譯，需看完整個句子、整個段落，了解意思後再譯出，需配合英語的動詞時態變化、名詞單複數。不要執著在每個英語單字的意思，要譯其意。

主題短文 Article

Afghanistan is a remote, mountainous, and land-locked country in southwestern Asia.

The total population of Afghanistan is about 22 million. In the mid-1990s, about 3 million were nomads, and millions more were refugees living beyond Afghanistan's borders. There are two major ethnic groups in Afghanistan are Pashtun and Hazara.

The two principal languages spoken in Afghanistan are Dari, a form of Persian, and Pashto（also spelled Pashtu）, which is also spoken in some areas of the neighboring country, Pakistan. Dari and Pashto are the official languages of Afghanistan, and most educated Afghanis can speak both. The majority of Afghani names are Islamic. It is only recently that Afghanis have started begun to use surnames（last names）.

Part 4

＊Afghanistan n. 阿富汗（指國家）
＊nomad n. 遊牧民族
＊Pushtun 普什圖人
＊Dari 達利語
＊Pakistan 巴基斯坦
＊Afghanis n. 阿富汗人
＊ethnic adj. 種族的；人種的
＊Hazara 哈扎拉族
＊Pashto 普什圖語
＊Islamic adj. 伊斯蘭的

中文譯文對照
Chinese Translation

阿富汗（Afghanistan）是位於亞洲西南部一個多山、內陸的國家。

總人口數約 2 千 2 百萬人。在 1990 年代中期，約有 300 萬人口為遊牧民，還有數百萬人口為居住在阿富汗國境外的難民。阿富汗主要種族為普什圖人（Pushtun）和哈札拉族（Hazara）。

阿富汗主要說兩種語言：達利語（Dari），一種波斯語，以及普什圖語（Pashto，亦寫作 Pashtu）；鄰近國家巴基斯坦（Pakistan）的一些地區亦使用該語言。達利語和普什圖語皆為阿富汗的官方語言，而且多數受過教育的阿富汗人（Afghanis）都能說這兩種語言。多數阿富汗人的姓名是伊斯蘭教的方式。阿富汗人只有最近才開始用姓氏。
、

D 英譯中譯文討論 iscussions

1. 原　文「The total population is about 22 million. In the mid-1990s, about 3 million were nomads, and millions more were refugees living beyond Afghanistan's borders.」，金額以阿拉伯數字合併金額單位表示，年代文皆以阿拉伯數字表示，譯為「總人口數約 2 千 2 百萬人。在 1990 年代中期，約有 300 萬人口為遊牧民，還有數百萬人口為居住在阿富汗國境外的難民。」。

2. 原文「The two principal languages spoken in Afghanistan are Dari, a form of Persian, and Pashto（also spelled Pashtu), which is also spoken in some areas of the neighboring country, Pakistan.」這裡不需在譯文中刻意強調「spoken」的譯出文字，因為語言本來就是用說的，所以這裡亦可譯作「阿富汗有兩種主要語言」。

3. 原文「The majority of Afghani names are Islamic.」，為了譯文流暢度，可在不更改原意的前提下，適時加入譯出文，亦可譯作「多數阿富汗人的姓名為伊斯蘭教式的。」

Unit 16

16.2 中英筆譯互譯要點【中譯英】

Tips 中譯英要點提示

1. 本身為英文名的專有名詞直接譯回原文，不需再附上中文譯文。

2. 冒號「：」用於引語、解釋、範例。分號「；」用於連接獨立的子句，可以逗號取代。

3. 年分、數字、數值僅以阿拉伯數字譯出即可。

4. 易誤譯的常見金額數值單位，「one million- 一百萬」;「one billion- 十億」。

5. 英語語法有時態、詞性變化，中翻英時必須看完整個句子、段落，了解其意思之後再譯出，每個句子皆需選擇文法與時態。**特別留意中文不易在文字中看出英語語法的時態與被動語態。**

6. 其它：內陸是「land-locked」。

阿富汗（Afghanistan）是位於亞洲西南部一個多山、內陸的國家。

總人口數約 2 千 2 百萬人。在 1990 年代中期，約有 300 萬人口為遊牧民，還有數百萬人口為居住在阿富汗國境外的難民。阿富汗主要種族為普什圖人（Pushtun）和哈札拉族（Hazara）。

阿富汗主要說兩種語言：達利語（Dari）， 一種波斯語，以及普什圖語（Pashto，亦寫作 Pashtu）；鄰近國家巴基斯坦（Pakistan）的一些地區亦使用該語言。達利語和普什圖語皆為阿富汗的官方語言，而且多數受過教育的阿富汗人（Afghanis）都能說這兩種語言。多數阿富汗人的姓名是伊斯蘭教的。阿富汗人只有最近才開始用姓氏。

■ 請試著翻劃底線的部分。

Part 4

Afghanistan is a remote, mountainous, land-locked country in southwestern Asia.

The total population is about 22 million. In the mid-1990s, about 3 million were nomads, and millions more were refugees living beyond Afghanistan's borders.（詳見下頁討論 1） There are two ethnic groups in Afghanistan are Pashtun and Hazara.

The two principal languages spoken in Afghanistan are Dari, a form of Persian, and Pashto（also spelled Pashtu）, which is also spoken in some areas of the neighboring country, Pakistan.（詳見下頁討論 2） Dari and Pashto are the official languages of Afghanistan, and most educated Afghanis can speak both.（詳見下頁討論 3） The majority of Afghani names are Islamic. It is only recently that Afghanis have started to use surnames（last names）.（詳見下頁討論 4）

D 中譯英譯文討論
Discussions

1. 原文「在 1990 年代中期，約有 300 萬人口為遊牧民，還有數百萬人口為居住在阿富汗國境外的難民。」由於敘述的時間背景為「1990 年代中期」，故需使用過去式文法，亦可譯作「There were about 3 million nomads, and millions of refugees lived outside Afghanistan in the mid-1990s.」。

2. 原文「阿富汗主要說兩種語言」，此句為現在式被動語態（主詞＋現在式 be 動詞＋過去分詞），譯作「There are two principal languages spoken in Afghanistan」。原文「（Pashto，亦寫作 Pashtu）」，因為英文字是用「拼」出來的，所以在這裡必須以過去式譯作「spelled 或 spelt」。「鄰近國家巴基斯坦（Pakistan）的一些地區亦使用該語言」，表示所說的語言，需使用被動語態且以關係代名詞 which 代領形容詞子句，亦可譯作「which is also spoken in some areas of neighboring Pakistan.」。

3. 「達利語和普什圖語皆為阿富汗的官方語言，而且多數受過教育的阿富汗人（Afghanis）都能說這兩種語言。」主詞可使用代名詞「they」表示「Dari and Pashto」，以「both」表示「兩者皆是」，亦可譯作「They are both official languages of Afghanistan. Most educated Afghanis can speak both.」。

4. 原文「阿富汗人只有最近才開始用姓氏。」，時間片語「最近」用在現在完成式（主詞 +have＋過去分詞），所以需翻譯為「Afghanis have only recently begun to use surnames.」「姓氏」有三種英語寫法，可以譯作「surname、last name、family name」。

Unit 17

17.1 中英筆譯互譯要點【英譯中】

Tips 英譯中要點提示

1. 翻譯時，為了流暢度並讓讀者充分了解文章要表達的意思，可在不更改原意的前提下，適時加入譯出文。避免錯字、異體字。

2. 國家名、以及專有名詞若有固定譯名皆需譯出，若是十分普遍常見的譯名，可不需再加註原文，否則第一次出現於文中時需以圓括號引註原文，其後則以譯名表示即可。

3. 在英語原文中有以引號「“ ”」標註的文字，在譯文加上單引號強調譯文，再以圓括弧加註原文。

4. 計量的次數請勿以阿拉伯數字譯出。

Afghani life centers around the family, including the extended family. Extended families often live together in the same household, or in separate households clustered together. Large cities are made up of numerous small "villages" of extended family units. The women of the family households form a single work group to raise the children. The senior male member, usually the grandfather, controls the finances. The grandmother organizes and controls all domestic chores.

Women have a high level of power in the home, but little authority in public. Islamic tradition requires that they be veiled and kept separate from men in public.

Divorce is fairly simple in Islamic law. To divorce his wife, a man merely has to say "I divorce you" three times in front of witnesses. A woman has to appear before a judge and give reasons for divorcing her husband. However, divorce is rare in Afghanistan.

Children are cherished in Afghani society, especially boys. Girls are not mistreated, but their brothers' needs always come first. Children are expected to grow up quickly and learn how to take care of themselves at a young age.

---

* Afghani 阿富汗的
* domestic chore n. 家庭日常事務
* veil v. 戴面紗
* raise v. 養育
* require that 需要

C 中文譯文對照
Chinese Translation

阿富汗的（Afghani）生活以家庭為中心，包括整個大家族。大家族通常住在同一戶，不然就是毗鄰群聚的個別戶中。大型的城市也是以大家族為單位的眾多小型「村落」（villages）構成。家族裡的女人組成一支勞動團體養育小孩。掌管開銷的通常是地位較高的爺爺輩男性成員。奶奶輩安排並管理所有家庭的日常事務。

女人在家中掌大權，但是對外卻不然。伊斯蘭的傳統要求女人們在公共場合戴面紗，並與男人隔開。

離婚在伊斯蘭的法律中相當簡單。要跟老婆離婚，男人僅需在見証人群面前說「我要跟你離婚」三次即可。女人則必需在法官面前提出跟丈夫離婚的理由。儘管如此，離婚在阿富汗很罕見。

在阿富汗的社會裡，小孩備受寵愛，尤其是男孩。女孩並未受到虐待，只不過兄弟的需求總是優先。在阿富汗，小孩被期待要很快長大，年幼時就要學會如何照顧自己。

1. 原文「The senior male member, usually the grandfather, controls the finances. The grandmother organizes and controls all domestic chores.」，把「爺爺」和「奶奶」的譯文加上一個「輩」字，會使譯文更加通暢，亦可譯作「掌管開銷的是地位較高的男性成員，通常是爺爺輩。奶奶輩則是安排和管理所有家庭的日常事務。」。

2. 原 文「Women have a high level of power in the home, but little authority in public.」，亦可譯作「女人在家中擁有極高的權力，但是對外只有極少權力。」。

3. 原文「Girls are not mistreated」，亦可譯作「女孩並未受到不當的對待。」

4. 原文「Children are expected to grow up quickly and learn how to take care of themselves at a young age.」，在中文譯文加入敘述的背景，更有助讀者了解，本句為接續「阿富汗的社會」敘述，亦可譯作「在阿富汗，小孩被期待要很快長大，年紀輕輕就要學會如何照顧自己。」。

Unit 17

17.2 中英筆譯互譯要點【中譯英】

Tips 中譯英要點提示

1. 本身為英文名的專有名詞直接譯回原文，不需再附上中文譯文。

2. 計量的次數勿以阿拉伯數字譯出。

3. 在中文原文中有以單引號「」標註的文字，在譯文加上引號“”表示強調。

4. 譯文前後的連貫性與流暢度需符合英語語法，主詞在隨後接續的敘述中盡量皆以代名詞／指示代名詞／其他名詞表示，不要一直重複名詞主詞。

5. 英語語法有時態、詞性變化，中翻英時必須看完整個句子、段落，了解其意思之後再譯出，每個句子皆需選擇文法與時態。

6. 要特別留意英語語法中的時態、被動語態、倒裝句，譯文需符合英語語法，不可直譯。

7. 其它：

   a 大家族是「extended family」。
   b 家庭的日常事務是「domestic chore」。
   c 戴面紗是「veil」。
   d 寵愛是「cherish」。
   e 伊斯蘭的是「Islamic」。

主題短文 Article

阿富汗的（Afghani）生活以家庭為中心，包括整個大家族。大家族通常住在同一戶，不然就是毗鄰群聚的個別戶中。大型的城市也是以大家族為單位的眾多小型「村落」（villages）構成。家族裡的女人組成一支勞動團體養育小孩。掌管開銷的通常是地位較高的爺爺輩男性成員。奶奶輩安排並管理所有家庭的日常事務。

女人在家中掌大權，但是對外卻不然。伊斯蘭的傳統要求女人們在公共場合戴面紗，並與男人隔開。

離婚在伊斯蘭的法律中相當簡單。要跟老婆離婚，男人僅需在見証人群面前說「我要跟你離婚」三次即可。女人則必需在法官面前提出跟丈夫離婚的理由。儘管如此，離婚在阿富汗很罕見。

在阿富汗的社會裡，小孩備受寵愛，尤其是男孩。女孩並未受到虐待，只不過兄弟的需求總是優先。在阿富汗，小孩被期待要很快長大，年幼時就要學會如何照顧自己。

■ 請試著翻劃底線的部分。

Afghani life centers around the family, including the extended family. Extended families often live together in the same household, or in separate households clustered together. Large cities are made up of numerous small "villages" of extended family units. The women of the family households form a single work group, to raise the children. The senior male member, usually the grandfather, controls the finances. The grandmother organizes and controls all domestic chores.

Women have a high level of power in the home, but little authority in public.（詳見下頁討論 1） Islamic tradition requires that they be veiled and kept separate from men in public.（詳見下頁討論 2）

Children are cherished in Afghani society, especially boys. Girls are not mistreated, but their brothers' needs always come first. Children are expected to grow up quickly and learn how to take care of themselves at a young age.（詳見下頁討論 4）

D 中譯英譯文討論
iscussions

1. 原文「女人在家中掌大權，但是對外卻不然。」，亦可譯作「Women have a great deal of power in the home, but not in public.」，在這裡，「家中」必須譯成「**in the home**」，指的是所有阿富汗人的家。

2. 原文「伊斯蘭的傳統要求女人們在公共場合戴面紗，並與男人隔開。」，亦可譯作「Islamic tradition **requires that women wear a veil and keep distance from men in public.**」。

3. 原文「離婚在伊斯蘭的法律中相當簡單。要跟老婆離婚，男人僅需在見証人群面前說「我要跟你離婚」三次即可。」亦可譯作，「Divorce is quite easy under in Islamic law. If a man wants to divorce his wife, he simply has to say "I divorce you" three times in front of witnesses.」第一個「divorce」是名詞，第二個「divorce」是動詞。

4. 原文「在阿富汗，小孩被期待要很快長大，年幼時就要學會如何照顧自己。」，由於本文是在敘述阿富汗的生活，故可省略「在阿富汗」的譯文接續敘述即可，或是譯出「在阿富汗」的譯文，亦可譯作「In Afghanistan, expectations are for children to grow up fast and to look after themselves from a young age.」。

Unit 18

18.1 中英筆譯互譯要點【英譯中】

Tips 英譯中要點提示

1. 圓括弧用於引註原文、修飾詞句。
2. 譯文以白話文為主，以正常速度唸文章時，該停頓換氣時，原則上就是需要下逗號的位置，但仍視原文而定。
3. 翻譯時要留意譯文前後的連貫性與流暢度，一些主詞／代名詞／指示代名詞可在隨後接續的譯文中省略或譯出完整主詞。
4. 年分、數字皆以阿拉伯數字表示，百分比以符號代替即可，金額以阿拉伯數字合併金額單位表示。
5. 專有名詞、國家名若有固定譯名皆需譯出，第一次出現於文中時需以圓括號引註原文，其後則以譯名表示即可。在無固有譯名的情況下，直接以原文譯出。
6. 英語人名的譯文要在姓氏與名字之間以音界號「・」分隔，且採直譯的方式，不可將姓氏與名字的順序調換，英語人名的寫法為名字在前，姓氏在後。

Jamaica is a predominantly Christian country with more than 80 percent identifying themselves as Christian. Therefore, religion has a significant place in Jamaicans lives.

Of Jamaican's Christians, nearly one hundred thousand are members of a Jamaican messianic movement（based on the belief in a savior）called Rastafarians. According to Rastafarian belief, which started in the 1930s, Ethiopia is the true holy land and the late Ethiopian emperor Haile Sellassie（previously Ras Tafari）is the only true God.

Rastafarians are famous for wearing their hair in dreadlocks, carrying Bibles and growing beards as a sign of their pact with God. Rastafarianism has become known outside of Jamaica largely because of the late reggae musician Bob Marley, who was its most famous follower.

---

* Jamaicans 牙買加人
* Christian 基督教徒
* Rastafarians 拉斯塔法里教徒」；Rastafarianism 拉斯塔法里派教義
* messianic adj. 有關救世主的
* late adj. 已故的；已過世的
* Haile Sellassie 海爾．塞拉西
* Ras Tafari 拉斯．塔法里
* Ethiopia 衣索比亞
* dreadlocks 長 綹
* reggae 雷鬼音樂
* Bob Marley 巴布．馬利

中文譯文對照 Chinese Translation

牙買加（Jamaica）是個多數人為基督教徒的國家，超過 80% 的人將自己視為基督教徒（Christian）。因此，宗教信仰在牙買加人的生活中有十分重要的地位。

牙買加的基督教徒有將近 10 萬人是篤信牙買加救世主群眾運動（基於篤信有救世主）的成員，稱作拉斯塔法里教徒（Rastafarians）。根據拉斯塔法里教徒源自 1930 年代的信仰，衣索比亞（Ethiopia）才是真正的神聖之地，而唯一真神是衣索比亞的（Ethiopian）已故皇帝海爾．塞拉西（Haile Selassie）（原名拉斯．塔法里（Ras Tafari））。

拉斯塔法里教徒以將頭髮蓄成長髮綹聞名，並將隨身攜帶聖經（Bible）與蓄鬍視為與神做協定的象徵。牙買加以外的會知道拉斯塔法里派教義（Rastafarianism），主要是因為有位最有名的信徒，已故雷鬼（reggae）音樂家巴布．馬利（Bob Marley）。

1. 翻譯時，為了譯文流暢度並讓讀者充分了解文章要表達的意思，可在不更改原意的前提下，適時加入譯出文。

2. 原　文「nearly one hundred thousand are members of a Jamaican messianic movement（based on the belief in a savior）called Rastafarians.」，數值的部分必須格外留意，很容易誤譯，是「10 萬人」。

3. 原　文「Rastafarians are famous for wearing their hair in dreadlocks, carrying Bibles and growing beards as a sign of their pact with God.」，「grow」在身體毛髮當動詞用時，譯成「蓄」，也就是「留長」的意思，表示「蓄」、「蓄鬍」，亦可譯作「拉斯塔法里教徒以蓄長髮綹著名，且將蓄鬍與隨身攜帶聖經（Bible）視為與神做協定的象徵。」。

4. 原　文「Rastafarianism has become know outside of Jamaica largely because of the late reggae musician Bob Marley, who was its most famous follower.」，句中有以形容詞子句代表在那之前的名詞的敘述，也就是補述 Bob Marley 的敘述，譯文需符合中文語法並完整呈現人物角色的敘述，亦可譯作「牙買加以外的人知道拉斯塔法里派教義（Rastafarianism）全是因這位最有名的信徒，已故雷鬼（reggae）音樂家巴布 · 馬利（Bob Marley）。」。

Unit 18

18.2 中英筆譯互譯要點【中譯英】

Tips 中譯英要點提示

1. 圓括號標註插入語或修飾評論。
2. 英語語法有時態、詞性變化，中翻英時必須看完整個句子、段落，了解其意思之後再譯出，每個句子皆需選擇文法與時態。
3. 譯文前後的連貫性與流暢度需符合英語語法，主詞在隨後接續的敘述中盡量皆以代名詞／指示代名詞／其他名詞表示，不要一直重複名詞主詞。
4. 年分、數字、數值僅以阿拉伯數字譯出即可，百分比可譯出或以符號表示皆可。
5. 本身為英文名的專有名詞直接譯回原文，不需再附上中文譯文。
6. 牙買加人「Jamaican」是單數名詞，複數要加「s」。
7. 拉斯塔法里教徒「Rastafarian」是單數名詞，複數要加「s」。
8. 基督教徒「Christian」單複數寫法相同。

主題短文 Article

牙買加（Jamaica）是個多數人為基督教徒的國家，超過 80% 的人將自己視為基督教徒（Christian）。因此，宗教信仰在牙買加人的生活中有十分重要的地位。

牙買加的基督教徒有將近 10 萬人是篤信牙買加救世主群眾運動（基於篤信有救世主）的成員，稱作拉斯塔法里教徒（Rastafarians）。根據拉斯塔法里教徒源自 1930 年代的信仰，衣索比亞（Ethiopia）才是真正的神聖之地，而唯一真神是衣索比亞的（Ethiopian）已故皇帝海爾．塞拉西（Haile Selassie）（原名拉斯．塔法里（Ras Tafari））。

拉斯塔法里教徒以將頭髮蓄成長髮綹聞名，並將隨身攜帶聖經（Bible）與蓄鬍視為與神做協定的象徵。牙買加以外的會知道拉斯塔法里派教義（Rastafarianism），主要是因為有位最有名的信徒，已故雷鬼（reggae）音樂家巴布．馬利（Bob Marley）。

■ 請試著翻劃底線的部分。

英文譯文對照 English Translation

Religion is a significant part of life for Jamaicans. More than 80 percent are Christian.（詳見下頁討論 1）

Nearly one hundred thousand Jamaicans are Rastafarians. Rastafarians are members of a Jamaican messianic（based on the belief in a savior）movement that began in the 1930s.（詳見下頁討論 2）According to Rastafarian belief, the only true God is the late Ethiopian emperor Haile Sellassie（originally known as Ras Tafari）and Ethiopia is the true holy land.

Rastafarians are famous for wearing their hair in dreadlocks, growing beards as a sign of a pact with God and carrying Bibles.（詳見下頁討論 3）Rastafarianism is best known outside of Jamaica because its famous believer, the late reggae musician Bob Marley, was an international star.（詳見下頁討論 4）

D 中譯英譯文討論
Discussions

1. 原文「牙買加（Jamaica）是個多數人為基督教徒的國家，超過 80% 的人將自己視為基督教徒（Christian）。因此，宗教信仰在牙買加人的生活中有十分重要的地位。」，亦可譯作「Most Jamaicans are Christian. Religion is an important part of life for Jamaicans of whom more than 80% are Christian.」

2. 原文「牙買加的基督教徒有將近 10 萬人是篤信牙買加救世主群眾運動（基於篤信有救世主）的成員，稱作拉斯塔法里教徒（Rastafarians）。」，亦可譯作「Nearly one hundred thousand of Jamaican's Christians are Rastafarians which is a messianic（based on a belief in a savior）movement.」。

3. 原文「拉斯塔法里教徒以將頭髮蓄成長髮綹聞名，並將隨身攜帶聖經（Bible）與蓄鬍視為與神做協定的象徵。」，亦可譯作「Rastafarians are known for having their hair in dreadlocks, growing beards to signify a pact with God and carrying Bibles.」。

4. 原文「牙買加以外的會知道拉斯塔法里派教義（Rastafarianism），主要是因為有位最有名的信徒，已故雷鬼（reggae）音樂家巴布．馬利（Bob Marley）。」，亦可譯作「The late Reggae musician, Bob Marley, was responsible for bringing Rastafarianism to the wider world, as he was its most high profile believer.」。

Part 4

Unit 19

19.1 中英筆譯互譯要點【英譯中】

Tips 英譯中要點提示

1. 年代譯文皆以阿拉伯數字表示。
2. 表示幾世紀的譯文，以阿拉伯數字和中文字表示皆可。
3. 專有名詞國家名、人名，以及專有名詞若有固定譯名皆需譯出，若是十分普遍常見的譯名，可不需再加註原文，否則第一次出現於文中時需以圓括號引註原文，其後則以譯名表示即可。在無固有譯名的情況下，直接以原文譯出。
4. 英語圓括號用於標註插入語或修飾評論，譯文也以圓括號表示。
5. 音界號用於區隔外國人名的姓氏與名字，且採直譯的方式，不可將姓氏與名字的順序調換，英語人名的寫法為名字在前，姓氏在後。

The most popular sport in Jamaica is cricket. The game dates back to sixteenth century England and has some similarities to baseball. A cricket match can go on for days. One legendary Jamaican cricket player from the 1930s was George Headley. The young and old from all over the island both play and watch the sport.

Track and field, boxing and basketball are also sports which Jamaicans have excelled at. They also enjoy all types of water sports.

Jamaicans have a passion for enjoying life. They are well known for their casual, laid-back attitude, but they are not ones to be found sitting at home watching television. There are in fact only two television stations on the island. For Jamaicans entertainment and recreation means live music, most likely reggae; metting friends; sports or simply enjoying a day of food and fun at the beach.

Along the tourist areas, crafts by Jamaican artisans are displayed including bankras（baskets) and yabbas（clay bowls).

---

* cricket n. 板球運動
* date back（to) 追溯到…
* track and field 田徑
* laid-back adj. 悠然自得的
* reggae n. 雷鬼（為一種音樂型態）
* Jamaica n. 牙買加；Jamaican n./adj 牙買加人；牙買加的

C 中文譯文對照
Chinese Translation

板球是牙買加（Jamaica）最受觀迎的體育活動。這個略像棒球的板球運動可追溯到英國十六世紀。一場比賽可進行數日。喬治．海德利（George Headley）是 1930 年代的牙買加傳奇板球運動員。整座島上無論大人或小孩，從事板球運動與觀看板球賽事的程度相當。

牙買加人在田徑、拳擊和籃球上有傑出表現。他們也享受所有水上運動。

牙買加人樂於享受生活。他們以隨興、悠然自得的生活態度聞名，但是不會發現有人會呆坐在家裡看電視。島上僅有兩個電視台。對牙買加人來說，娛樂和消遣就是聽現場演奏的音樂，通常是雷鬼（reggae）音樂；跟朋友碰面、體育活動，或是單純在海灘吃喝玩樂享受一天。

牙買加的藝術家們沿著觀光客駐足的地區陳列自製手工藝品，有「bankras」（籃簍）和「yabbas」（陶碗）。

1. 原　文「The most popular sport in Jamaica is cricket. The game dates back to sixteenth century England and has some similarities to baseball.」，亦可譯作「牙買加 (Jamaica) 最受觀迎的體育活動是板球。這個跟棒球有點相似的運動可追溯到英國十六世紀。

2. 原　文「Track and field, boxing and basketball are also sports which Jamaicans have excelled at. They also enjoy all types of water sports.」，譯文以白話文為主，以正常速度唸文章時，該停頓換氣時，原則上就是需要下逗號的位置，但仍視原文而定，亦可譯成單一句完整的譯文，譯作「牙買加人在田徑、拳擊和籃球上有傑出表現，同時也享受所有水上運動。」。

3. 原　文「Jamaicans have a passion for enjoying life. They are well known for their casual, laid-back attitude, but they are not ones to be found sitting at home watching television.」，亦可譯作「牙買加人享受生活。那隨興、悠然自得的生活態度廣為人知，但是你不會發現他們有人呆坐在家裡看電視。」。

4. 原文「For Jamaicans entertainment and recreation means live music, most likely reggae; metting friends; sports or simply enjoying a day of food and fun at the beach.」，亦可譯作「休閒娛樂對牙買加人來說就是聽現場演奏的音樂，通常是雷鬼 (reggae) 音樂；跟三五好友聚在一塊；從事體育活動，或是就在海灘吃喝玩樂享受一天。」。

Part 4

Unit 19

19.2 中英筆譯互譯要點【中譯英】

Tips 中譯英要點提示

1. 年分僅以阿拉伯數字譯出即可。

2. 譯文前後的連貫性與流暢度需符合英語語法，主詞在隨後接續的敘述中盡量皆以代名詞／指示代名詞／其他名詞表示，不要一直重複名詞主詞。

3. 本身為英文名的專有名詞直接譯回原文，不需再附上中文譯文。

4. 英語的引號主要用於標註章節的開始與結束，引述人物言語，強調內容。也用於指明意涵和單字有不尋常含糊不清意涵的狀態。

板球是牙買加（Jamaica）最受觀迎的體育活動。這個略像棒球的板球運動可追溯到英國十六世紀。一場比賽可進行數日。喬治・海德利（George Headley）是 1930 年代的牙買加傳奇板球運動員。整座島上無論大人或小孩，從事板球運動與觀看板球賽事的程度相當。

牙買加人在田徑、拳擊和籃球上有傑出表現。他們也享受所有水上運動。

牙買加人樂於享受生活。他們以隨興、悠然自得的生活態度聞名，但是不會發現有人會呆坐在家裡看電視。島上僅有兩個電視台。對牙買加人來說，娛樂和消遣就是聽現場演奏的音樂，通常是雷鬼（reggae）音樂；跟朋友碰面、體育活動，或是單純在海灘吃喝玩樂享受一天。

牙買加的藝術家們沿著觀光客駐足的地區陳列自製手工藝品，有「bankras」（籃簍）和「yabbas」（陶碗）。

■ 請試著翻劃底線的部分。

E 英文譯文對照
English Translation

The most popular sport in Jamaica is cricket.（詳見下頁討論 1） The game dates back to sixteenth century England and has some similarities to baseball. （詳見下頁討論 2）A cricket match can go on for days. One legendary Jamaican cricket player from the 1930s was George Headley. The young and old from all over the island both play and watch the sport.（詳見下頁討論 3）

Track and field, boxing and basketball are also sports which Jamaicans have excelled at. They also enjoy all types of water sports.（詳見下頁討論 4）

Jamaicans have a passion for enjoying life. They are well known for their casual, laid-back attitude, but they are not ones to be found sitting at home watching television. There are in fact only two television stations on the island. For Jamaicans entertainment and recreation means live music, most likely reggae; metting friends; sports or simply enjoying a day of food and fun at the beach.

Along the tourist areas, crafts by Jamaican artisans are displayed including bankras（baskets）and yabbas（clay bowls）.（詳見下頁討論 5）

1. 原文「板球是牙買加（Jamaica）最受觀迎的體育活動」，亦可譯作「Cricket is the most popular sport in Jamaica.」

2. 原文「這個略像棒球的板球運動可追溯到英國十六世紀。」，亦可譯作「It is a little like baseball, and can be dated from 16th century England.」。

3. 原文「整座島上無論大人或小孩，從事板球運動與觀看板球賽事的程度相當。」，亦可譯作「Children and adults on the island are equally into playing and watching cricket.」。

4. 原文「牙買加人在田徑、拳擊和籃球上也有傑出表現。他們也享受所有水上運動。」，亦可譯作「Jamaicans have also excelled in athletics, boxing and basketball, and enjoy all types of water sports as well.」。

5. 原文「牙買加的藝術家們沿著觀光客駐足的地區陳列自製手工藝品」，有「bankras」（籃簍）和「yabbas」（陶碗），亦可譯作「Jamaican artisans display their crafts including “bankras”（baskets） and “yabbas”（clay bowls）around the tourist areas.」。

Part 4

Unit 20

20.1 中英筆譯互譯要點【英譯中】

Tips 英譯中要點提示

1. 英語的分號用於連接獨立的子句。比起句號更能顯示出兩個子句之間的相關性，譯文可直譯出分號。
2. 譯文以白話文為主，以正常速度唸文章時，該停頓換氣時，原則上就是需要下逗號的位置，但仍視原文而定。
3. 日期譯文皆以阿拉伯數字表示。
4. 計量的次數請勿以阿拉伯數字譯出，要以中文字譯出。
5. 國家名和專有名詞若有固定譯名皆需譯出，若是十分普遍常見的譯名，可不需再加註原文，否則第一次出現於文中時需以圓括號引註原文，其後則以譯名表示即可。

A 主題短文 Article

Afghanistan is a predominantly Muslim country with most of its major holidays being Islamic holy days according to the lunar calendar. The most important is Ramadan. The start of the ninth lunar month signals the beginning of a month of fasting from dawn to dust.

Afghanistan also has a number of secular holidays including Revolution Day on April 27, Workers' Day on May 1 and Independence Day on August 18.

Weddings in Afghanistan are traditionally spread over three days of festivities. They involve feasting and dancing paid for by the groom's family. In the official ceremony a mullah reads from the Koran and the marriage contract is signed in front of witnesses. Finally sugared almonds and walnuts are tossed onto the bridegroom.

The birth of the first child, especially if it's a boy, is greeted with day-long celebrations. It is usual for children to be named on the third day after their birth. Boys are usually circumcised at seven, after which they begin wearing turbans.

Part 4

---

* Afghanistan 阿富汗
* Islamic adj. 伊斯蘭教的
* Muslin 穆斯林
* Ramadan 萊麥丹日
* Revolution Day 革命日
* Independence Day 獨立日
* Workers' Day 勞動節
* circumcise v. 割禮；割包皮
* mullah n. 毛拉（伊斯蘭教對神學家的敬稱）
* Koran 可蘭經
* turban n. 頭巾

中文譯文對照
Chinese Translation

阿富汗（Afghanistan）是個穆斯林（Muslim）居多的國家，重要假日大多是依據農曆的伊斯蘭教（Islamic）宗教節日。最重要的一個節日是萊麥丹月（Ramadan），從農曆第九個月開始，表示從月初開始為期整個月，從日出到日落禁食。

阿富汗也有幾個非宗教性質的假日，包括4月27日的革命日（Revolution Day），5月1日的勞動節（Workers' Day）和8月18日的獨立日（Independence Day）。

傳統的阿富汗婚禮會一連舉行三天慶典。包括費用皆由新郎家庭支付的盛宴和舞蹈。在公證結婚儀式裡，毛拉（mullah）會朗誦可蘭經（Koran），且結婚證書要在眾多見證人面前簽立。最後再將加了糖衣的杏仁和核桃往新郎身上丟。

第一個小孩誕生後，尤其如果是個男孩，會舉行一整天的慶祝。孩子通常在出生後的第三天取名。阿富汗的男孩通常在7歲左右行割禮，在這之後就開始包頭巾。

1. 翻譯時，為了流暢度並讓讀者充分了解文章要表達的意思，可在不更改原意的前提下，適時加入譯出文。

2. 原文「Afghanistan also has a number of secular holidays including Revolution Day on April 27, Workers' Day on May 1 and Independence Day on August 18.」，在譯文加入「性質」，讓譯文更通暢，英語原文的分號也可以中文的逗號取代，亦可譯作「阿富汗幾個非宗教性質的假日有4月27日的革命日（Revolution Day），5月1日的勞動節（Workers' Day），或是8月18日的獨立日（Independence Day）。」。

3. 原文「In the official ceremony a mullah reads from the Koran and the marriage contract is signed in front of witnesses.」，其「official ceremony」指的就是「official wedding ceremony」，在譯文完整譯出「公證結婚儀式」，有助讀者理解。

4. 原文「Boys are usually circumcised at seven, after which they begin wearing turbans.」，其「boys」指的就是「阿富汗的男孩們 」，故在譯文加入「阿富汗」使譯文更通順。中文語法中無明顯或必須使用的被動語態，若直譯為「男孩通常在7歲左右被割除包皮。在這之後，他們開始包頭巾。」並不通順，需稍加潤飾用詞，譯作「阿富汗的男孩通常在7歲左右行割禮。在這之後，就會開始包頭巾。」。

Unit 20

20.2 中英筆譯互譯要點【中譯英】

Tips 中譯英要點提示

1. 英語的分號是用於連接獨立的子句，顯示出兩個子句之間的相關性。

2. 日期的月份需以英文字譯出，不可以阿拉伯數字取代，日的部分則皆可。

3. 特別留意中文不易在文字中看出英語語法的時態與被動語態，譯文需符合英語語法，必須看完整個句子、段落，了解其意思之後再譯出，每個句子皆需選擇文法與時態。

4. 本身為英文名的專有名詞直接譯回原文，不需再附上中文譯文。

5. 其它：

   a 非宗教性質是「secular」。
   b 公證結婚儀式是「official ceremony」。
   c 割禮是「circumcise」。
   d 結婚證書是「marriage contract」。
   e 禁食是「fasting」。

A 主題短文 Article

阿富汗（Afghanistan）是個穆斯林（Muslim）居多的國家，重要假日大多是依據農曆的伊斯蘭教（Islamic）宗教節日。最重要的一個節日是萊麥丹月（Ramadan），從農曆第九個月開始，表示從月初開始為期整個月，從日出到日落禁食。

阿富汗也有幾個非宗教性質的假日，包括 4 月 27 日的革命日（Revolution Day），5 月 1 日的勞動節（Workers' Day）和 8 月 18 日的獨立日（Independence Day）。

傳統的阿富汗婚禮會一連舉行三天慶典。包括費用皆由新郎家庭支付的盛宴和舞蹈。在公證結婚儀式裡，毛拉（mullah）會朗誦可蘭經（Koran），且結婚證書要在眾多見證人面前簽立。最後再將加了糖衣的杏仁和核桃往新郎身上丟。

第一個小孩誕生後，尤其如果是個男孩，會舉行一整天的慶祝。孩子通常在出生後的第三天取名。阿富汗的男孩通常在 7 歲左右行割禮，在這之後就開始包頭巾。

■ 請試著翻劃底線的部分。

英文譯文對照 English Translation

Afghanistan is a predominantly Muslim country with most of its major holidays being Islamic holy days according to the lunar calendar.（詳見下頁討論 1）The most important is Ramadan. The start of the ninth lunar month signals the beginning of a month of fasting from dawn to dust.（詳見下頁討論 2）

Afghanistan also has a number of secular holidays including Revolution Day on April 27, Workers' Day on May 1 and Independence Day on August 18.

Weddings in Afghanistan are traditionally spread over three days of festivities. They involve feasting and dancing paid for by the groom's family. In the official ceremony a mullah reads from the Koran and the marriage contract is signed in front of witnesses.（詳見下頁討論 3）Finally sugared almonds and walnuts are tossed onto the bridegroom.

The birth of the first child, especially if it's a boy, is greeted with day-long celebrations. It is usual for children to be named on the third day after their birth.（詳見下頁討論 4）Boys are usually circumcised at seven, after which they begin wearing turbans.（詳見下頁討論 5）

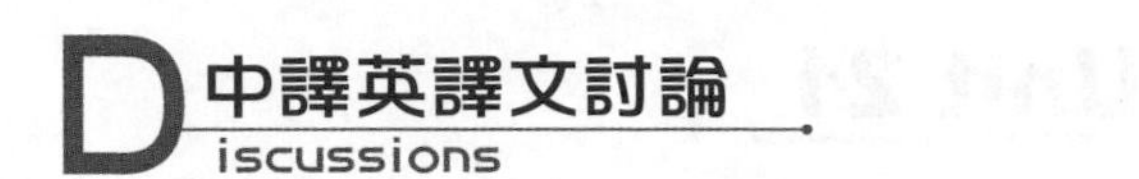

D 中譯英譯文討論 Discussions

1. 原文「阿富汗（Afghanistan）是個穆斯林（Muslim）居多的國家，重要假日大多是依據農曆的伊斯蘭教（Islamic）宗教節日。」，譯文需使用現在式被動語態，亦可譯作「In Afghanistan, most major holidays are Islamic holy days and are reckoned by a lunar calendar.」。

2. 原文「最重要的一個節日是萊麥丹月（Ramadan），從農曆第九個月開始，表示從月初開始為期整個月，從日出到日落禁食。」亦可譯作「The most important holiday is the month of Ramadan, which starts at the beginning of the ninth lunar month, with fasting from dawn to dusk.」

3. 原文「結婚證書要在眾多見證人面前簽立」，譯文使用現在式被動語態，亦可譯作「The marriage contract is signed in front of witnesses」。

4. 原文「孩子通常在出生後的第三天取名。」，譯文需使用現在式被動語態，而「孩子」即泛指所有阿富汗小孩，譯作「Children are usually named on the third day after birth.」。

5. 原文「阿富汗的男孩通常在 7 歲左右行割禮，在這之後就開始包頭巾。」，由於整篇文章敘述背景為阿富汗，譯文可省略「阿富汗」接續敘述即可，這裡使用現在式被動語態，亦可譯作「Boys are usually circumcised at the age of seven, then they begin to wear turbans.」。

Unit 21

21.1 中英筆譯互譯要點【英譯中】

Tips 英譯中要點提示

1. 翻譯時，為了流暢度並讓讀者充分了解文章要表達的意思，可在不更改原意的前提下，適時加入譯出文。避免錯字、異體字。

2. 專有名詞若有固定譯名皆需譯出，若是十分普遍常見的譯名，可不需再加註原文，否則第一次出現於文中時需以圓括號引註原文，其後則以譯名表示即可。在無固有譯名的情況下，直接以原文譯出。

3. 機構名稱需查證固有譯名，本文的 NASA 亦可不譯出譯名，因為 NASA 是眾所皆知的一個機構。

The human body is a purpose built machine, designed for the one G Earth environment. When we venture into the zero-G of space or the 0.38 G of Mars, things start to come undone. Bones get brittle, eyeballs lose their shape, hearts no longer have to pump against gravity and beat less efficiently, and balance goes awry. At least, that's what we know up till now.

NASA is looking for subjects to venture out and run long-duration tests. In a perfect world, every participant would also have a control subject on the ground—someone with the exact same genes and a very similar temperament, so that the changes that come from being aloft for 12 months could be teased apart from those that are just the results of growing one year older on Earth.

* G是「重力」的意思，數值的部分以阿拉伯數字譯出。
* venture into 冒險做
* awry [əˋraɪ] adj. 不對勁
* tease apart 梳理
* aloft adv. 在高空

中文譯文對照
Chinese Translation

人體是座專為特定目的建造的機器，特別為地球的 1G（重力單位）環境所設計。當我們冒險進入零 G（無重力）的太空或是 0.38G 的火星（Mars），事情就會開始不對勁。骨骼脆化，眼球變形，心臟再也不需對抗地心引力將血液抽運至全身，所以也就沒那麼有效率的跳動，平衡感也全亂了套。至少，那是我們直至目前所了解的。

美國太空總署（NASA）正在尋求受試者冒險進行長期的測試。在完美的生活環境裡，每位參與者都會配有一名控制組的受試者留在地面，有著完全相同基因與十分相似的性情，所以就可以拿那些在地球上變老一年的結果，梳理出在高空中生活 12 個月的改變。

D 英譯中譯文討論
iscussions

1. 原文「G」是「重力單位」的意思，若是在譯文中譯為 1G 的重力、0G 的重力、0.38G 的重力雖然不算錯誤，但求譯文通順，就顯得有些多餘。

2. 原文「When we venture into the zero-G of space or the 0.38 G of Mars, things start to come undone. Bones get brittle, eyeballs lose their shape, hearts no longer have to pump against gravity and beat less efficiently, and balance goes awry.」，文中的代名詞 things，表示「我們所知的一切事情」，為求譯文通順，譯作「當我們冒險進入零 G（無重力）的太空或是 0.38G 的火星（Mars），事情就會開始不對勁。」。**原文「zero-G」是「零重力」也就是「無重力」的意思。**

3. 原文「Bones get brittle, eyeballs lose their shape, hearts no longer have to pump against gravity and beat less efficiently, and balance goes awry.」，其「no longer」是「再也不」的意思，**「awry」是出錯的意思，譯文以白話文及通順為原則，不照單字片面意思直譯**，故整句譯作「骨骼脆化，眼球變形，心臟再也不需對抗地心引力將血液抽運至全身，所以也就沒那麼有效率的跳動，平衡感也全亂了套。」。

4. 原文「run the long-duration tests」，這裡的 run 是「從事；進行某事」的意思，譯為「從事長期的測試」。

Unit 21

21.2 中英筆譯互譯要點【中譯英】

Tips 中譯英要點提示

1. 英語中用於敘述事實、常識、研究成果時，通常使用現在式語法。

2. 數字以阿拉伯數字譯出即可。1G、0.38G、零 G，以阿拉伯數字與單位符號譯出即可。

3. 本身為英文名的專有名詞直接譯回原文，不需再附上中文譯文。

4. 英語語法在敘述同一事件時，名詞主詞出現過之後，後續敘述通常慣以代名詞和指示代名詞「**it／they／she／he／we／these／those／this…**」表示。

5. 英語中有被動語態，現在式語法基礎結構為主詞＋動詞／be 動詞…，骨骼脆化、眼球變形這兩句在譯文中必須加入動詞「get」，以符合英語語法。

6. 其它：

   a 冒險進入是「venture into」。
   b 地心引力是「gravity」。
   c 冒險去做（進行）是「venture out」。
   d 受試者是「subject」。
   e 參與者是「participant」。
   f 脾氣是「temperament」。
   g 在高空是「aloft」。
   h 梳理是「tease apart」。

人體是座專為特定目的建造的機器，特別為地球的 1G（重力單位）環境所設計。當我們冒險進入零 G（無重力）的太空或是 0.38G 的火星（Mars），事情就會開始不對勁。骨骼脆化，眼球變形，心臟再也不需對抗地心引力將血液抽運至全身，所以也就沒那麼有效率的跳動，平衡感也全亂了套。至少，那是我們直至目前所了解的。

美國太空總署（NASA）正在尋求受試者冒險進行長期的測試。在完美的生活環境裡，每位參與者都會配有一名控制組的受試者留在地面，有著完全相同基因與十分相似的性情，所以就可以拿那些在地球上變老一年的結果，梳理出在高空中生活 12 個月的改變。

■ 請試著翻劃底線的部分。

Part 5

E 英文譯文對照
English Translation

The human body is a purpose built machine, designed for the one G Earth environment.（詳見下頁討論 1）When we venture into the zero-G of space or the 0.38 G of Mars things start to come undone.（詳見下頁討論 2）Bones get brittle, eyeballs lose their shape, hearts no longer have to pump against gravity and beat less efficiently, and balance goes awry. At least that's what we know up till now.

NASA is looking for subjects to venture out and run long-duration tests. In a perfect world, every participant would also have a control subject on the ground — someone with the exact same genes and a very similar temperament,（詳見下頁討論 3） so that the changes that come from being aloft for 12 months could be teased apart from those that are just the results of growing one year older on Earth.

D 中譯英譯文討論
Discussions

1. 原文「人體是座專為特定目的建造的機器」，是現在式被動語態，主詞＋現在式 be 動詞＋過去分詞，亦可譯作「The human body is a purpose built machine, and it is designed for the one G environment of Earth.」。

2. 原文「當我們冒險進入零 G（無重力）的太空或是 0.38G 的火星（Mars），事情就會開始不對勁。」，亦可譯作「Take us into the zero-G of space or the 0.38 G of Mars and things start to come unsprung.」。

3. 原文「有著完全相同基因與十分相似的性情」，亦可譯作「for example someone with the exact same genes and a very similar temperament」，或是「someone with, let's say, the exact same genes and a very similar temperament」。

Unit 22

22.1 中英筆譯互譯要點【英譯中】

Tips 英譯中要點提示

1. 國家名、人名、著作名、公司組織名，以及專有名詞若有固定譯名皆需譯出，若是十分普遍常見的譯名，可不需再加註原文，否則第一次出現於文中時需以圓括號引註原文，其後則以譯名表示即可。在無固有譯名的情況下，直接以原文譯出。
2. 數字、數值的譯文皆以阿拉伯數字表示即可。
3. 翻譯時，為了流暢度並讓讀者充分了解文章要表達的意思，可在不更改原意的前提下，適時加入譯出文。
4. 英語的引號用於引述人物言語，中文則以單引號表示。

主題短文 Article

Fleas carry bacteria, and bacteria cause plague. "A warmer climate increases the activity of fleas and their ability to spread bacteria from individual to individual," said Nils Christian Stenseth, head of Center of Ecological and Evolutionary Synthesis at the University of Oslo. "We have previously shown that an increase of 1 degree Celsius doubles the prevalence of plague in wild rodents in central Asia."

In historic cases researchers have concluded that while there was no connection between European plague outbreaks and European temperature patterns, plague outbreaks were proceeded by warmer temperatures in Asia. Temperature spikes in Asia appear around 15 years before plague outbreaks in Europe. Travel between Europe and Asia was much slower back then, so researchers attribute the time lag to the length of the Silk Road trade routes.

Part 5

---

* Celsius 是「溫度的單位，攝氏」，譯文以代表溫度單位的符號「℃」表示即可。
* prevalence n. 盛行
* plague n. 瘟疫
* rodent n. 嚙齒動物
* outbreak n. 大爆發

中文譯文對照
Chinese Translation

跳蚤帶有細菌，而細菌會導致瘟疫。奧斯陸大學（University of Oslo）生態學與演化綜論中心長 Nils Christian Stenseth 說，「較溫暖的氣候會提高跳蚤活動力，以及由個體至個體傳播細菌的能力，我們先前已證實氣溫上升 1℃，就會加倍中亞地區野生囓齒動物瘟疫流行程度。」

在歷史案例中，研究者推斷瘟疫大爆發與歐洲氣溫模式無相互關聯性，是由於亞洲氣溫上升接著才發生瘟疫大爆發。亞洲氣溫急升是發生在歐洲瘟疫大爆發的 15 年前。以往旅行於歐洲與亞洲之間的速度要比現今慢得多，所以研究者把這個延遲時間歸因於貿易路線絲路（Silk Road）的長度。

1. 原 文「"We have previously shown that an increase of 1 degree Celsius doubles the prevalence of plague in wild rodents in central Asia"」，要注意其「double」是「「我們先前已證實氣溫上升 1℃，就會加倍中亞地區野生嚙齒動物瘟疫流行程度。」，直接在譯文中說明哪一種事情的流行，並加入「氣溫」、「地區」與「程度」來使語意更為通順。

2. 原文「Temperature spikes in Asia appear around 15 years before plague outbreaks in Europe.」，譯文先說明地點、時間、主詞才符合中文語法，亦可譯作「在歐洲瘟疫大爆發前 15 年，亞洲已出現氣溫急升現象。」。

3. 原文「Travel between Europe and Asia was much slower back then, so researchers attribute the time lag to the length of the Silk Road trade routes.」譯文需符點中文語法，必須先說明敘述的時間、地點，譯文加入「現今」和「back then」呼應，亦可譯作「以往旅行於歐洲與亞洲之間的速度要比現今慢得多，所以研究者將歐洲瘟疫大爆發時間的延遲，歸因於絲路（Silk Road）貿易路線的長度」。

Unit 22

22.2 中英筆譯互譯要點【中譯英】

Tips 中譯英要點提示

1. 年代、數值譯文皆以阿拉伯數字表示即可。
2. 單位可以符號表示，亦可譯出。
3. 英語語法有時態，中翻英時必須看完整個句子、段落，了解其意思之後再譯出，每個句子皆需選擇文法與時態。
4. 本身為英文名的專有名詞直接譯回原文，不需再附上中文譯文。
5. 中文以單引號引述人物言語，英語以引號表示。
6. 中文語法慣用先表明說話者為何，但在英語語法中，敘述人常放在敘述內容之後。
7. 其它：

   a 細菌是「bacteria」。

   b 囓齒動物是「rodent」。

   c 瘟疫是「plague」。

   d 流行程度「prevalence」。

   e 大爆發是「outbreak」。

跳蚤帶有細菌，而細菌會導致瘟疫。奧斯陸大學（University of Oslo）生態學與演化綜論中心長 Nils Christian Stenseth 說，「較溫暖的氣候會提高跳蚤活動力，以及由個體至個體傳播細菌的能力，我們先前已證實氣溫上升 1℃，就會加倍中亞地區野生囓齒動物瘟疫流行程度。」

在歷史案例中，研究者推斷瘟疫大爆發與歐洲氣溫模式無相互關聯性，是由於亞洲氣溫上升接著才發生瘟疫大爆發。亞洲氣溫急升是發生在歐洲瘟疫大爆發的 15 年前。以往旅行於歐洲與亞洲之間的速度要比現今慢得多，所以研究者把這個延遲時間歸因於貿易路線絲路（Silk Road）的長度。

請試著翻劃底線的部分。

E 英文譯文對照
English Translation

Fleas carry bacteria, and bacteria cause plague. “A warmer climate increases the activity of fleas and their ability to spread bacteria from individual to individual,” said Nils Christian Stenseth, head of Center of Ecological and Evolutionary Synthesis at the University of Oslo. “We have previously shown that an increase of 1 degree Celsius doubles the prevalence of plague in wild rodents in central Asia.”（詳見下頁討論 2）

In historic cases researchers have concluded that while there was no connection between European plague outbreaks and European temperature patterns, plague outbreaks were proceeded by warmer temperatures in Asia.（詳見下頁討論 3） Temperature spikes in Asia appear around 15 years before plague outbreaks in Europe. Travel between Europe and Asia was much slower back then, so researchers attribute the time lag to the length of the Silk Road trade routes.（詳見下頁討論 4）

1. 敘述過去發生過的事，常使用英語中的過去式／現在完成式。敘述常態的事件，僅以簡單現在式表達。

2. 「Celsius」是十分普遍常見的單位符號，譯文中亦可以單位符號「℃」譯出即可。原文「我們先前已證實氣溫上升 1℃，就會加倍中亞地區野生囓齒動物瘟疫流行程度。」，亦可譯為「We have previously shown that if the temperature increased 1 ℃, the prevalence of plague in wild rodents in central Asia doubled.」。

3. 原文「在歷史案例中，研究者推斷瘟疫大爆發與歐洲氣溫模式無相互關聯性，是由於亞洲氣溫上升接著才發生瘟疫大爆發。」，亦可譯作「In historic cases the researchers found that the plague outbreaks were preceded by warmer temperatures in Asia, but there was no correlation with temperature patterns in Europe.」，連接詞「**while**」有同時；然而的意思，根據前後文意，在這裡使用連接詞「**but**，但」也符合意思。

4. 原文「研究者把這個延遲時間歸因於貿易路線絲路（Silk Road）的長度」，亦可譯作「researchers believe that the length of the Silk Road trade routes account for this lag.」。

Unit 23

23.1 中英筆譯互譯要點【英譯中】

Tips 英譯中要點提示

1. 國家名、組織名，以及專有名詞若有固定譯名皆需譯出，若是十分普遍常見的譯名，可不需再加註原文，否則第一次出現於文中時需以圓括號引註原文，其後則以譯名表示即可。在無固有譯名的情況下，直接以原文譯出。
2. 譯文以白話文為主，以正常速度唸文章時，該停頓換氣時，原則上就是需要下逗號的位置，但仍視原文而定。
3. 英語語法與中文語法不同，不可用直譯方式逐字翻譯，需看完整個句子、整個段落，了解意思後再譯出。不可省略或誤譯，更不可更改原意。

A 主題短文 Article

For the first time, the chytrid fungus, which is fatal to amphibians, has been detected in Madagascar. This means that the chytridiomycosis pandemic, which has already decimated the US, Central American and Australian salamander, frog and toad populations has now come ashore in this biodiversity hotspot. The Indian Ocean island is home to around 290 species of amphibians that cannot be found anywhere else in the world. A further 200 frog species that are yet to be classified are also thought to live on the island. Researchers from the Helmholtz Centre for Environmental Research（UFZ） and TU Braunschweig, together with international colleagues, have therefore put forward an emergency plan.

＊ chytrid fungus 蛙壺菌

＊ amphibian 兩棲生物

＊ chytridiomycosis 蛙壺菌傳染病

＊ decimate [ˋd s͵met] v. 毀滅

＊ biodiversity 生態多樣性

＊ Helmholtz Centre for Environmental Research（UFZ）是「Helmholtz 環境研究中心（UFZ）」。

＊ TU Braunschweig 是「Braunschweig 科技大學」

C 中文譯文對照
Chinese Translation

蛙壺菌（chytrid fungus）首次在馬達加斯加（Madagascar）偵測到，是一種兩棲生物的致命黴菌。這表示蛙壺菌傳染病（chytridiomycosis）的大流行，已使得美國、中美洲以及澳洲的蠑螈、青蛙和蟾蜍大量死亡，此地也因而達到生物多樣性熱點的狀況。這個位於印度洋的小島，是將近 290 種兩棲生物的棲息地，全世界其他地方找不到這些生物。另外還有 200 種尚未被歸類的青蛙，也被認為棲息於該島。Helmholtz 環境研究中心（Helmholtz Centre for Environmental Research, UFZ）與 Braunschweig 科技大學（TU Braunschweig）研究人員連同國際研究者同仁們，皆為此提出緊急應變計劃。

D 英譯中譯文討論 Discussions

1. 原文「For the first time, the chytrid fungus, which is fatal to amphibians, has been detected in Madagascar.」，由於知道「chytrid fungus」為一種黴菌，在譯文加入「黴菌」使得譯文更為完整，亦可譯作「蛙壺菌（chytrid fungus）是一種兩棲生物的致命黴菌，已首次在馬達加斯加（Madagascar）偵測到。」。

2. 原　文「which has already decimated the US, Central American and Australian salamander, frog and toad populations」，其「populations」用在某種領或的生物時，譯為「族群數量」，**「decimated」為「大量毀滅」的意思**，譯作「已使得美國、中美洲以及澳洲的蠑螈、青蛙和蟾蜍大量死亡」。

3. 英語常用代名詞 / 指示代名詞 / 名詞連貫敘述來代替主詞，原文「The Indian Ocean island is home to around 290 species of amphibians that cannot be found anywhere else in the world.」，其「home」在本文用於形容兩棲類生物的家，需配合中文說法為「棲息地」而不是「家」，**其「The Indian Ocean island」指的是「馬達加斯加」，由於本文就是在敘述該島，所以接敘的譯文不需再重覆提述「馬達加斯加」**，譯作「這個位於印度洋的小島，是將近 290 種兩棲生物的棲息地，全世界其他地方找不到這些生物。」。

4. 原　文「A further 200 frog species that are yet to be classified are also thought to live on the island.」， 其**「live」用於兩棲生物時，要符合一般中文說法以「棲息」而不是「居住」來表示**，譯作「另外還有 200 種尚未被歸類的青蛙，也被認為棲息於該島。」

Unit 23

23.2 中英筆譯互譯要點【中譯英】

Tips 中譯英要點提示

1. 譯文前後的連貫性與流暢度需符合英語語法，主詞在隨後接續的敘述中盡量皆以代名詞／指示代名詞／其他名詞表示，不要一直重複名詞主詞。

2. 特別留意中文並沒有英語語法中的被動語態、倒裝句，翻譯時需符合英語語法。

3. 本身為英文名的專有名詞直接譯回原文，不需再附上中文譯文。

4. 數值譯文皆以阿拉伯數字表示。

5. 每個領域的專有名詞、術語、特定用詞皆需查證，相同字彙在不同領域意涵不盡相同。

6. 其它：

   a 兩棲生物是「amphibian」。

   b 大流行是「pandemic」。

   c 蠑螈是「salamander」。

   d 蟾蜍是「toad」。

   e 生物多樣性熱點是「biodiversity hotspot」。

A 主題短文 Article

蛙壺菌（chytrid fungus）首次在馬達加斯加（Madagascar）偵測到，是一種兩棲生物的致命黴菌。這表示蛙壺菌傳染病（chytridiomycosis）的大流行，已使得美國、中美洲以及澳洲的蠑螈、青蛙和蟾蜍大量死亡，此地也因而達到生物多樣性熱點的狀況。這個位於印度洋的小島，是將近 290 種兩棲生物的棲息地，全世界其他地方找不到這些生物。另外還有 200 種尚未被歸類的青蛙，也被認為棲息於該島。Helmholtz 環境研究中心（Helmholtz Centre for Environmental Research, UFZ）與 Braunschweig 科技大學（TU Braunschweig）研究人員連同國際研究者同仁們，皆為此提出緊急應變計劃。

■ 請試著翻劃底線的部分。

E 英文譯文對照
English Translation

For the first time, the chytrid fungus, which is fatal to amphibians, has been detected in Madagascar.（詳見下頁討論1） This means that the chytridiomycosis pandemic, which has already decimated the US, Central American and Australian salamander, frog and toad populations has now come ashore in this biodiversity hotspot. The Indian Ocean island is home to around 290 species of amphibians that cannot be found anywhere else in the world.（詳見下頁討論2） A further 200 frog species that are yet to be classified are also thought to live on the island.（詳見下頁討論3） Researchers from the Helmholtz Centre for Environmental Research（UFZ） and TU Braunschweig, together with international colleagues, have therefore put forward an emergency plan.

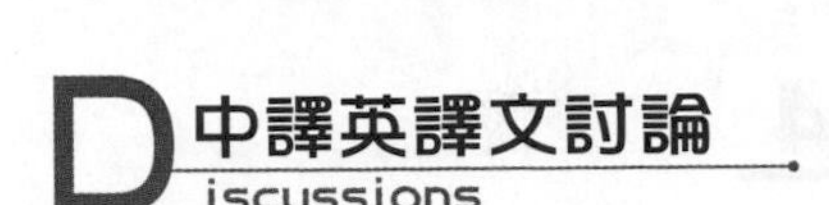

中譯英譯文討論 Discussions

1. 原文「蛙壺菌（chytrid fungus）首次在馬達加斯加（Madagascar）偵測到，是一種兩棲生物的致命黴菌。」，亦可譯作「For amphibians, the chytrid fungus is fatal, and it has been detected in Madagascar for the first time.」，**中文語法看不出英語的被動語態，蛙壺菌「已首次在馬達加斯加偵測到」譯文需使用被動語態。**

2. 原文「這個位於印度洋的小島，是將近 290 種兩棲生物的棲息地，全世界其他地方找不到這些生物。」，亦可譯作「The island which is located in the Indian Ocean is home to around 290 species of amphibians that are not found anywhere else in the world.」。

3. 原文「另外還有 200 種尚未被歸類的青蛙，也被認為棲息於該島。」，譯文為被動語態，亦可譯作「Also another 200 frog species that have not been classified yet are thought to live on the island」或是「A further 200 frog species that have not been classified yet are also thought to live on the island」，以及「Furthermore another 200 frog species that have not been classified yet are also thought to live on the island」。

Unit 24

24.1 中英筆譯互譯要點【英譯中】

Tips 英譯中要點提示

1. 英語的年代、數字譯文皆以阿拉伯數字表示。文章來源為史料、研究文件、官方文件時「西元」需譯出，若為一般文章通常不譯。

2. 翻譯時，為了流暢度並讓讀者充分了解文章要表達的意思，可在不更改原意的前提下，適時加入譯出文。

3. 專有名詞公司機構名稱需查證固有譯名。

4. **英語的引號用於強調內容。也用於指明意涵和單字有不尋常含糊不清意涵的狀態。中文則以單引號表示。**

5. 國家名、公司組織名，以及專有名詞若有固定譯名皆需譯出，若是十分普遍常見的譯名，可不需再加註原文，否則第一次出現於文中時需以圓括號引註原文，其後則以譯名表示即可。

A 主題短文 Article

There has been a dramatic increase in the number of Americans with peanut allergies. Between 1997 and 2003 rates have quadrupled. The American Academy of Pediatrics created guidelines in 2005 to try to combat this dramatic surge. It was suggested that peanuts should not be eaten by children under the age of three. However, in 2008 when these guidelines seemed to be having no effect on the rising number of peanut allergies, the AAP retracted the recommendation. Further studies by allergists having now been published fly in the face of the original recommendation, and instead conclude that it is beneficial to give peanuts to children at a young age, even those who are judged as "high risk" of allergies.

The team of researchers from the UK studied a group of 640 "high risk" infants aged between 4 months and 11 months, who had already shown signs of eczema and / or an allergy to eggs. Peanut-containing food was fed to half of the infants at least twice a week up until the age of five, while the other half had all peanut-containing food excluded from their diet until the same age.

---

* quadruple [ˋkwadrʊpl̩] v. 變四倍
* American Academy of Pediatrics 是「美國小兒科學會（APP）」，第一次出現時在譯文後以圓括弧引註原文，第二次出現時，則直接以譯名表示，不再引註。
* refrain from 節制；避免
* fly in the face of 公然違抗
* eczema [ˋɛksɪmə] n. 濕疹
* exclude v. 不包括

中文譯文對照
Chinese Translation

美國人花生過敏人數爆增。在 1997 年和 2003 年之間，美國人花生過敏比例

增加了四倍。美國小兒科學會（American Academy of Pediatrics; AAP）在 2005 年訂出一個指導方針來對抗花生過敏人數急劇攀升。建議 3 歲以下兒童不該食用花生。然而在 2008 年，當這個建議看似並未對花生過敏人數攀升產生影響時，美國小兒科學會撤回該項建議。過敏專家團隊進一步研究，並發表了公然違抗原先的建議，除了推斷出給予年幼兒童食用花生有益之外，甚至也對那些被判斷為有過敏「高風險」的人有益。

來自英國的一組研究者研究 640 名年齡層介於 4 到 11 個月，已發展出濕疹以及／或對蛋過敏的過敏「高風險」嬰幼兒。其中半數嬰幼兒一週至少兩次食用含有花生的食物至 5 足歲，而另一半嬰幼兒的飲食中則不能含有花生直至相同年齡。

D 英譯中譯文討論 iscussions

1. 原文「to combat this dramatic surge」，依前文可知道「this dramatic surge」指的是過敏人數的劇烈增加，故在在譯文加入「過敏人數」，亦可譯作「為了防止過敏人數激增」。

2. 英語原文中有以引號「“ ”」標註的文字，在譯文加上單引號表示強調譯文。

3. 原文「a group of 640 “high risk” infants aged between 4 months and 11 months, who had already shown signs of eczema and ／ or an allergy to eggs. Peanut-containing food was fed to half of the infants at least twice a week up until the age of five, while the other half had all peanut-containing food excluded from their diet until the same age.」，亦可譯作「這些年齡層介於 4~11 個月的嬰幼兒已出現濕疹以及／或對蛋過敏。受試的 640 名嬰幼兒中，半數一週至少食用二次含有花生的食物直到 5 足歲，同時另外半數的嬰幼兒則是必須避免食用含花生的食物至 5 足歲。」。

Unit 24

24.2 中英筆譯互譯要點【中譯英】

Tips 中譯英要點提示

1. 年分、數字僅以阿拉伯數字譯出即可。
2. 英語語法有時態，中翻英時必須看完整個句子、段落，了解其意思之後再譯出，每個句子皆需選擇文法與時態。
3. 本身為英文名的專有名詞直接譯回原文，不需再附上中文譯文。
4. 中文以單引號表示強調內容，也用於指明意涵和單字有不尋常含糊不清意涵的狀態。英語則以引號表示。
5. 特別留意中文不易在文字中看出英語語法的時態與被動語態、倒裝句，翻譯時需符合英語語法。
6. 每個專業領域裡的術語、特有名詞皆需查證譯名。
7. 其它：
   a 花生過敏是「peanut allergies」。
   b 變四倍是「quardrupled」。
   c 主張；認為是「argue that」。
   d 濕疹是「eczema」。
   e 公然違抗是「fly in the face of」。
   f 5 足歲是「age of five; age of 5; turn 5; turn five」。

A 主題短文 Article

美國人花生過敏人數爆增。在 1997 年和 2003 年之間，美國人花生過敏比例增加了四倍。美國小兒科學會（American Academy of Pediatrics; AAP）在 2005 年訂出一個指導方針來對抗花生過敏人數急劇攀升。建議 3 歲以下兒童不該食用花生。然而在 2008 年，當這個建議看似並未對花生過敏人數攀升產生影響時，美國小兒科學會撤回該項建議。過敏專家團隊進一步研究，並發表了公然違抗原先的建議，除了推斷出給予年幼兒童食用花生有益之外，甚至也對那些被判斷為有過敏「高風險」的人有益。

來自英國的一組研究者研究 640 名年齡層介於 4 到 11 個月，已發展出濕疹以及／或對蛋過敏的過敏「高風險」嬰幼兒。其中半數嬰幼兒一週至少兩次食用含有花生的食物至 5 足歲，而另一半嬰幼兒的飲食中則不能含有花生直至相同年齡。

■ 請試著翻劃底線的部分。

E 英文譯文對照
English Translation

There has been a dramatic increase in the number of Americans with peanut allergies. Between 1997 and 2003 rates have quadrupled.（詳見下頁討論 1）The American Academy of Pediatrics created guidelines in 2005 to try to combat this dramatic surge.（詳見下頁討論 2）It was suggested that peanuts should not be eaten by children under the age of three. However, in 2008 when these guidelines seemed to be having no effect on the rising number of peanut allergies, the AAP retracted the recommendation.（詳見下頁討論 3）Further studies by allergists having now been published fly in the face of the original recommendation, and instead conclude that it is beneficial to give peanuts to children at a young age, even those who are judged as "high risk" of allergies.（詳見下頁討論 4）

The team of researchers（詳見下頁討論 5）from the UK studied a group of 640 "high risk" infants aged between 4 months and 11 months, who had already shown signs of eczema and / or an allergy to eggs. Peanut-containing food was fed to half of the infants at least twice a week up until the age of five, while the other half had all peanut-containing food excluded from their diet until the same age.（詳見下頁討論 6）

1. 原文「在 1997 年和 2003 年之間，美國人花生過敏比例增加了四倍。」，亦可譯作「From 1997 to 2003, Americans with peanut allergies rates increased four fold.」，也可譯為「From 1997 to 2003, there was a four-fold increase in Americans with peanut allergies.」。

2. 原文「美國小兒科學會（American Academy of Pediatrics; AAP）」在第一次出現於文章時以全名譯出，第二次以後以譯名或英文縮寫表示皆可。

3. 原文「然而在 2008 年，當這個建議看似並未對花生過敏人數攀升產生影響時，美國小兒科學會撤回該項建議。」，亦可譯作「When, in 2008, this didn't seem to be having any impact on the rising number of peanut allergies, the AAP retracted the recommendations.」。

4. 原文「過敏專家團隊進一步研究，並發表了公然違抗原先的建議，除了推斷出給予年幼兒童食用花生有益之外，甚至也對那些被判斷為有過敏「高風險」的人有益。」，其「公然違抗」亦可譯作「**contradict**」，「發表」用於研究、文章、書籍時，使用「**publish**」。亦可譯作「Now, a team of allergists has published a study that contradicts those recommendations, arguing that it is actually beneficial to feed peanuts to infants with a "high risk" of developing the allergy.」。

5. 原文「英國研究者們」，亦可譯為「Researchers based in the U.K.」。

6. 原文「其中半數嬰幼兒一週至少兩次食用含有花生的食物至 5 足歲，而另一半嬰幼兒的飲食中則不能含有花生直至相同年齡。」，需使用英語語法中的被動語態，亦可譯作「**Half** were asked to eat peanut-containing foods at least two times a week until they turned 5, **meanwhile** the other half had to avoid eating peanuts in any form until they also turned 5.」。

Unit 25

25.1 中英筆譯互譯要點【英譯中】

Tips 英譯中要點提示

1. 英語常用代名詞／指示代名詞／名詞連貫敘述，需適時在不容易了解該代名詞指向何者時，在譯文中把代名詞／其他名詞換成主詞名詞。翻譯時要留意譯文前後的連貫性與流暢度。

2. 年份以阿拉伯數字表示即可。

3. 專業術語／名詞之字詞譯名需查證，同樣的字詞在不同專業領域表達的意涵不同。

4. **英語的破折號「-」用於介紹某種說法，加入強調語氣、定義，或是解釋。也用於隔開兩個子句。**

5. 專有名詞若有固定譯名皆需譯出，若是十分普遍常見的譯名，可不需再加註原文，否則第一次出現於文中時需以圓括號引註原文，其後則以譯名表示即可。在無固有譯名的情況下，直接以原文譯出。

It's common knowledge that leaves are loaded with chlorophyll, which makes them green. But less well known is that all green plants also carry a set of chemicals called carotenoids. On their own, these look yellow or orange − carotenoids give color to corn and carrots, for example - but they're invisible beneath the chlorophyllic green of a leaf for most of the year. However in the fall, when leaves are nearing the end of their life cycle, the chlorophyll breaks down, and the yellow-orange is revealed. "The color of a leaf is subtractive, like crayons on a piece of paper," says David Lee, Director of the national Tropical Botanical Garden, who has been studying leaf color for over forty years.

Most trees also evolved to produce a different set of chemicals during autumn when it's bright and cold. These chemicals, which have a reddish tint are called anthocyanins. They're sometimes produced in sprouting leaves and are even responsible for the color of a blueberry.

Part 5

---

* chlorophyll [ˋklɔrə͵fɪl] 葉綠素
* carotenoids [kəˋratɪ͵nɔɪd] 類胡蘿蔔素
* Florida International University 是「美國佛羅里達州國際大學」。
* anthocyanin [͵ænθəˋsaɪənɪn] 花青素

C 中文譯文對照
Chinese Translation

葉子富含葉綠素（chlorophyll）大家都知道的知識，就是這個物質讓葉子呈綠色。但是比較少人知道所有綠色植物也帶有一組稱作類胡蘿蔔素（carotenoids）的化學物質。類胡蘿蔔素單獨存在時看起來呈黃或橘——舉例來說，玉米和胡蘿蔔的顏色。只不過，一年中的大部分時間裡，類胡蘿蔔素都存在於跟葉綠素有關的綠葉下，所以才讓人看不出來。然而秋天時，葉子正接近生命週期的結束，葉綠素分解之後，就換黃橘色現形。已研究葉子顏色超過 40 年的美國國立熱帶植物園（National Tropical Botanical Garden）園長 David Lee 說，「葉子的顏色飽合度是會減少的，就跟用蠟筆著色於紙上一樣。」

秋季當天氣晴朗且寒冷時，大多數的樹木已演化成會產出一組不同的化學物質。這些有淡紅色調的化學物質稱作花青素（anthocyanins）。花青素有時在新發芽的嫩葉裡產出，甚至也是藍莓顏色的原由。

1. 專有名詞若有固定譯名皆需譯出，第一次出現於文中時需以圓括號引註原文，其後則以譯名表示即可。

2. 原　文「－ carotenoids give color to corn and carrots, for example － but they're invisible beneath the chlorophyllic green of a leaf for most of the year.」，英語倒裝句（強調動作／事情發生的時間、主詞的狀態或當句中的主詞帶有一長串的修飾語，也常常將「時間副詞」或「形容詞」放在句首）在翻譯時需符合中文語法，譯作「——舉例來說，玉米和胡蘿蔔的顏色。只不過，一年中的大部分時間裡，類胡蘿蔔素都存在於跟葉綠素有關的綠葉下，所以才讓人看不出來」。

3. 原文「The color of a leaf is subtractive, like crayons on a piece of paper」，用於形容色澤亮度深淺，故在譯文中加上「飽合度」有助譯文流暢度，譯作「葉子的顏色飽合度是會減少的，就跟用蠟筆著色於紙上一樣」

4. 原　文「They're sometimes produced in sprouting leaves and are even responsible for the color of a blueberry.」，其「they」指的是「花青素」，將其代名詞主詞完整譯出所指何物，有利文章完整性，亦可譯作「有時花青素會在新發芽的嫩葉裡產生，也是藍莓顏色的原由。」。

Unit 25

25.2 中英筆譯互譯要點【中譯英】

Tips 中譯英要點提示

1. 本身為英文名的專有名詞直接譯回原文，不需再附上中文譯文。
2. 破折號「-」用於介紹某種説法，加入強調語氣、定義，或是解釋。引號「 “” 」用於引述人物言語。
3. **英語語法有時態、詞性變化，中翻英時必須看完整個句子、段落，了解其意思之後再譯出，每個句子皆需選擇文法與時態。**
4. 譯文前後的連貫性與流暢度需符合英語語法，主詞在隨後接續的敘述中盡量皆以代名詞／指示代名詞／其他名詞表示，不要一直重複名詞主詞。

主題短文 Article

葉子富含葉綠素（chlorophyll）大家都知道的知識，就是這個物質讓葉子呈綠色。但是比較少人知道所有綠色植物也帶有一組稱作類胡蘿蔔素（carotenoids）的化學物質。類胡蘿蔔素單獨存在時看起來呈黃或橘一舉例來說，玉米和胡蘿蔔的顏色。只不過，一年中的大部分時間裡，類胡蘿蔔素都存在於跟葉綠素有關的綠葉下，所以才讓人看不出來。然而秋天時，葉子正接近生命週期的結束，葉綠素分解之後，就換黃橘色現形。已研究葉子顏色超過 40 年的美國國立熱帶植物園（National Tropical Botanical Garden）園長 David Lee 說，「葉子的顏色飽合度是會減少的，就跟用蠟筆著色於紙上一樣。」

秋季當天氣晴朗且寒冷時，大多數的樹木已演化成會產出一組不同的化學物質。這些有淡紅色調的化學物質稱作花青素（anthocyanins）。花青素有時在新發芽的嫩葉裡產出，甚至也是藍莓顏色的原由。

■ 請試著翻劃底線的部分。

英文譯文對照
English Translation

It's common knowledge that leaves are loaded with chlorophyll, which makes them green. But less well known is that all green plants also carry a set of chemicals called carotenoids. On their own, these look yellow or orange − carotenoids give color to corn and carrots, for example − but they're invisible beneath the chlorophyllic green of a leaf for most of the year.（詳見下頁討論 2）However in the fall, when leaves are nearing the end of their life cycle, the chlorophyll breaks down, and the yellow-orange is revealed. "The color of a leaf is subtractive, like crayons on a piece of paper," says David Lee, Director of the national Tropical Botanical Garden, who has been studying leaf color for over forty years.

Most trees also evolved to produce a different set of chemicals during autumn when it's bright and cold.（詳見下頁討論 3） These chemicals, which have a reddish tint are called anthocyanins. They're sometimes produced in sprouting leaves and are even responsible for the color of a blueberry.

D 中譯英譯文討論
Discussions

1. 中文不易在文字中看出英語語法的時態與被動語態、倒裝句（除了「場所副詞」放在句首，需使用倒裝句外，當強調動作／事情發生的時間、主詞的狀態或當句中的主詞帶有一長串的修飾語，也常常將「時間副詞」或「形容詞」放在句首，形成倒裝句），翻譯時需符合英語語法。

2. 原文「類胡蘿蔔素單獨存在時看起來呈黃或橘——舉例來說，玉米和胡蘿蔔的顏色。只不過，一年中的大部分時間裡，類胡蘿蔔素都存在於跟葉綠素有關的綠葉下，所以才讓人看不出來。」，亦可譯作「Carotenoids on their own look yellow or orange. For example, they give color to corn and carrots, but most of the year they're invisible beneath the green of chlorophyll.」。

3. 原文「秋季當天氣晴朗且寒冷時，大多數的樹木已演化成會產出一組不同的化學物質。這些有淡紅色調的化學物質稱作花青素（anthocyanins）。」，亦可譯作「When it's bright and cold in autumn, most trees have evolved to produce a different set of chemicals called anthocyanins.」。

Unit 26

26.1 中英筆譯互譯要點【英譯中】

Tips 英譯中要點提示

1. 專有名詞、人名如有固定譯名皆需譯出，若是十分普遍常見的譯名，可不需再加註原文，否則第一次出現於文中時需以圓括號引註原文，其後則以譯名表示即可。

2. 圓括弧「（）」用於引註原文、修飾詞句。

3. 英語人名的譯文要在姓氏與名字之間以音界號「・」分隔，且採直譯的方式。

4. 英語常用代名詞／指示代名詞／名詞連貫敘述，需適時在不容易了解該代名詞指向何者時，在譯文中把「你（的）／我／他（她）／其／那些／這／那」…等代名詞／其他名詞換成主詞名詞。一些主詞／代名詞／指示代名詞可在隨後接續的譯文中省略。

5. 年分、年齡皆以阿拉伯數字表示。

Alzheimer's disease is an irreversible, progressive brain disease that slowly destroys memory and thinking skills, and eventually even the ability to perform the simplest tasks of daily living. Symptoms of Alzheimer's usually appear in people after the age of 65, and it is the most common cause of dementia in older people.

The disease is named after Dr. Alois Alzheimer. In 1906, Dr. Alzheimer noticed changes within the brain tissue of a woman who had died of an unusual mental illness. Her symptoms included memory loss, communication difficulties, and unpredictable behavior. After her death, he examined her brain and discovered many abnormal clumps（now known as amyloid plagues） and tangled bundles of fibers（now known as neurofibrillary tangles）.

The plaques and tangles discovered by Dr. Alzheimer are two of the features of Alzheimer's disease. The third is the degradation of connections between nerve cells（neurons） in the brain.

---

* Alzheimer's disease 是「阿茲海默症」。
* be named after 按…命名
* amyloid plaques 澱粉蛋白質斑
* neurofibrillary tangles 神經纖維纏結
* degradation n. 下降；降低　　　* neurons 神經元

中文譯文對照
Chinese Translation

阿茲海默症（Alzheimer's disease）是個無法復元的腦部疾病，會慢慢地破壞記憶和思考能力，最後甚至喪失完成日常生活簡單事務的能力。阿茲海默症的症狀通常好發於 65 歲後，也是造成老年人痴呆的一種最常見疾病。

這項疾病以愛羅斯．阿茲海默博士（Dr. Alois Alzheimer）命名。1906 年，阿茲海默博士注意到一名死於罕見精神疾病女性的腦部組織變化。該名女性患者的症狀包括喪失記憶、溝通障礙，以及無法預測的行為表現。在她過世之後，阿茲海默博士檢查她的腦部，發現了許多異常塊狀物質（現在稱為澱粉蛋白質斑（amyloid plaques）），還有大量糾結在一起的纖維（現在稱為神經纖維纏結（neurofibrillary tangles））。

由阿茲海默博士發現的兩個阿茲海默症主要特徵是腦部斑化與纏結。第三個特徵就是腦神經細胞（神經元（neurons））之間的連結降低。

1. 原文「Symptoms of Alzheimer's usually appear in people after the age of 65, and it is the most common cause of dementia in older people.」在醫學領域提到症狀「appear」，意指「發病、出現症狀」，亦可譯作「阿茲海默症的症狀通常好發於 65 歲以上的老年人，也是造成老年人痴呆的一種最常見疾病。」。

2. 原　文「Her symptoms included memory loss, communication difficulties and unpredictable behavior.」，代名詞所有格「her」，在譯文加入「患者」兩字，能讓譯文更清楚所指的「她」為何者，譯作「該名女性患者的症狀包括喪失記憶、溝通障礙，以及無法預測的行為表現。」。

3. 原　文「After her death, he examined her brain and discovered many abnormal clumps（now known as amyloid plagues） and tangled bundles of fibers（now known as neurofibrillary tangles）.」，上一句已詳加敘述該女性患者的症狀以及死於罕見精神疾病，接續的譯文以代名詞主詞「她」來表示不影響譯文清晰度，但第二句的代名詞主詞「he」若只直譯為「他」，會讓譯文完整度略顯不足，在這裡譯出「he」所指為何者，會讓譯文更通暢，亦可譯作「阿茲海默博士在她過世後檢查她的腦部，發現到許多異常塊狀物質〔現在稱為澱粉蛋白質斑（amyloid plaques）〕，以及大量糾結在一起的纖維〔現在稱為神經纖維纏結（neurofibrillary tangles）〕。」。

Unit 26

26.2 中英筆譯互譯要點【中譯英】

Tips 中譯英要點提示

1. 本身為英文名的專有名詞直接譯回原文，不需再附上中文譯文。
2. 年分、年齡僅以阿拉伯數字譯出即可。
3. 英語語法有時態、詞性變化，中翻英時必須看完整個句子、段落，了解其意思之後再譯出，每個句子皆需選擇文法與時態。
4. 譯文前後的連貫性與流暢度需符合英語語法，主詞在隨後接續的敘述中盡量皆以代名詞／指示代名詞／其他名詞表示，不要一直重複名詞主詞
5. 圓括號「（ ）」用於標註插入語或修飾評論。
6. 其它：

   a 好發於「appear」。

   b 以（按）…命名「named after」。

   c 死於…「died of」。

   d 塊狀「clump」。

主題短文 Article

阿茲海默症（Alzheimer's disease）是個無法復元的腦部疾病，會慢慢地破壞記憶和思考能力，最後甚至喪失完成日常生活簡單事務的能力。阿茲海默症的症狀通常好發於 65 歲後，也是造成老年人痴呆的一種最常見疾病。

這項疾病以愛羅斯．阿茲海默博士（Dr. Alois Alzheimer）命名。1906 年，阿茲海默博士注意到一名死於罕見精神疾病女性的腦部組織變化。該名女性患者的症狀包括喪失記憶、溝通障礙，以及無法預測的行為表現。在她過世之後，阿茲海默博士檢查她的腦部，發現了許多異常塊狀物質（現在稱為澱粉蛋白質斑（amyloid plaques）），還有大量糾結在一起的纖維（現在稱為神經纖維纏結（neurofibrillary tangles））。

由阿茲海默博士發現的兩個阿茲海默症主要特徵是腦部斑化與纏結。第三個特徵就是腦神經細胞（神經元（neurons））之間的連結降低。

■ 請試著翻劃底線的部分。

Part 6

Alzheimer's disease is an irreversible, progressive brain disease that slowly destroys memory and thinking skills, and eventually even the ability to perform the simplest tasks of daily living. Symptoms of Alzheimer's usually appear in people after the age of 65, and it is the most common cause of dementia in older people.（詳見下頁討論 1）

The disease is named after Dr. Alois Alzheimer. In 1906, Dr. Alzheimer noticed changes within the brain tissue of a woman who had died of an unusual mental illness.（詳見下頁討論 2） Her symptoms included memory loss, communication difficulties and unpredictable behavior. After her death, he examined her brain and discovered many abnormal clumps（now known as amyloid plagues） and tangled bundles of fibers（now known as neurofibrillary tangles）.

The plaques and tangles discovered by Dr. Alzheimer are two of the features of Alzheimer's disease. The third is the degradation of connections between nerve cells（neurons） in the brain.（詳見下頁討論 3）

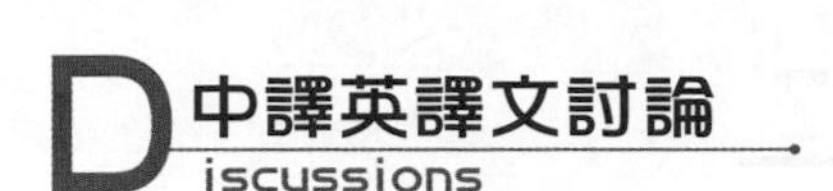

中譯英譯文討論 Discussions

1. 原文「阿茲海默症的症狀通常好發於 65 歲後，也是造成老年人痴呆的一種最常見疾病。」，其中「好發於」是醫學敘述中常見的詞，可以「first appear」表示，亦可譯作「Symptoms first appear in most people who have Alzheimer's after age 65. It is the most common cause of elderly people's dementia.」。

2. 原文「1906 年，阿茲海默博士注意到一名死於罕見精神疾病女性的腦部組織變化。」，當強調事情發生的時間，常常將「時間副詞」或「形容詞」放在句首，形成倒裝句。亦可譯作「After a woman died of an unusual mental illness in 1906, Dr. Alzheimer noticed changes in her brain tissue.」。

3. 原文「現在稱為」，亦可譯作「now called」。原文「第三個特徵就是腦神經細胞（神經元（neurons））之間的連結降低。」，亦可譯作「The third main symptom is the loss of connections between nerve cells（neurons） in the brain.」。

Unit 27

27.1 中英筆譯互譯要點【英譯中】

Tips 英譯中要點提示

1. 英文標點符號的單引號表示已在引號中的引述。譯文為中文時以用於引述人物言語、強調內容的單引號表示。

2. 專有名詞若有固定譯名皆需譯出，若是十分普遍常見的譯名，可不需再加註原文，否則第一次出現於文中時需以圓括號引註原文，其後則以譯名表示即可。在無固有譯名的情況下，直接以原文譯出。

3. 英語語法中，敘述人常放在敘述內容之後，但中文語法慣用先表明説話者為何。

4. 專業術語／名詞之字詞譯名需查證，同樣的字詞在不同專業領域表達的意涵不同。

Fruit and vegetables contaminated with pesticides may result in men with lower sperm counts of poorer quality, researchers have warned.

Sperm count for men who ate fruit and vegetables with high levels of pesticide residue had only half the count of men who consumed the least.

Consuming pesticide residue also lead to a one-third reduction in normally-formed sperm, a new study in the US has reported. The study showed that there was no link between semen quality and total consumption of fruit and vegetables. The link was with fruit and vegetables containing 'high' levels of the residue.

The researchers said that their finding "suggest exposure to pesticides used in agricultural production through diet may be sufficient to affect sperm in humans."

---

* pesticides 農藥
* contaminate 污染
* one-third 三分之一
* pesticide residue 農藥殘留物
* sperm 精子
* semen 精液

中文譯文對照
Chinese Translation

研究人員提出警告，受農藥污染的水果和蔬菜可能導致男性精子品質更差及數量減少。

食用含高劑量農藥殘留物水果和蔬菜的男性，精子數量只有攝取最少農藥殘留物男性的一半。

一項美國的新研究也指出，攝取農藥殘留物也會導致正常情況下產出精子的數量減少三分之一。該研究顯示，攝取水果和蔬菜的總量與精液品質之間並無關聯。而是跟攝取含有「高」劑量農藥殘留物的水果和蔬菜有關。

研究人員表示，他們的研究發現「暗指藉由飲食暴露在用於生產農作物的農藥中，可能足以影響人類精子。」

1. 原文「Fruit and vegetables contaminated with pesticides may result in men with lower sperm counts of poorer quality, researchers have warned.」，在譯文中先明確表明敘述者，再接續其內容，較符合中文語法，有助讀者理解文其意。亦可譯作「受農藥污染的水果和蔬菜可能導致精子品質更差且數量減少，研究人員提出警告。」。

2. 原文「Sperm count for men who ate fruit and vegetables with high levels of pesticide residue had only half the count of men who consumed the least.」，要先讀完整段文字了解其中的比較關係，再整彙譯文，亦可譯作「食用到含高劑量農藥殘留物水果和蔬菜的男性，精子數量比攝取到最少農藥殘留物的男性少了一半。」。

3. 原　文「Consuming pesticide residue also lead to a one-third reduction in normally-formed sperm, a new study in the US has reported.」，在譯文加入「數量」來呼應「**a one-third drop**」，亦可譯作「一項美國的新研究顯示，攝取農藥殘留物也導致男性在正常情況下所產生的精子數量只有原本的三分之二。」。

Unit 27

27.2 中英筆譯互譯要點【中譯英】

Tips 中譯英要點提示

1. 本身為英文名的專有名詞直接譯回原文，不需再附上中文譯文。

2. 英文標點符號的單引號「‘ ’」表現已在引號中的引述。

3. 譯文為英語時，則儘量避免以阿拉伯數字和符號來表示幾分之幾，盡量以英語表示。

4. 英語語法有時態、詞性變化，中翻英時必須看完整個句子、段落，了解其意思之後再譯出，每個句子皆需選擇文法與時態。

5. 其它：
   a 農藥是「pesticides」。
   b 農藥殘留物是「pesticide residue」。
   c 精子是「sperm」。
   d 精液是「semen」。

研究人員提出警告，受農藥污染的水果和蔬菜可能導致男性精子品質更差及數量減少。

食用含高劑量農藥殘留物水果和蔬菜的男性，精子數量只有攝取最少農藥殘留物男性的一半。

一項美國的新研究也指出，攝取農藥殘留物也會導致正常情況下產出精子的數量減少三分之一。該研究顯示，攝取水果和蔬菜的總量與精液品質之間並無關聯。而是跟攝取含有「高」劑量農藥殘留物的水果和蔬菜有關。

研究人員表示，他們的研究發現「暗指藉由飲食暴露在用於生產農作物的農藥中，可能足以影響人類精子。」

■ 請試著翻劃底線的部分。

Part 6

E 英文譯文對照
English Translation

Fruit and vegetables contaminated with pesticides may result in men with lower sperm counts of poorer quality, researchers have warned.（詳見下頁討論 1）

Sperm count for men who ate fruit and vegetables with high levels of pesticide residue had only half the count of men who consumed the least.（詳見下頁討論 2）

Consuming pesticide residue also lead to a one-third reduction in normally-formed sperm, a new study in the US has reported.（詳見下頁討論 3）The study showed that there was no link between semen quality and total consumption of fruit and vegetables.（詳見下頁討論 4）The link was with fruit and vegetables containing 'high' levels of the residue.

The researchers said that their finding "suggest exposure to pesticides used in agricultural production through diet may be sufficient to affect sperm in humans."

1. 原文「研究人員提出警告，受農藥污染的水果和蔬菜可能導致男性精子品質更差及數量減少。」，亦可譯作「Researchers have warned that pesticides in fruit and vegetables may lead to lower sperm counts of poorer quality.」。

2. 原文「食用含高劑量農藥殘留物水果和蔬菜的男性，精子數量只有攝取最少農藥殘留物男性的一半。」，亦可譯作「Comparison of the men who had consumed the most pesticide residue with those who consumed the least, showed the former to have a 50% lower sperm count.」。

3. 原文「一項美國的新研究也指出，攝取農藥殘留物也會導致正常情況下產出精子的數量減少三分之一。」，亦可譯作「A new US study also shows a decrease of one-third in normally-formed sperm among men consuming pesticide residue.」。

4. 原文「該研究顯示，攝取水果和蔬菜的總量與精液品質之間並無關聯。而是跟攝取含有「高」劑量農藥殘留物的水果和蔬菜有關。」，亦可譯作「Total consumption of fruit and vegetables had nothing to do with semen quality. The correlation was with fruit and vegetables which were ranked as containing 'high' residues of pesticides.」。

Unit 28

28.1 中英筆譯互譯要點【英譯中】

Tips 英譯中要點提示

1. 英語常用代名詞／指示代名詞／名詞連貫敘述，需適時在不容易了解該代名詞指向何者時，在譯文譯出主詞名詞。翻譯時要留意譯文前後的連貫性與流暢度，一些主詞／代名詞／指示代名詞亦可在隨後接續的譯文中省略。

2. 專有名詞、公司組織名若有固定譯名皆需譯出，若是十分普遍常見的譯名，可不需再加註原文，否則第一次出現於文中時需以圓括號引註原文，其後則以譯名表示即可。在無固有譯名的情況下，直接以原文譯出。

3. 英語語法中，敘述人常放在敘述內容之後，但中文語法慣用先表明說話者為何。

4. 金額以阿拉伯數字合併金額單位表示。

Japanese pharmaceutical company Daiichi Sankyo Co Ltd has agreed to pay the US government US$39 million over kickbacks it paid physicians to prescribe its drugs, the US Department of Justice announced on Wednesday last week.

The payment to the US federal government and to state Medicaid programs are to be made by the group's US subsidiary, Daiichi Sankyo Inc, to settle allegations which were first raised by a former company sales representative who provided evidence of the kickbacks.

According to the US government, the company would invite multiple physicians to lavish dinners to speak on often identical topics, and then pay them for the speeches.

The doctors were expected to favor the company's treatments and medicines over its rivals, the prescription of which increased costs for federal and state healthcare programs.

Part 6

---

* kickbacks 回扣
* US Department of Justice 美國司法部
* Medicaid programs 醫療援助制度計劃
* ubsidiary [səbˋsɪdˏɛrɪ] n. 子公司
* state healthcare programs 國家健康照護計劃

中文譯文對照
Chinese Translation

美國司法部（US Department of Justice）上週三公開表示，日商 Daiichi Sankyo 製藥有限公司同意支付美國政府 3,900 萬美元，以彌平支付醫師開立該公司藥品回扣的事件。

付給美國聯邦政府和國家醫療援助制度計劃（Medicaid programs）的錢是由 Daiichi Sankyo 集團的美國子公司支付，解決該公司前銷售代表提出的首波支付回扣證據指控。

根據美國政府的調查，Daiichi Sankyo 公司會邀請各界醫師共進鋪張的晚宴，並讓醫師們發表些一模一樣的主題，然後再支付他們演講酬勞。

所以這些受邀醫師被認定為會偏好開立 Daiichi Sankyo 公司的治療與藥物，而這些處方則會造成聯邦政府和國家健康照護計劃（state healthcare programs）成本增加。

D 英譯中譯文討論 iscussions

1. 原文「Japanese pharmaceutical company Daiichi Sankyo Co Ltd has agreed to pay the US government US$39 million over kickbacks it paid physicians to prescribe its drugs, the US Department of Justice announced on Wednesday last week.」，要符合中文語法，在譯文先說明發表以下敘述的來源為何，再接續敘述句中表達的事件前因後果，亦可譯作「美國司法部（US Department of Justice）上週三表示，日商 Daiichi Sankyo 製藥有限公司同意支付美國政府 3,900 萬美元，以彌平支付醫師回扣的事件。」。

2. 原　文「According to the US government, the company would invite multiple physicians to lavish dinners to speak on often identical topics, and then pay them for the speeches.」，依其後敘述內容在譯文加入「調查」兩字，亦可譯作「根據美國政府的調查，Daiichi Sankyo 公司會邀請各界醫師共進鋪張的晚宴，讓醫師們發表些一模一樣主題，然後再付錢給他們作為演講酬勞。」。

3. 原文「The doctors were expected to favor the company's treatments and medicines over its rivals, the prescription of which increased costs for federal and state healthcare programs.」，句中的名詞代名詞「The doctors」，指的就是前段提到的那些被邀請的各界醫師，譯文若直譯「醫師們」，就無法清楚表示出所指的是哪些「醫師」，故在譯文加入譯文「這些受邀的」，亦可譯作「所以這些受邀醫師被認定為會偏好開立 Daiichi Sankyo 公司的治療與藥物，造成聯邦政府和國家健康照護計劃（state healthcare programs）的成本增加。」。

Unit 28

28.2 中英筆譯互譯要點【中譯英】

Tips 中譯英要點提示

1. 譯文前後的連貫性與流暢度需符合英語語法，主詞在隨後接續的敘述中盡量皆以代名詞／指示代名詞／其他名詞表示，不要一直重複名詞主詞。
2. 本身為英文名的專有名詞直接譯回原文，不需再附上中文譯文。
3. 金額以阿拉伯數字合併金額單位表示。
4. 其它：

   a 3,900 萬的單位是「million 百萬」。

   b 回扣是「kickbacks」。

   c 鋪張是「lavish」。

   d 醫師是「physicians」、「doctors」。

美國司法部（US Department of Justice）上週三公開表示，日商 Daiichi Sankyo 製藥有限公司同意支付美國政府 3,900 萬美元，以彌平支付醫師開立該公司藥品回扣的事件。

付給美國聯邦政府和國家醫療援助制度計畫（Medicaid programs）的錢是由 Daiichi Sankyo 集團的美國子公司支付，解決該公司前銷售代表提出的首波支付回扣證據指控。

根據美國政府的調查，Daiichi Sankyo 公司會邀請各界醫師共進鋪張的晚宴，並讓醫師們發表些一模一樣的主題，然後再支付他們演講酬勞。

所以這些受邀醫師被認定為會偏好開立 Daiichi Sankyo 公司的治療與藥物，而這些處方則會造成聯邦政府和國家健康照護計劃（state healthcare programs）成本增加。

■ 請試著翻劃底線的部分。

Japanese pharmaceutical company Daiichi Sankyo Co Ltd has agreed to pay the US government US$39 million over kickbacks it paid physicians to prescribe its drugs, the US Department of Justice announced on Wednesday last week.（詳見下頁討論 1）

The payment to the US federal government and to state Medicaid programs are to be made by the group's US subsidiary, Daiichi Sankyo Inc, to settle allegations which were first raised by a former company sales representative who provided evidence of the kickbacks.

According to the US government, the company would invite multiple physicians to lavish dinners to speak on often identical topics, and then pay them for the speeches.（詳見下頁討論 2）

The doctors were expected to favor the company's treatments and medicines over its rivals, the prescription of which increased costs for federal and state healthcare programs.（詳見下頁討論 3）

1. 原文「美國司法部（US Department of Justice）上週三公開表示，日商Daiichi Sankyo製藥有限公司同意支付美國政府3,900萬美元，以彌平支付醫師開立該公司藥品回扣的事件。」，亦可以倒裝句譯作「Last Wednesday, the US Department of Justice reported that Japanese pharmaceutical company Daiichi Sankyo has agreed to pay US$39million to the US government over kickbacks it paid physicians to prescribe its drugs.」。

2. 原文「根據美國政府的調查，Daiichi Sankyo公司會邀請各界醫師共進鋪張的晚宴，常讓醫師們發表些一模一樣的主題，然後再支付他們演講酬勞。」，亦可譯作「According to the US government's investigation, multiple doctors would be invited to lavish dinners by Daiichi Sankyo at which they were paid to speak on often identical topics.」。

3. 原文「所以這些受邀醫師被認定為會偏好開立Daiichi Sankyo公司的治療與藥物，而這些處方則會造成聯邦政府和國家健康照護計劃（state healthcare programs）成本增加。」，**譯文使用過去式被動語態**，亦可譯作「The doctors were expected to prescribe more of the company's treatments and medicines, which could add costs to federal and state healthcare programs.」。

Unit 29

29.1 中英筆譯互譯要點【英譯中】

Tips 英譯中要點提示

1. 年代、數字譯文皆以阿拉伯數字表示，單獨表示月份時，譯文需使用中文字。
2. 英語中的破折號用於介紹某種說法，加入強調語氣、定義，或是解釋。也用於隔開兩個子句。
3. 英語常用代名詞／指示代名詞／名詞連貫敘述，需適時在不容易了解該代名詞指向何者時，在譯文中把這些代名詞／其他名詞，換成主詞名詞。

A doctor meets a dying patient's relatives—It's a scene repeated countless times in hospitals up and down the country.

Life and death may be routine for the medical staff, but for the rest of us it's, well, life and death.

For the next of kin, it's frightening. For the doctors it may seem a distraction from what they see as their appallingly busy work load. They'd love to give the relatives more of their time, but it's a distraction, and they need to maintain their emotional distance.

But there's another story—The same hospital, the same patient, the same pressure, but a different consultant. His approach was so full of kindness and compassion that it made me wonder whether the disparity between the doctors with an understanding bedside manner and those without is really more about the individual than the pressure of the job.

This man became our rock when our son's illness, whatever caused it in the first place, took a turn for the worst leaving doctors chasing the problems around his body for a year after he was admitted in April 2011.

---

* up and down 到處；上上下下
* appallingly adv. 極為困難地
* disparity n. 不同；不等
* take a turn（情勢；情況）轉變
* next of kin 直系親屬；近親
* consultant n. 會診醫生
* in the first place 究竟
* admit v. 入院治療

中文譯文對照
Chinese Translation

醫生與來日不多的病患家屬會面一是在全國上下所有醫院重覆上演無數次的場景。

對醫療人員來説，生與死稀鬆平常，但對我們這些非醫療人員而言，可是攸關至親的生與死。

對直系親屬來説，這是十分可怕的一件事。從醫生那極為困難與忙碌的工作量看來，與來日不多病患家屬會面是種令人分心的事。醫生很樂意付出更多時間在家屬身上，只不過這是種分心的事，況且醫生還得維持情感上的距離。

可是，在同一間醫院，同一病患，同等的壓力之下，只不過換了不同的會診醫生，事情就有了不同的局面。這位醫生對待病患的方式充滿仁慈和同理心，這讓我不禁納悶，這兩名醫生對待病人的態度在同理心程度上的不同，以及那些沒有同理心醫生的態度，其實是跟個人比較有關，而不是身為醫生的工作壓力。

這位對待病患充滿仁慈和同理心的醫生，在我們的兒子於 2011 年四月入院治療時，成了我們的定心石一不論究竟是什麼原因造成他患病，我兒子的病情突然惡化，這一年的時間，醫生只能努力找出他全身上下有什麼毛病。

D 英譯中譯文討論
iscussions

1. 原　文「A doctor meets a dying patient's relatives」，其「**dying**」「快死了」若直譯在譯文裡不太適合，應稍加修飾說法，譯作「醫生與來日不多的病患家屬會面」。

2. 原　文「Life and death may be routine for the medical staff, but for the rest of us it's, well, life and death.」，在譯文加入「至親」，更能顯現兩種角色對生與死的對比感受，譯作「對醫療人員來說，生與死稀鬆平常，但對我們這些非醫療人員而言，可是攸關至親的生與死。」。

3. 原　文「But there's another story. The same hospital, the same patient, the same pressure, but a different consultant.」，亦可譯作「不過事情也能有不同局面，在同一間醫院，同一病患，同等的壓力之下，只不過換了不同的會診醫生。」，屬直譯方式，沒有錯誤，**但前後文的關係與脈絡不夠顯而易見，建議將敘述放在結果之前，譯作「可是，在同一間醫院，同一病患，同等的壓力之下，只不過換了不同的會診醫生，事情就有了不同的局面。」**。

4. 原文「This man became our rock when our son's illness, whatever caused it in the first place, took a turn for the worst leaving doctors chasing the problems around his body for a year after he was admitted in April 2011.」，其「this man」指的是「對待病患充滿仁慈和同理心的醫生」，補充譯出名詞主詞，才能讓譯文更加清楚流暢，譯作「這位對待病患充滿仁慈和同理心的醫生，在我們的兒子於 2011 年四月入院治療時，成了我們的定心石一不論究竟是什麼原因造成他患病，我兒子的病情突然惡化，這一年的時間，醫生只能努力找出他全身上下有什麼毛病。

Part 6

Unit 29

29.2 中英筆譯互譯要點【中譯英】

Tips 中譯英要點提示

1. 破折號用於介紹某種説法，加入強調語氣、定義，或是解釋。也用於隔開兩個子句。

2. 譯文前後的連貫性與流暢度需符合英語語法，主詞在隨後接續的敘述中盡量皆以代名詞／指示代名詞／其他名詞表示，不要一直重複名詞主詞。

3. 月份需以英文字譯出，不可以阿拉伯數字取代。

4. 英語語法有時態、詞性變化，中翻英時必須看完整個句子、段落，了解其意思之後再譯出，每個句子皆需選擇文法與時態。

5. 其它：

   a 生與死是「life and death」。

   b 直系親屬是「next of kin」。

   c 工作量是「work load」。

   d 令人分心的事「distraction」。

   e 會診醫生是「consultant」。

   f 同理心是「compassion」。

   g 定心石「rock」。

醫生與來日不多的病患家屬會面一是在全國上下所有醫院重覆上演無數次的場景。

對醫療人員來説，生與死稀鬆平常，但對我們這些非醫療人員而言，可是攸關至親的生與死。

對直系親屬來説，這是十分可怕的一件事。從醫生那極為困難與忙碌的工作量看來，與來日不多病患家屬會面是種令人分心的事。醫生很樂意付出更多時間在家屬身上，只不過這是種分心的事，況且醫生還得維持情感上的距離。

可是，在同一間醫院，同一病患，同等的壓力之下，只不過換了不同的會診醫生，事情就有了不同的局面。這位醫生對待病患的方式充滿仁慈和同理心，這讓我不禁納悶，這兩名醫生對待病人的態度在同理心程度上的不同，以及那些沒有同理心醫生的態度，其實是跟個人比較有關，而不是身為醫生的工作壓力。

這位對待病患充滿仁慈和同理心的醫生，在我們的兒子於 2011 年四月入院治療時，成了我們的定心石一不論究竟是什麼原因造成他患病，我兒子的病情突然惡化，這一年的時間，醫生只能努力找出他全身上下有什麼毛病。

■ 請試著翻劃底線的部分。

英文譯文對照 English Translation

A doctor meets a dying patient's relatives—It's a scene repeated countless times in hospitals up and down the country.（詳看下頁討論 1）

Life and death may be routine for the medical staff, but for the rest of us it's, well, life and death.

For the next of kin, it's frightening. For the doctors it may seem a distraction from what they see as their appallingly busy work load.（詳看下頁討論 2） They'd love to give the relatives more of their time, but it's a distraction, and they need to maintain their emotional distance.

But there's another story—The same hospital, the same patient, the same pressure, but a different consultant.（詳看下頁討論 3） His approach was so full of kindness and compassion that it made me wonder whether the disparity between the doctors with an understanding bedside manner and those without is really more about the individual than the pressure of the job.（詳看下頁討論 4）

This man became our rock when our son's illness, whatever caused it in the first place, took a turn for the worst leaving doctors chasing the problems around his body for a year after he was admitted in April 2011.（詳看下頁討論 5）

D 中譯英譯文討論 iscussions

1. 原文「對醫療人員來說，生與死稀鬆平常，但對我們這些非醫療人員而言，可是攸關至親的生與死。」，亦可譯作「For medical staff, life and death may be routine, but for us, it's about our loved one's life and death.」。

2. 原文「從醫生那極為困難與忙碌的工作量看來，與來日不多病患家屬會面是種令人分心的事。」，用代名詞主詞「it」表示「與來日不多病患家屬會面」這件事，亦可譯作「Due to the doctors appallingly busy work load, it may seem a distraction to them.」。

3. 原文「可是，在同一間醫院，同一病患，同等的壓力之下，只不過換了不同的會診醫生，事情就有了不同的局面。」，亦可譯作「But in the same hospital, the same patient, and the same pressure, but under a different consultant, things turned out differently.」。

4. 原文「這位醫生對待病患的方式充滿仁慈和同理心，這讓我不禁納悶，這兩名醫生對待病人的態度在同理心程度上的不同，以及那些沒有同理心醫生的態度，其實是跟個人比較有關，而不是身為醫生的工作壓力。」，亦可譯作「The way he treated his patients was so full of kindness and compassion. It made me wonder if the disparity between the doctors with an understanding bedside manner and those without is really nothing to do with the pressure of the job, but more about the individual.」。

5. 原文「這位對待病患充滿仁慈和同理心的醫生，在我們的兒子於 2011 年四月入院治療時，成了我們的定心石一不論究竟是什麼原因造成他患病，我兒子的病情突然惡化，這一年的時間，醫生只能努力找出他全身上下有什麼毛病。」，亦可譯作「Regardless of what caused my son's illness, when, after he was admitted in April 2011, he took a turn for the worst, leaving doctors chasing the problems around his body for a year, this man became our rock.」。

Unit 30

30.1 中英筆譯互譯要點【英譯中】

Tips 英譯中要點提示

1. 國家名若有固定譯名需譯出，若是十分普遍常見的譯名，可不需再加註原文，否則第一次出現於文中時需以圓括號引註原文，其後則以譯名表示即可。

2. 數字以阿拉伯數字表示，百分比以符號譯出即可。

3. 數值可直接以阿拉伯數字表示，亦可合併單位使用。

4. 破折號用於介紹某種説法，加入強調語氣、定義，或是解釋。也用於隔開兩個子句。

5. 英語語法與中文語法不同，不可用直譯方式逐字翻譯，需看完整個句子、整個段落，了解意思後再譯出。不要執著在每個英語單字的意思，在不同內容下，會有不同的詮釋方式，要譯其意。不可省略或誤譯重點文字、數值，更不可更改原意。

Many dream of an early retirement. A middle age spent taking it easy—perhaps a bit of light pottering around the garden or strolling the decks of a cruise ship.

Those enjoying this relaxing lifestyle may want to avert their eyes from the latest health advice.

It might make uncomfortable reading for the early afternoon snoozers and occasional gardeners, but working up a sweat in middle age may mean that you live longer than those of the same age who prefer a more gentle form of exercise.

A study in Australia which followed 204,000 men and women over the age of 45 for six years has concluded that for those whose lives included a work-out mortality rates were lowered by 9 to 13 percent. The more vigorous the exercise, the greater the benefit there is, especially for men.

Current guidelines in the UK are for adults to spend 150 minutes a week doing moderate activity, or 75 minutes of strenuous activity.

Part 6

---

* take it easy 從容
* mortality rate n. 死亡率
* moderate adj. 中等的；適度的
* strenuous [ˋstrɛnjʊəs] adj. 劇烈的
* avert from v. 避開
* vigorous [ˋvɪgərəs] adj. 強健的

中文譯文對照 Chinese Translation

許多人夢想提早退休。中年人從容渡過退休生活一也許在花園做點瑣碎的事，或是在郵輪甲板上蹓躂。那些享受這般愜意生活型態的人，也許會想把目光避開最新的健康建議。

對午後打盹片刻，以及偶爾整理一下花園的人來說，也許讀到這個會不太自在，但是一直努力工作至中年，可能表示你會比同年齡但偏好較溫和運動型態的人活得更久。

澳洲進行了一項為期六年，涉及 20 萬 4000 名 45 歲男女的研究，結論出在生活中有運動的人，死亡率低了 9%~13%。運動強度愈強，就愈有益，尤其對男性更是如此。

英國目前給予成人的健康指南是每週從事中等強度活動 150 分鐘，或是每週從事劇烈活動 75 分鐘。

D 英譯中譯文討論 iscussions

1. 原文「Many dream of an early retirement.」，其「many」指的是「many people」，譯作「許多人夢想提早退休。」。

2. 原文「A middle age spent taking it easy—perhaps a bit of light pottering around the garden or strolling the decks of a cruise ship.」，其「spend」表示「渡過」，譯作「中年人從容渡過退休生活一也許在花園做點瑣碎的事，或是在郵輪甲板上蹓躂。」。

3. 原　文「A study in Australia which followed 204,000 men and women over the age of 45 for six years has concluded that for those whose lives included a work-out mortality rates were lowered by 9 to 13 percent.」，譯文要符合中文語法的敘述前後順序，譯文才會通順，亦可譯作「澳洲一項為期六年涉及 204,000 名 45 歲男女的研究，結論出在生活中有運動的人，死亡率低了 9%~13%。」。

4. 原　文「The more vigorous the exercise, the greater the benefit there is, especially for men.」，亦可譯作「運動強度愈強益處就愈大，尤其男性。」。

Unit 30

30.2 中英筆譯互譯要點【中譯英】

Tips 中譯英要點提示

1. 數值僅以阿拉伯數字譯出即可，百分比可譯出或以符號表示皆可。
2. 數量以阿拉伯數字或合併量詞單位譯出皆可。
3. 譯文前後的連貫性與流暢度需符合英語語法，主詞在隨後接續的敘述中盡量皆以代名詞／指示代名詞／其他名詞表示，不要一直重複名詞主詞。
4. 英語中的破折號用於介紹某種説法，加入強調語氣、定義，或是解釋。也用於隔開兩個子句。
5. 國家名若有固定譯名皆需查證並譯出。
6. 其它：
   - a 蹓躂是「strolling」。
   - b 死亡率是「mortality rate」。
   - c 運動強度是「vigorous」。
   - d 中等運動強度是「moderate」。
   - e 劇烈運動強度是「strenuous」。

A主題短文
rticle

許多人夢想提早退休。中年人從容渡過退休生活—也許在花園做點瑣碎的事，或是在郵輪甲板上蹓躂。那些享受這般愜意生活型態的人，也許會想把目光避開最新的健康建議。

對午後打盹片刻，以及偶爾整理一下花園的人來說，也許讀到這個會不太自在，但是一直努力工作至中年，可能表示你會比同年齡但偏好較溫和運動型態的人活得更久。

澳洲進行了一項為期六年涉及 20 萬 4000 名 45 歲男女的研究，結論出在生活中有運動的人，死亡率低了 9%~13%。運動強度愈強，就愈有益，尤其對男性更是如此。

英國目前給予成人的健康指南是每週從事中等強度活動 150 分鐘，或是每週從事劇烈活動 75 分鐘。

■ 請試著翻劃底線的部分。

英文譯文對照 English Translation

Many dream of an early retirement.（詳看下頁討論 1）A middle age spent taking it easy—perhaps a bit of light pottering around the garden or strolling the decks of a cruise ship.

Those enjoying this relaxing lifestyle may want to avert their eyes from the latest health advice.（詳看下頁討論 2）

It might make uncomfortable reading for the early afternoon snoozers, and occasional gardeners, but working up a sweat in middle age may mean that you live longer than those of the same age who prefer a more gentle form of exercise.（詳看下頁討論 3）

A study in Australia which followed 204,000 men and women over the age of 45 for six years has concluded that for those whose lives included a work-out mortality rates were lowered by 9 to 13 percent. The more vigorous the exercise, the greater the benefit there is, especially for men.

Current guidelines in the UK are for adults to spend 150 minutes a week doing moderate activity, or 75 minutes of strenuous activity.（詳看下頁討論 4）

1. 原文「許多人夢想提早退休。」，亦可譯作「Many people dream of an early retirement.」。

2. 原文「那些享受這般愜意生活型態的人，也許會想把目光避開最新的健康建議。」，亦可譯作「Those who enjoy such a relaxing lifestyle may want to avert their eyes from the newest health advice.」。

3. 原文「但是一直努力工作至中年，可能表示你會比同年齡但偏好較溫和運動型態的人活得更久。」，亦可譯作「but a moderate workout throughout middle age may mean that you live longer than those of the same age group who are inclined to gentler forms of exercise.」。

4. 原文「英國目前給予成人的健康指南是每週從事中等強度活動 150 分鐘，或是每週從事劇烈活動 75 分鐘。」，亦可譯作「British guidelines currently urge adults to spend 150 minutes a week doing moderate activity, or 75 minutes of vigorous activity.」。

Unit 31

31.1 中英筆譯互譯要點【英譯中】

Tips 英譯中要點提示

1. 國家名、公司組織名，若有固定譯名皆需譯出，若是十分普遍常見的譯名，可不需再加註原文，否則第一次出現於文中時需以圓括號引註原文，其後則以譯名表示即可。在無固有譯名的情況下，直接以原文譯出。
2. 年代、數值以阿拉伯數字表示，百分比以符號代替即可。
3. 金額以阿拉伯數字合併金額單位表示。
4. 各國貨幣符號盡量譯出譯名，不要只用符號表示，若是常用且辨識率高的貨幣，只以符號譯出亦可。
5. 翻譯時，為了流暢度並讓讀者充分了解文章要表達的意思，可在不更改原意的前提下，適時加入譯出文。避免錯字、異體字。

The Home Office has admitted that its £1.2 billion upgrade to the mobile communications network that emergency services rely on is in trouble leaving dead zones that potentially put police, paramedics, firemen and the public at risk.

The Home Office is effectively betting on Britain's big mobile network providers to live up to the promises they made to put the necessary technology in place to eliminate a 10 percent coverage gap by 2020 when the new service will be in full operation.

Britain's 300,000 strong emergency services currently use a dedicated radio-based network for mobile communication. The current system covers almost the entire UK.

Part 7

* billion 十億
* at risk 冒風險
* in place 準備就緒
* dead zone n. 無手機訊號的地區
* live up to 達到；符合

中文譯文對照 Chinese Translation

Home Office 公司坦承以 12 億英鎊升級的行動通訊網絡，也就是緊急服務機構仰賴的網絡，留有手機收不到訊號的問題，而這可能會將警方、醫務輔助人員、消防員和大眾，置於極大的風險中。

實際上 Home Office 全賭在英國最大行動網絡提供商會兑現承諾，把必要的科技準備就緒，排除在 2020 年前新服務達到完全運作之前的 10% 收訊覆蓋範圍缺口。

英國有多達 30 萬個緊急服務機構，目前以專用的無線電做為行動通訊。目前使用的系統幾乎涵蓋整個英國。

D 英譯中譯文討論 iscussions

1. 原文「The Home Office has admitted that its £1.2 billion upgrade to the mobile communications network that emergency services rely on is in trouble leaving dead zones that potentially put police, paramedics, firemen and the public at risk.」，其「in trouble leaving dead zones」直譯為「留下盲區的問題」無法讓讀者了解其意思，需以平常的白話方式表達，譯作「留有手機收不到訊號的問題」，翻譯時，為了流暢度並讓讀者充分了解文章要表達的意思，可在不更改原意的前提下，適時加入譯出文。

2. 原文「The Home Office is effectively betting on Britain's big mobile network providers to live up to the promises they made to put the necessary technology in place to eliminate a 10 percent coverage gap by 2020 when the new service will be in full operation.」，其「by 2020」是「不遲於；在…之前」的意思，「coverage gap」是「涵蓋範圍的缺口」，加入「收訊」使文意更清楚，「provider」用於商業性質的內容，以「提供商」詮釋較為恰當，譯作「實際上 Home Office 全賭在英國最大行動網絡提供商會兌現承諾，把必要的科技準備就緒，排除在 2020 年前新服務達到完全運作之前的 10% 收訊覆蓋範圍缺口。」。

3. 原　文「Britain's 300,000 strong emergency services currently use a dedicated radio-based network for mobile communication. The current system covers almost the entire UK.」，其「300,000 strong」是「多達 300,000 個」的意思，數值的部份亦可以阿拉伯數字直譯，亦可譯作「英國有多達 300,000 個緊急服務機構，目前以專用的無線電做為行動通訊。目前使用的系統幾乎涵蓋整個英國。」。

Unit 31

31.2 中英筆譯互譯要點【中譯英】

Tips 中譯英要點提示

1. 年代、數值以阿拉伯數字表示，百分比以符號或英文字表示皆可。

2. 金額以阿拉伯數字或英文字表示皆可。

3. **常見且辨識率高的各國貨幣符號僅以符號表示。辨識率不高的貨幣則需譯出英語名稱。**

4. 本身為英文名的專有名詞直接譯回原文，不需再附上中文譯文。

5. 譯文前後的連貫性與流暢度需符合英語語法，主詞在隨後接續的敘述中盡量皆以代名詞／指示代名詞／其他名詞表示，不要一直重複名詞主詞。

6. 其它：

   a 十億是「billion」。

   b 行動通訊網絡是「mobile communication network」。

   c 手機收不到訊號是「dead zone」。

   d 醫務輔助人員是「paramedic」。

Home Office 公司坦承以 12 億英鎊升級的行動通訊網絡，也就是緊急服務機構仰賴的網絡，留有手機收不到訊號的問題，而這可能會將警方、醫務輔助人員、消防員和大眾，置於極大的風險中。

實際上 Home Office 全賭在英國最大行動網絡提供商會兌現承諾，把必要的科技準備就緒，排除在 2020 年前新服務達到完全運作之前的 10% 收訊覆蓋範圍缺口。

英國有多達 30 萬個緊急服務機構，目前以專用的無線電做為行動通訊。目前使用的系統幾乎涵蓋整個英國。

■ 請試著翻劃底線的部分。

英文譯文對照
English Translation

The Home Office has admitted that its £1.2 billion upgrade to the mobile communications network that emergency services rely on is in trouble leaving dead zones that potentially put police, paramedics, firemen and the public at risk.（詳看下頁討論 1）

The Home Office is effectively betting on Britain's big mobile network providers to live up to the promises they made to put the necessary technology in place to eliminate a 10 percent coverage gap by 2020 when the new service will be in full operation.（詳看下頁討論 2）

Britain's 300,000 strong emergency services currently use a dedicated radio-based network for mobile communication. The current system covers almost the entire UK.（詳看下頁討論 3）

中譯英譯文討論 Discussions

1. 原文「Home Office 公司坦承以 12 億英鎊升級的行動通訊網絡，也就是緊急服務機構仰賴的網絡，留有手機收不到訊號的問題，而這可能會將警方、醫務輔助人員、消防員和大眾，置於極大的風險中。」，以所有格代名詞「its」表示「Home Office」這間公司，亦可譯作「The Home Office has admitted that its 1.2 billion pound upgrade to the mobile communications network used by the emergency services could have a dead zone problem putting police, paramedics, firemen and the public at risk.」。

2. 原文「實際上 Home Office 全賭在英國最大行動網絡提供商會兌現承諾，把必要的科技準備就緒，排除在 2020 年前新服務達到完全運作之前的 10% 收訊覆蓋範圍缺口。」，亦可譯作「The Home Office is confident that the commitments given by Britain's biggest mobile communication network providers to install the necessary technology to eliminate a 10% coverage gap by 2010 will be honored.」。

3. 原文「英國有多達 30 萬個緊急服務機構，目前以專用的無線電做為行動通訊。目前使用的系統幾乎涵蓋整個英國。」，亦可譯作「Currently a dedicated radio-based network is used for mobile communication by the 300,000 members of the Britain's emergency services. The current system covers almost the entire UK.」。

Unit 32

32.1 中英筆譯互譯要點【英譯中】

Tips 英譯中要點提示

1. 專業術語／名詞之字詞譯名需查證，同樣的字詞在不同專業領域表達的意涵不同。
2. 在英語原文中有以引號「“ ”」標註的文字，在譯文加上單引號強調譯文，再以圓括弧加註原文。
3. 專有名詞若有固定譯名皆需譯出，若是十分普遍常見的譯名，可不需再加註原文，否則第一次出現於文中時需以圓括號引註原文，其後則以譯名表示即可。
4. **譯文以白話文為主，以正常速度唸文章時，該停頓換氣時，原則上就是需要下逗號的位置，但仍視原文而定。**

＊ Internet of Things 物聯網；簡稱 IoT　　＊ identifier 標誌號
＊ micro-electromechanical systems 微機電系統；簡稱 MEMS
＊ biochip 生物晶片　　＊ convergence 聚合
＊ smart node 智慧節點　　＊ back and forth 來來回回

A主題短文 rticle

The Internet of Things（IoT）is predicted to be the next big step in information technology. It is a scenario in which objects, animals and people all have unique identifiers and the ability to transfer data back and forth over a wireless network without any human interaction. It is the convergence of previous unrelated technologies from wireless technology and micro-electromechanical systems（MEMS）to the Internet that has evolved into the IoT.

A thing, in the Internet of Things, can be a heart monitoring implant, a biochip in dairy cows, a sensor in the cement of a bridge, the washing machine in the home or any object that can be given a unique IP address and the ability to transfer data over a network. It is with machine-to-machine（M2M）communications in large scale industrial manufacturing and in the power, oil and gas utilities that the IoT has been most closely associated with so far.

"Smart" is the name that is usually given to products with M2M communication capabilities.

Everything on the planet could easily be assigned an IP address. However, with the increase in the number of smart nodes, as well as the amount of data they generate, there are increasing worries over data privacy, data sovereignty and security.

C 中文譯文對照
Chinese Translation

物聯網（Internet of Things; IoT）被預測為資訊科技接下來的一大進展。物聯網是個物體、動物和人類全擁有獨特標記號，以及擁有不需人力介入就能透過無線網路來回傳送資料能力的情境。是把先前互不相關的科技聚合在一起進化成為物聯網，從無線技術（wireless technology）和微機電系統（micro-electromechanical systems）到網際網路（Internet）。

在物聯網裡，物件可以是個心臟監測植入器、家畜體內的生物晶片、橋樑水泥內的感測器、家裡的洗衣機，或是任何其他能夠給予網路位址（IP address）且有能力在網路傳送資料的物件。目前為止，與物聯網最緊密關聯的是大型工業製造業中的機器對機器（machine-to-machine; M2M）通訊，以及電力、石油和瓦斯公用事業。

「智慧型」（smart）通常用於以機器對機器通訊能力打造的產品。

可以輕易指定給每個地球物件一個網路位址。然而智慧節點（smart nodes）的數量增加，產生的資料也跟著增加，這增添對於資料保密（data privacy）、資料主權（data sovereignty）與安全性（security）的憂慮。

D 英譯中譯文討論 iscussions

1. 原　文「The Internet of Things（IoT）is predicted to be the next big step in information technology. It is a scenario in which objects, animals and people all have unique identifiers and the ability to transfer data back and forth over a wireless network without any human interaction.」，其代名詞主詞「It」表示「The Internet of Things」為文符合中文語法與譯文通順，譯文應完整譯出主詞所指為何，在主詞很明顯的狀態下，亦省略譯出，亦可譯作「物聯網（Internet of Things; IoT）被預測為資訊科技接下來的一大進展。是個物體、動物和人類全擁有獨特標記號，以及擁有不需人力介入就能透過無線網路來回傳送資料能力的情境。」。

2. 原　文「It is with machine-to-machine（M2M）communications in large scale industrial manufacturing and in the power, oil and gas utilities that the IoT has been most closely associated with so far.」，其「has been most closely associated with」是被動語態，若直譯為「被拿來最緊密地跟製造業中的機器對機器通訊，以及電力、石油和瓦斯公用事業有關聯」，並不符合中文語法，譯文要譯其意而非其英語文法，亦可譯作「目前為止，與物聯網最緊密關聯的是大型工業製造業中的機器對機器（machine-to-machine; M2M）通訊，以及電力、石油和瓦斯公用事業。」。

3. 原文「However, with the increase in the number of smart nodes, as well as the amount of data they generate, there are increasing worries over data privacy, data sovereignty and security.」，亦可譯作「隨著智慧節點（smart nodes）數量增加，產生的資料也就跟著增加，這加劇對於資料保密（data privacy）、資料主權（data sovereignty）與安全性（security）問題的憂慮。」。

Unit 32

32.2 中英筆譯互譯要點【中譯英】

Tips 中譯英要點提示

1. 英語的引號用於指明意涵和單字有不尋常含糊不清意涵的狀態。

2. 英語語法有時態、詞性變化，中翻英時必須看完整個句子、段落，了解其意思之後再譯出，每個句子皆需選擇文法與時態。特別留意中文不易在文字中看出英語語法的時態與被動語態。

3. 本身為英文名的專有名詞直接譯回原文，不需再附上中文譯文。

4. 其它：
   a 標記號是「identifier」。
   b 監測器是「monitor」。
   c 轉發器是「transponder」。
   d 感測器是「sensor」。
   e 電力、石油和瓦斯公用事業是「power, oil and gas utilities」。
   f 上游資料流是「upstream data」。

物聯網（Internet of Things; IoT）被預測為資訊科技接下來的一大進展。物聯網是個物體、動物和人類全擁有獨特標記號，以及擁有不需人力介入就能透過無線網路來回傳送資料能力的情境。是把先前互不相關的科技聚合在一起進化成為物聯網，從無線技術（wireless technology）和微機電系統（micro-electromechanical systems）到網際網路（Internet）。

在物聯網裡，物件可以是個心臟監測植入器、家畜體內的生物晶片、橋樑水泥內的感測器、家裡的洗衣機，或是任何其他能夠給予網路位址（IP address）且有能力在網路傳送資料的物件。目前為止，與物聯網最緊密關聯的是大型工業製造業中的機器對機器（machine-to-machine; M2M）通訊，以及電力、石油和瓦斯公用事業。

「智慧型」（smart）通常用於以機器對機器通訊能力打造的產品。

可以輕易指定給每個地球物件一個網路位址。然而智慧節點（smart nodes）的數量增加，產生的資料也跟著增加，這增添對於資料保密（data privacy）、資料主權（data sovereignty）與安全性（security）的憂慮。

■ 請試著翻劃底線的部分。

Part 7

E 英文譯文對照
English Translation

The Internet of Things（IoT）is predicted to be the next big step in information technology. It is a scenario in which objects, animals and people all have unique identifiers and the ability to transfer data back and forth over a wireless network without any human interaction. It is the convergence of previous unrelated technologies from wireless technology and micro-electromechanical systems（MEMS）to the Internet that has evolved into the IoT.（詳見下頁討論 1）

A thing, in the Internet of Things, can be a heart monitoring implant, a biochip in dairy cows, a sensor in the cement of a bridge, the washing machine in the home or any object that can be given a unique IP address and the ability to transfer data over a network. It is with machine-to-machine（M2M）communications in large scale industrial manufacturing and in the power, oil and gas utilities that the IoT has been most closely associated with so far.（詳見下頁討論 2）

"Smart" is the name that is usually given to products with M2M communication capabilities.（詳見下頁討論 3）

Everything on the planet could easily be assigned an IP address. However, with the increase in the number of smart nodes, as well as the amount of data they generate, there are increasing worries over data privacy, data sovereignty and security.（詳見下頁討論 4）

D 中譯英譯文討論 Discussions

1. 原文「是把先前互不相關的科技聚合在一起進化成為物聯網，從無線技術（wireless technology）和微機電系統（micro-electromechanical systems）到網際網路（Internet）。」，使用現在完成式，因此譯作「It's the convergence of previous unrelated technologies from wireless technology and micro-electromechanical systems（MEMS）to the Internet that has evolved into the IoT.」。

2. 原文「目前為止，與物聯網最緊密關聯的是大型工業製造業中的機器對機器（machine-to-machine; M2M）通訊，以及電力、石油和瓦斯公用事業。」，亦可譯作「It's with machine-to-machine（M2M）communication in large scale industrial manufacturing and power, oil and gas utilities that the Internet of Things has been the most closely associated with up till now.」。

3. 原文「「智慧型」（smart）通常用於以機器對機器通訊能力打造的產品。」，亦可譯作「Products which have M2M communication capabilities built into them are often said to be smart.」。

4. 原文「然而智慧節點（smart nodes）的數量增加，產生的資料也跟著增加，這增添對於資料保密（data privacy）、資料主權（data sovereignty）與安全性（security）的憂慮。」，亦可譯作「But concerns about data privacy, data sovereignty and security are predicted to increase as the number of smart nodes as well as the amount data they generate increases.」。

Part 7

Unit 33

33.1 中英筆譯互譯要點【英譯中】

Tips 英譯中要點提示

1. 專有名詞、公司組織名若有固定譯名皆需譯出，若是十分普遍常見的譯名，可不需再加註原文，否則第一次出現於文中時需以圓括號引註原文，其後則以譯名表示即可，若無固定譯名，則以原文表示。

2. 專業術語／名詞之字詞譯名需查證，同樣的字詞在不同專業領域表達的意涵不同。

3. 在英語原文中有圓括號「（ ）」，表示標註插入語或修飾評論。若無固有譯名即以原文表示。

4. 翻譯時，為了流暢度並讓讀者充分了解文章要表達的意思，可在不更改原意的前提下，適時加入譯出文。

---

* quantum computer 全量子電腦
* sophisticated 精密的；尖端的
* revolutionize 革新；變動
* circuitry 電路圖
* prowess 本領
* quantum bit 量子位元
* superconducting quantum computer 超導量子電腦
* hurdle 難關；障礙

The first ever quantum device that detects and corrects its own errors has arrived.

When scientists finally deliver on the promise of a full quantum computer, the world of computing will be revolutionized. The promised improvements in speed and energy efficiency will make today's most sophisticated machines look like something from the stone age.

But to take advantage of this marvelous increase in computing prowess, quantum physicists have a major hurdle to overcome, for these quantum bit（qubit）devices are highly vulnerable to environmentally-induced errors.

Keeping quibits error-free and stable enough to reproduce the same result time after time, is one of the major challenges faced by scientists.

In what is being called a major milestone, researchers at the Martinis Lab have created quantum circuitry with the ability to self check for errors and suppress them. These circuits are able to preserve the qubits' state giving the system the stability and reliability that has long been sought. It is hoped that the lab's work will provide the foundation for the building of the world's first superconducting quantum computer.

C 中文譯文對照
Chinese Translation

第一個可偵測並自行更正錯誤的量子裝置已經到來。

當科學家們終於兌現對全量子電腦（quantum computer）的承諾，電腦計算的世界將會有徹底的大變動。在速度和能量效率上產生的大好進步，相較之下會讓現今最尖端的機器看起來就像來自石器時代的物品。

不過，要利用這個卓越的計算本領，量子物理學家必須克服一個重要的關卡，也就是這些量子位元（quantum bit;「qubit」）裝置高度易受環境引發出錯。

要保持量子位元零出錯，而且要穩定性夠好到足以一再產生相同結果，是科學家們面臨的其中一項重要挑戰。

在這個被稱為重要的里程碑裡，Martinis Lab 實驗室裡的研究人員已研發出能自行檢測和抑制出錯的電路圖。這些電路圖能保存量子位元狀態，給予系統一直以來所追求的穩定性和可靠性。希望實驗室的研究工作將提供打造全世界第一台超導量子電腦（superconducting quantum computer）的基礎。

D 英譯中譯文討論
Discussions

1. 原文「When scientists finally deliver on the promise of a full quantum computer, the world of computing will be revolutionized. The promised improvements in speed and energy efficiency will make today's most sophisticated machines look like something from the stone age.」，譯文需符合中文語法，看完整段後找出脈絡再譯出，不可以直譯的方式逐句譯出，會讓人摸不著頭緒，其「**machine**」指的是「電腦」，「**stone age**」是「石器時代」的意思，是以現代科技產物和舊時的石器時代物品相對應，在譯文加入「相較之下」更為通暢，亦可譯作「當科學家們終於兑現對全量子電腦（quantum computer）的承諾，電腦計算的世界將會進入一場革命。在速度和能量效率上產生的大好進步，相較之下會讓現今最尖端的電腦看起來就像來自石器時代的物品。」。

2. 原　文「Keeping quibits error-free and stable enough to reproduce the same result time after time, is one of the major challenges faced by scientists.」，其「error-free」亦可譯作「零失誤；零出錯；無失誤」，其「hurdle」是「難關；障礙」的意思，亦可譯作「要保持量子位元無出錯，以及穩定性夠高足以一再產生相同結果，是科學家們在量子計算（quantum computing）所面臨的其中一大挑戰。」。

3. 原文「These circuits are able to preserve the qubits' state giving the system the stability and reliability that has long been sought.」，其「sought」是「尋找」的意思，亦可譯作「一直以來所追求的系統穩定性與可靠性，能藉由這些可保存量子位元狀態的電路圖達成。」。

Unit 33

33.2 中英筆譯互譯要點【中譯英】

Tips 中譯英要點提示

1. 英語的引號用於強調內容。指明意涵和單字有不尋常含糊不清意涵的狀態，中文以單引號強調內容。

2. 譯文前後的連貫性與流暢度需符合英語語法，主詞在隨後接續的敘述中盡量皆以代名詞／指示代名詞／其他名詞表示，不要一直重複名詞主詞。

3. 本身為英文名的專有名詞直接譯回原文，不需再附上中文譯文。

4. 其它：

   a 電路圖是「circuitry」。
   b 計算是「computing」。
   c 里程碑是「mile stone」。
   d 零出錯是「error-free」。

第一個可偵測並自行更正錯誤的量子裝置已經到來。

當科學家們終於兌現對全量子電腦（quantum computer）的承諾，電腦計算的世界將會有徹底的大變動。在速度和能量效率上產生的大好進步，相較之下會讓現今最尖端的機器看起來就像來自石器時代的物品。

不過，要利用這個卓越的計算本領，量子物理學家必須克服一個重要的關卡，也就是這些量子位元（quantum bit;「qubit」）裝置高度易受環境引發出錯。

要保持量子位元零出錯，而且要穩定性夠好到足以一再產生相同結果，是科學家們面臨的其中一項重要挑戰。

在這個被稱為重要的里程碑裡，Martinis Lab 實驗室裡的研究人員已研發出能自行檢測和抑制出錯的電路圖。這些電路圖能保存量子位元狀態，給予系統一直以來所追求的穩定性和可靠性。希望實驗室的研究工作將提供打造全世界第一台超導量子電腦（superconducting quantum computer）的基礎。

■ 請試著翻劃底線的部分。

E 英文譯文對照
English Translation

The first ever quantum device that detects and corrects its own errors has arrived.

When scientists finally deliver on the promise of a full quantum computer, the world of computing will be revolutionized. The promised improvements in speed and energy efficiency will make today's most sophisticated machines look like something from the stone age.（詳見下頁討論 1）

But to take advantage of this marvelous increase in computing prowess, quantum physicists have a major hurdle to overcome, for these quantum bit（qubit）devices are highly vulnerable to environmentally-induced errors.（詳見下頁討論 2）

Keeping quibits error-free and stable enough to reproduce the same result time after time, is one of the major challenges faced by scientists.

In what is being called a major milestone, researchers at the Martinis Lab have created quantum circuitry with the ability to self check for errors and suppress them. These circuits are able to preserve the qubits' state giving the system the stability and reliability that has long been sought. It is hoped that the lab's work will provide the foundation for the building of the world's first superconducting quantum computer.（詳見下頁討論 3）

中譯英譯文討論 Discussions

1. 原文「當科學家們終於兌現對全量子電腦（quantum computer）的承諾，電腦計算的世界將會有徹底的大變動。在速度和能量效率上產生的大好進步，相較之下會讓現今最尖端的機器看起來就像來自石器時代的物品。」，亦可譯作「A revolution of speed and energy efficiency will transform the world of computing when scientists finally fulfill the promise of a full quantum computer, then even our most sophisticated present day machines will look like they are from the stone age.」。

2. 原文「不過，要利用這個卓越的計算本領，量子物理學家必須克服一個重要的關卡，也就是這些量子位元（quantum bit;「qubit」）裝置高度易受環境引發出錯。」，亦可譯作「But for all these marvelous advances in computer prowess promised by the quantum bit（qubit）to be realized, quantum physicists will have to create circuitry that overcomes its vulnerability to environmentally-induced errors.」。

3. 原文「在這個被稱為重要的里程碑裡，Martinis Lab 實驗室裡的研究人員已研發出能自行檢測和抑制出錯的電路圖。這些電路圖能保存量子位元狀態，給予系統一直以來所追求的穩定性和可靠性。希望實驗室的研究工作將提供打造全世界第一台超導量子電腦（superconducting quantum computer）的基礎。」，亦可譯作「Researchers in the Martinis Lab have developed quantum circuitry that self-checks for errors and suppresses them while preserving the qubits' state. This highly sought-after reliability will prove foundational for building the first superconducting quantum computers, and is being called a major milestone.」。

Unit 34

34.1 中英筆譯互譯要點【英譯中】

Tips 英譯中要點提示

1. 譯文以白話文為主，以正常速度唸文章時，該停頓換氣時，原則上就是需要下逗號的位置，但仍視原文而定。
2. 翻譯時，為了流暢度並讓讀者充分了解文章要表達的意思，可在不更改原意的前提下，適時加入譯出文。
3. 專有名詞若有固定譯名皆需譯出，若是十分普遍常見的譯名，可不需再加註原文，否則第一次出現於文中時需以圓括號引註原文，其後則以譯名表示即可。
4. 專業術語／名詞之字詞譯名需查證。

Cloud computing is a new way of delivering, consuming and producing IT resources via the Internet. The forging of new standards will only continue to boost its potential and make the technology even more promising.

Cloud computing is quite possibly the hottest, most discussed and often misunderstood concept in information technology（IT） today. This revolutionary concept has reached unexpected heights in the last decade and is recognized by both government and private-sector organizations as a major game-changing technology.

Organizations and individuals alike are keen to store and process their data in the Cloud, to access the stored data and applications from anywhere, and to do this faster and at lower cost than through conventional means. Commercial enterprises and public-sector organizations are eager to gain the promised efficiency and agility, while the average user desires the Cloud's ubiquity and flexibility, but above all, it's all about reducing costs.

＊Cloud computing 雲端運算
＊IT 為資訊科技（Information Technology）的縮寫
＊game-changing 改變戰局
＊mean 平均值
＊agility 敏捷
＊application 應用程式
＊public-sector 政府資助的企（事）業
＊ubiquity 無所不在；普遍存在

中文譯文對照
Chinese Translation

雲端運算（Cloud computing）是一個透過網際網路（Internet）來遞送、消耗、產生 IT（資訊科技）資源的新方式。另創的新標準將只會繼續強化雲端運算的潛力，讓這項科技更加前景看好。

雲端運算可能是現今最熱門、討論度最高，以及在資訊科技（IT）裡最常被誤解的概念。這個革命性的概念在過去十年來已達出乎預期的巔峰，政府及私營企業機構也都意識到這是個開創新局的重要科技。

機構和個人皆樂於在雲端儲存和處理他們的資料，從任何地方皆可存取儲存的資料和應用程式（applications），比透過傳統方式的平均值更快速且成本更低。商業企業跟政府資助的機構渴望獲得這個掛保證的效率和敏捷度，而一般使用者則是想要雲端的普遍性和變通性，但是最重要的是關乎降低成本花費。

1. 原　文「Cloud computing is a new way of delivering, consuming and producing IT resources via the Internet. The forging of new standards will only continue to boost its potential and make the technology even more promising.」，其「**promising**」是「有希望；有前途」的意思，但是「有前途」較適合用於形容人在未來和事業上的發展，用於形容該科技，將譯文改為「前景看好」較為適當。

2. 原　文「Cloud computing is quite possibly the hottest, most discussed and often misunderstood concept in information technology（IT） today.」，其「most discussed」若直譯為「最被討論的；被拿來做討論最多的」，使得譯文不順暢，以「討論度最高」來表達，不影響原意，亦符合中文語法。

3. 原文「This revolutionary concept has reached unexpected heights in the last decade and is recognized by both government and private-sector organizations as a major game-changing technology.」，亦可譯作「這個革命性的概念在過去十年來已達出乎預期的高點，政府及私營企業機構也都意識到這是個改變戰局的重要科技。」。

4. 原　文「Commercial enterprises and public-sector organizations are eager to gain the promised efficiency and agility, while the average user desires the Cloud's ubiquity and flexibility, but above all, it's all about reducing costs.」其「**eager to**」和「**desire**」都有「渴望」的意思，但是「**eager to**」有比較迫切的意思，為顯出差異性，譯作「渴望」和「想要」。

Unit 34

34.2 中英筆譯互譯要點【中譯英】

Tips 中譯英要點提示

1. 英語語法有時態、詞性變化，中翻英時必須看完整個句子、段落，了解其意思之後再譯出，每個句子皆需選擇文法與時態。**特別留意中文不易在文字中看出英語語法的時態與被動語態、倒裝句。**

2. 本身為英文名的專有名詞直接譯回原文，不需再附上中文譯文。

3. 譯文前後的連貫性與流暢度需符合英語語法，主詞在隨後接續的敘述中盡量皆以代名詞／指示代名詞／其他名詞表示，不要一直重複名詞主詞

4. 其它：
   a 私營企業機構是「private-sector organization」。
   b 平均值是「mean」。
   c 普遍性是「ubiquity」。

雲端運算（Cloud computing）是一個透過網際網路（Internet）來遞送、消耗、產生 IT（資訊科技）資源的新方式。另創的新標準將只會繼續強化雲端運算的潛力，讓這項科技更加有希望。

雲端運算可能是現今最熱門、討論度最高，以及在資訊科技（IT）裡最常被誤解的概念。這個革命性的概念在過去十年來已達出乎預期的巔峰，政府及私營企業機構也都意識到這是個開創新局的重要科技。

機構和個人皆樂於在雲端儲存和處理他們的資料，從任何地方皆可存取儲存的資料和應用程式（applications），比透過傳統方式的平均值更快速且成本更低。商業企業跟政府資助的機構渴望獲得這個掛保證的效率和敏捷度，而一般使用者則是想要雲端的普遍性和變通性，但是最重要的是關乎降低成本花費。

■ 請試著翻劃底線的部分。

Cloud computing is a new way of delivering, consuming and producing IT resources via the Internet. The forging of new standards will only continue to boost its potential and make the technology even more promising.（詳見下頁討論 1）

Cloud computing is quite possibly the hottest, most discussed and often misunderstood concept in information technology（IT） today.（詳見下頁討論 2） This revolutionary concept has reached unexpected heights in the last decade and is recognized by both government and private-sector organizations as a major game-changing technology.

Organizations and individuals alike are keen to store and process their data in the Cloud, to access the stored data and applications from anywhere, and to do this faster and at lower cost than through conventional means. Commercial enterprises and public-sector organizations are eager to gain the promised efficiency and agility, while the average user desires the Cloud's ubiquity and flexibility, but above all, it's all about reducing costs.（詳見下頁討論 3）

D 中譯英譯文討論
Discussions

1. 原文「另創的新標準將只會繼續強化雲端運算的潛力，讓這項科技更加前景看好。」，亦可譯作「Its potential will continue to be boosted by the creation of new standards making the technology even more promising.」。

2. 原文「雲端運算可能是現今最熱門、討論度最高，以及在資訊科技（IT）裡最常被誤解的概念。」，亦可譯作「Quite possibly the hottest, most discussed and often misunderstood concept in information technology（IT）today is Cloud computing.」。

3. 原文「商業企業跟政府資助的機構渴望獲得這個掛保證的效率和敏捷度，而一般使用者則是想要雲端的普遍性和變通性，但是最重要的是關乎降低成本花費。」，亦可譯作「While the average user desires the ubiquity and flexibility of the Cloud, commercial enterprises and public-sector organizations are eager to gain the promised efficiency and agility, but above all it's all about costs.」。

Unit 35

35.1 中英筆譯互譯要點【英譯中】

Tips 英譯中要點提示

1. 翻譯時，為了流暢度並讓讀者充分了解文章要表達的意思，可在不更改原意的前提下，適時加入譯出文。
2. 數值譯文可以阿拉伯數字或合併單位表示，百分比以符號代替即可。
3. 人名、城市名、公司組織名，以及專有名詞若有固定譯名皆需譯出，若是十分普遍常見的譯名，可不需再加註原文，否則第一次出現於文中時需以圓括號引註原文，其後則以譯名表示即可。在無固有譯名的情況下，直接以原文譯出。
4. 專業術語／名詞之字詞譯名需查證，同樣的字詞在不同專業領域表達的意涵不同。
5. 為求譯文清楚通暢，需適時將代名詞主詞完整譯出。

---

* story 層；樓
* hydroelectric [ˌhaɪdroɪˋlɛktrɪk] 水力發電
* reinforce [ˌriɪnˋfɔrs] v. 加強；使更強烈
* renewable energy source 可再生能源
* megawatts [ˋmɛgəˌwɑt] n. 百萬瓦特
* free air-cooling 機房自然冷卻法
* square foot 平方英尺

Communications and data services provider CenturyLink has opened a new data center which uses nearby dams to provide 85 percent of its power needs.

The three-story 50,000-square-foot data center, located in Moses Lake, Wash., will have 8 megawatts（MW) of hydroelectric power available on site at start-up, but this will increase to an eventual 30MW.

The facility, which is leased to CenturyLink by Server Farm Realty, is powered by the Wanapum Dam and Priest Rapids Dam on the Columbia River.

Cloud and disaster recovery services will be supported by the new facility, which CenturyLink claim is reinforced by a more reliable renewable energy source than either wind or solar - both of which are dependent on daylight and weatherconditions.

"CenturyLink's new low-cost power data center services provide many benefits to our customers, including a highly resilient solution coupled with power costs and efficiency metrics that rank among the best in the industry, and the facility serves as an excellent disaster recovery location," David Meredith, senior vice president of CenturyLink, said in a statement.

Free air-cooling provided by the central Washington climate also drives power use down even further, according to the company.

C 中文譯文對照
Chinese Translation

通訊與資料服務提供者 CenturyLink 開設了一個 85% 電力來源為鄰近水壩的新資料中心。

這座三層共 5 萬平方英尺的資料中心坐落於華盛頓摩西湖（Moses Lake, Wash.），原先的水力發電最終將從 8 百萬瓦特（MW）變成支援現場相當 30 MW 的電量負載。

這個場所是 Server Farm Realty 所有並租給 CenturyLink，由哥倫比亞河（Columbia River）上的 Wanapum 水壩和 Priest Rapids 水壩提供電力。

這個新的資料中心將會用來支持雲端和災難復元（disaster recovery）服務，CenturyLink 表示該中心的電力是以比需要仰賴日光的太陽能發電，或是視氣象情況的風力發電還要更可靠的可再生能源支援。

CenturyLink 的資深副總裁 David Meredith 在聲明稿上表示，「CenturyLink 低電費成本的新資料中心，提供我們顧客許多好處，包括適應力高的解決辦法，加上低電費成本以及在該產業公制中評為最有效率等級，該中心也作為絕佳的災難復元地點。」

根據 CenturyLink 的說法，華盛頓中部的氣候也允許使用極有意義的機房自然冷卻法（free air-cooling），而這甚至讓用電量又更低。

1. 原　文「The facility, which is leased to CenturyLink by Server Farm Realty, is powered by the Wanapum Dam and Priest Rapids Dam on the Columbia River.」，其「the facility」指的是「設立新資料中心的場所」，在譯文適時加入譯出文，有助譯文通暢，亦可譯作「這個設立新資料中心的場所是 Server Farm Realty 所有並租給 CenturyLink，由哥倫比亞河（Columbia River）上的 Wanapum 水壩和 Priest Rapids 水壩提供電力。」。

2. 原　文「Cloud and disaster recovery services will be supported by the new facility, which CenturyLink claim is reinforced by a more reliable renewable energy source than either wind or solar - both of which are dependent on daylight and weather conditions.」，　其「the new facility」指的是「新資料中心」，譯出完整主詞使譯文更清楚，亦可譯作「這個新的資料中心將會用來支持雲端和作為災難復元（disaster recovery）服務，CenturyLink 宣稱該中心的電力來源是更可靠的可再生能源，而不是仰賴日光的太陽能發電，或是得視氣象情況的風力發電。」。

3. 原　文「Free air-cooling provided by the central Washington climate also drives power use down even further, according to the company.」，其「company」指的是「CenturyLink」，在譯文中譯出完整主詞有助讀者理解，中法語法通常會先表明説話的人為何者再接續敘述，亦可譯作「根據 CenturyLink 的説法，華盛頓中部的氣候也允許使用極有意義的機房自然冷卻法（Free air-cooling），而這甚至讓用電量又更低。」。

Unit 35

35.2 中英筆譯互譯要點【中譯英】

Tips 中譯英要點提示

1. 中文使用單引號引述人物言語，英語以引號表示。
2. 數值以阿拉伯數字譯出即可。
3. 本身為英文名的專有名詞直接譯回原文，不需再附上中文譯文。
4. 譯文前後的連貫性與流暢度需符合英語語法，主詞在隨後接續的敘述中盡量皆以代名詞／指示代名詞／其他名詞表示，不要一直重複名詞主詞。數值譯文可以阿拉伯數字或合併單位表示，百分比以符號或譯出英文皆可。
5. 其它：

   a 水壩是「dam」。
   b 雲端是「cloud」。
   c 資料服務是「data service」。
   d 水力發電是「hydroelectric」。
   e 平方英尺是「square-foot」。
   f 再生能源是「renewable energy source」。
   g 太陽能發電是「solar」。

通訊與資料服務提供者 CenturyLink 開設了一個 85% 電力來源為鄰近水壩的新資料中心。

這座三層共 5 萬平方英尺的資料中心坐落於華盛頓摩西湖（Moses Lake, Wash.），原先的水力發電最終將從 8 百萬瓦特（MW）變成支援現場相當 30 MW 的電量負載。

這個場所是 Server Farm Realty 所有並租給 CenturyLink，由哥倫比亞河（Columbia River）上的 Wanapum 水壩和 Priest Rapids 水壩提供電力。

這個新的資料中心將會用來支持雲端和災難復元（disaster recovery）服務，CenturyLink 表示該中心的電力是以比需要仰賴日光的太陽能發電，或是視氣象情況的風力發電還要更可靠的可再生能源支援。

CenturyLink 的資深副總裁 David Meredith 在聲明稿上表示，「CenturyLink 低電費成本的新資料中心，提供我們顧客許多好處，包括適應力高的解決辦法，加上低電費成本以及在該產業公制中評為最有效率等級，該中心也作為絕佳的災難復元地點。」

根據 CenturyLink 的說法，華盛頓中部的氣候也允許使用極有意義的機房自然冷卻法（free air-cooling），而這甚至讓用電量又更低。

■ 請試著翻劃底線的部分。

E 英文譯文對照
English Translation

Communications and data services provider CenturyLink has opened a new data center which uses nearby dams to provide 85 percent of its power needs.（詳見下頁討論 1）

The three-story 50,000-square-foot data center, located in Moses Lake, Wash., will have 8 megawatts（MW）of hydroelectric power available on site at start-up, but this will increase to an eventual 30MW.（詳見下頁討論 2）

The facility, which is leased to CenturyLink by Server Farm Realty, is powered by the Wanapum Dam and Priest Rapids Dam on the Columbia River.

Cloud and disaster recovery services will be supported by the new facility, which CenturyLink claim is reinforced by a more reliable renewable energy source than either wind or solar - both of which are dependent on daylight and weather conditions.（詳見下頁討論 3）

"CenturyLink'sprovide many benefits to our customers, including a highly resilient solution coupled with power costs and efficiency metrics that rank among the best in the industry, and the facility serves as an excellent disaster recovery location," David Meredith, senior vice president of CenturyLink, said in a statement.

Free air-cooling provided by the central Washington climate also drives power use down even further, according to the company.（詳見下頁討論 4）

1. 原文「通訊與資料服務提供者 CenturyLink 開設了一個 85% 電力來源為鄰近水壩的新資料中心。」，亦可譯作「CenturyLink, the communications and data services provider, has opened a new data center that gets 85 percent of its power from nearby dams.」。

2. 原文「這座三層共 5 萬平方英尺的資料中心坐落於華盛頓摩西湖（Moses Lake, Wash.），原先的水力發電最終將從 8 百萬瓦特（MW）變成支援現場相當 30 MW 的電量負載。」，亦可譯作「Hydroelectric power on site will eventually climb to 30 megawatts（MW） from an initial 8 MW for the three-story 50,000-square-foot data center, located in Moses Lake, Washington.」。

3. 原文「這個新的資料中心將會用來支持雲端和災難復元（disaster recovery）服務，CenturyLink 表示該中心的電力是以比需要仰賴日光的太陽能發電，或是視氣象情況的風力發電還要更可靠的可再生能源支援。」，亦可譯作「CenturyLink said that as the new facility has a more reliable renewable energy source than wind or solar, which are dependent on daylight or the weather, it will be used to support cloud and disaster recovery services.」。

4. 原文「根據 CenturyLink 的說法，華盛頓中部的氣候也允許使用極有意義的機房自然冷卻法（free air-cooling），而這甚至讓用電量又更低。」，亦可譯作「According to the company significant use of free air-cooling is allowed by the central Washington climate, driving even lower power usage.」。

Unit 36

36.1 中英筆譯互譯要點【英譯中】

Tips 英譯中要點提示

1. 新聞常出現地名、人名、組織名稱等專有名詞，皆必須引用已慣用的譯名，若是十分普遍常見的譯名，可不需再加註原文，否則第一次出現於文中時需以圓括號引註原文，其後則以譯名表示即可。

2. 本文有 Pakistani Taliban 是「巴基斯坦的塔利班組織」，以及 Pushtu 是「普什圖語」。

3. 新聞文章裡的數字，在中文譯文中，通常以阿拉伯數字的形式呈現，不須再另行譯為中文字，除非特定單位量詞，如 2 million、10 billion，會譯為以數字加中文字的方式「200萬」、「100億」。

Seven members of the Pakistani Taliban, dressed in the uniform of the local paramilitary force and speaking with the local Pushtu accent came over the wall from an adjacent graveyard and into a large, army-run school. They then moved systematically through it, murdering children and teachers alike with guns and grenades. Three or four attackers are thought to have blown themselves up.

At the latest count 141 had died, 132 of them children. Survivors told harrowing stories of children shot hiding behind desks and chairs. It is even reported that many died when the gunmen interrupted a first-aid training session in the school hall, while others fell in the playground.

Eyewitnesses spoke of children were lined up and shot. The local hospital was so overwhelmed with the injured that it ran out of blood.

---

* adjacent adj. 毗連的
* systematically adv. 按照部署執行
* grenade n. 手榴彈　　* blow up 炸死
* harrowing adj. 令人斷腸的；恐怖的
* run out of 用盡（某物）

中文譯文對照
Chinese Translation

7名巴基斯坦的塔利班組織成員（Pakistani Taliban）穿著當地軍隊制服，操著道地普什圖（Pushtu）口音，從毗鄰一間大規模軍事訓練學校的墓地翻牆進入校園。然後他們有系統地行動，以手槍和手榴彈在校園內殘殺孩童和教師。據說其中3或4名發動攻擊者被自己投出的手榴彈炸死。

最新統計這場攻擊共造成141人死亡，其中有132名孩童。生還者泣訴孩童躲在書桌和椅子後遭到射殺的恐怖敘述。甚至有報導指出，許多孩童在槍手闖入正在進行急救訓練講習的學校禮堂遭到射殺，然而其他孩童則在操場被射殺。

目擊者提到孩童們被排成一排射殺。當地醫院被排山倒海而來的傷者淹沒，以致於血庫存量已用盡。

D 英譯中譯文討論
Discussions

1. 原　文「They then moved systematically through it, murdering children and teachers alike with guns and grenades.」其「murdering」為「謀殺」的意思，依照前後文章脈絡敘述的事件，不直譯為「謀殺」，譯作「然後他們有系統地行動，以手槍和手榴彈在校園內殘殺孩童和教師。」。

2. 原　文「At the latest count 141 victims had died, 132 of them children.」中並無「攻擊」字眼，但從前文「attacker」得知這是場攻擊事件，故在譯文中加入「最新統計這場攻擊共造成 141 人死亡，其中有 132 名孩童。」，這句也可翻譯成「這起事件最新統計遇難人數達 141 人，其中有 132 名孩童。」也可把「攻擊」譯為「這起事件」，由於沒有說明是何種事件（如報復事件、臨時起意事件…等），且前文清楚表明一干人等為「攻擊者」，所以譯文採用「攻擊事件」為較好譯法。

3. 原　文「Survivors told harrowing stories of children shot hiding behind desks and chairs.」在譯文加入「泣訴」而不是直譯為「告訴」，以呼應「harrowing」，譯作「生還者泣訴孩童躲在書桌和椅子後遭到射殺的恐怖敘述。」。

4. 原　文「The local hospital was so overwhelmed with the injured that it ran out of blood.」，其「so…that」表明這句敘述的因果關係，亦可譯作「當地醫院湧入太多傷患，以致於血庫存量已用盡。」

Unit 36

36.2 中英筆譯互譯要點【中譯英】

Tips 中譯英要點提示

1. 本身為英文名的專有名詞直接譯回原文，不需再附上中文譯文。
2. 表示數值／數量不可譯錯，英文譯文常見譯法建議在 10 以下（不包括 10）的數字要以英文字表達，其餘僅以阿拉伯數字表達即可。
3. 特別留意中文不易在文字中看出英語語法的時態與被動語態。英語語法有時態、詞性變化，中翻英時必須看完整個句子、段落，了解其意思之後再譯出，每個句子皆需選擇文法與時態。

A 主題短文 Article

7名巴基斯坦的塔利班組織成員（Pakistani Taliban）穿著當地軍隊制服，操著道地普什圖（Pushtu）口音，從毗鄰一間大規模軍事訓練學校的墓地翻牆進入校園。然後他們有系統地行動，以手槍和手榴彈在校園內殘殺孩童和教師。據說其中3或4名發動攻擊者被自己投出的手榴彈炸死。

最新統計這場攻擊共造成141人死亡，其中有132名孩童。生還者泣訴孩童躲在書桌和椅子後遭到射殺的恐怖敘述。甚至有報導指出，許多孩童在槍手闖入正在進行急救訓練講習的學校禮堂遭到射殺，然而其他孩童則在操場被射殺。

目擊者提到孩童們被排成一排射殺。當地醫院被排山倒海而來的傷者淹沒，以致於血庫存量已用盡。

■ 請試著翻劃底線的部分。

英文譯文對照
English Translation

Seven members of the Pakistani Taliban, dressed in the uniform of the local paramilitary force and speaking with the local Pushtu accent came over the wall from an adjacent graveyard and into a large, army-run school. They then moved systematically through it, murdering children and teachers alike with guns and grenades. Three or four attackers are thought to have blown themselves up.

At the latest count 141 had died, 132 of them children.（詳看下頁討論 1） Survivors told harrowing stories of children shot hiding behind desks and chairs.（詳看下頁討論 2） It is even reported that many died when the gunmen interrupted a first-aid training session in the school hall,（詳看下頁討論 3） while others fell in the playground.

Eyewitnesses spoke of children lined up and shot.（詳看下頁討論 4） The local hospital was so overwhelmed with the injured that it ran out of blood.（詳看下頁討論 5）

D 中譯英譯文討論
iscussions

1. 原文「最新統計這場攻擊共造成 141 人死亡，其中有 132 名孩童」，這句的譯文亦可以現在完成式譯為「At the latest count 141 victims of which 132 were children have died.」。

2. 原文「生還者泣訴孩童躲在書桌和椅子後遭到射殺的令人斷腸敘述。」，亦可譯作「Survivors told harrowing stories of children shot as they tried to hide（themselves）behind desks and chairs.」。

3. 原文「目擊者提到孩童們被排成一排射殺。」，這裡也可以用被態語態表示孩子們被攻擊者排成一排並屠殺，「目睹」兩字就不需再多譯出，因為「目擊者」就表示目睹之意，這句亦可譯作「Witnesses also reported that children were lined up and shot.」。

4. 「槍手闖入正在進行急救講習的學校禮堂」其中的「闖入」若譯成 broke in 是表示在該場所沒有人的情況下強行進入，由於文中表明是正在進行急救講習的期間「闖入」，故用「interrupted」一詞才正確。

5. 原文「當地醫院被排山倒海而來的傷者淹沒，以致於血庫存量已用盡。」，亦可譯作「So many injured arrived at the local hospital that it ran out of blood.」。

Unit 37

37.1 中英筆譯互譯要點【英譯中】

Tips 英譯中要點提示

1. 專有名詞國名、城市名、人名，均需查證並以固有的譯名譯出。若城市名是較讀者較不熟悉的，便可加註所屬國家補充説明，且在譯名後於括號內附上原文的城市名。

2. 英語的破折號用於介紹某種説法，加入強調語氣、定義，或是解釋。也用於隔開兩個子句。

3. 城市名 Freetown 是「自由城」。

4. 沒有固有譯名的公司或機構名稱，僅以原文表示即可，Bureh Beach Surf Club 是「Bureh 海灘沖浪俱樂部」。

5. 在英文原文中有以引號「“ ”」標註的文字，在譯文加入引號並加註原文。

6. live out 是「以（某種）方式度過餘生」的意思。

7. trade hands 是「從事交易的手沒停過」之意，也就是「商業行為熱絡」的意思。

8. Ebola 是「伊波拉」。

Every morning, all the roads leading to Freetown, the capital, are teaming with thousands of people as they march in from the surrounding thick green hills. They take their places at their desks, or in their sheet metal kiosks, or along the main roads where so much of the economy – from mangoes and stacks of trousers to plastic pipes and buckets of gravel – trades hands.

On the outskirts of Freetown, along a perfect crescent of golden sand where little wooden shacks stare out at the sea and the palms hang heavy with fuzzy coconuts, the Bureh Beach Surf Club gives new meaning to the word "resilience". No one here is bowing to Ebola. Instead, the surfers seem determined to live out their passion as a way to cope.

---

* be teaming with 擠滿
* fuzzy adj. 模糊的
* live out 以（某種）方式度過餘生
* crescent n. 新月形
* resilience n. 適應力

C 中文譯文對照
Chinese Translation

每天早晨，每條通往首都自由城（Freetown）的道路都被數以千計的人擠滿，齊步從四面八方的草木茂盛山丘湧入。他們在自己的工作檯，或者是金屬製的售貨亭，又或者是沿著商業行為熱絡的主要道路開始做起生意 ── 商品從芒果和成堆疊好的褲子，到塑膠水管和成桶的礫石都有。

在自由城市郊，沿著完美新月形的金黃色沙灘，幾間既小又簡陋的棚屋凝視著大海，椰子樹上掛著結實纍纍的椰子，Bureh 海灘沖浪俱樂部給了「適應力」（resilience）一個全新的意思。在這裡沒有人向伊波拉病毒低頭。反倒是沖浪者們似乎決心用他們熱愛的活動渡過餘生，來做為對付伊波拉（Ebola）的方法。

D 英譯中譯文討論
iscussions

1. 原文雖然只有「Freetown, the capital」的敘述，但是為了讓讀者更了解，亦可在譯文加入國名「塞拉利昂」，譯作「塞拉利昂的首都自由城（Freetown）」。

2. 原　文「along the main roads where so much of the economy - from mangoes and stacks of trousers to plastic pipes and buckets of gravel – trades hands」，這部分的譯法要先將所敘述的事件譯出，中間詳述的部分才能有補充說明的功能，所以譯文時會變成「沿著商業行為熱絡的主要道路做生意」，再來才譯出補充內容「商品從芒果和成堆疊好的褲子，到塑膠水管和成桶的礫石都有」的部分。

3. 原文「palms hang heavy with fuzzy coconuts」，譯文直接譯成「椰子樹」，雖然「palm」僅指棕櫚樹，但因為是有椰子的棕櫚樹，固直接譯為「椰子樹」。

4. 原文「gives new meaning to the word "resilience"」，原文以引號標註的字詞，在譯文中也要附上原文，通常這些字會視該文章敘述的背景而有不同的意涵，翻譯時也必須將文章要表達的意思納入考慮。

Unit 37

37.2 中英筆譯互譯要點【中譯英】

Tips 中譯英要點提示

1. 英語語法有時態，中翻英時必須看完整個句子、段落，了解其意思之後再譯出，每個句子皆需選擇文法與時態。

2. 國家名、城市名、公司機構名稱，以及專有名詞均需查證並以固有的譯名譯出。沒有固有譯名的公司或機構名稱，僅以原文表示即可，在中譯英時，也可以羅馬拼音將中文的音譯出，並在括號內附上原文。

3. 在中文譯文裡，有用引號表示的文字即代表在翻譯為英語時，要以「“ ”」表示。

4. 英語的破折號用於介紹某種說法，加入強調語氣、定義，或是解釋。也用於隔開兩個子句。可以中文的逗號和句號代替。

5. 其它：

   a 售貨亭是「kiosk」。

   b 椰子樹是「coconut palm」。

   c 新月形狀是「crescent」。

   d 簡陋的棚屋是「shack」。

A 主題短文 Article

每天早晨，每條通往首都自由城（Freetown）的道路都被數以千計的人擠滿，齊步從四面八方的草木茂盛山丘湧入。他們在自己的工作檯，或者是金屬製的售貨亭，又或者是沿著商業行為熱絡的主要道路開始做起生意 —— 商品從芒果和成堆疊好的褲子，到塑膠水管和成桶的礫石都有。

在自由城市郊，沿著完美新月形的金黃色沙灘，幾間既小又簡陋的棚屋凝視著大海，椰子樹上掛著結實纍纍的椰子，Bureh 海灘沖浪俱樂部給了「適應力」（resilience）一個全新的意思。在這裡沒有人向伊波拉病毒低頭。反倒是沖浪者們似乎決心用他們熱愛的活動渡過餘生，來做為對付伊波拉（Ebola）的方法。

■ 請試著翻劃底線的部分。

Every morning, all the roads leading to Freetown, the capital, are teaming with thousands of people as they march in from the surrounding thick green hills.（詳看下頁討論 3） They take their places at their desks, or in their sheet metal kiosks, or along the main roads where so much of the economy － from mangoes and stacks of trousers to plastic pipes and buckets of gravel － trades hands.（詳看下頁討論 4）

On the outskirts of Freetown, along a perfect crescent of golden sand where little wooden shacks stare out at the sea（詳看下頁討論 5） and the palms hang heavy with fuzzy coconuts, the Bureh Beach Surf Club gives new meaning to the word "resilience". No one here is bowing to Ebola. Instead, the surfers seem determined to live out their passion as a way to cope.

D 中譯英譯文討論
iscussions

1. 本身為英文名的專有名詞直接譯回原文，不需再附上中文譯文。

2. 在文章中形容描述事件時，若該事件仍一直存在著，英語多以現在式文法呈現，若陳述的故事／事件已發生過，多以過去式／現在完式文法表示。

3. 原文「首都自由城（Freetown）」，亦可譯為「Freetown, the capital of Sierra Leone」。原文「每天早晨，每條通往首都自由城（Freetown）的道路都被數以千計的人擠滿，齊步從四面八方的草木茂盛山丘湧入。」，亦可譯作「Every morning, all the roads leading to Freetown, the capital, are packed with thousands of people. They swarm in from the thick green hills all around Freetown」。

4. 原文「沿著商業行為熱絡的主要道路做生意 ── 商品從芒果和成堆疊好的褲子，到塑膠水管和成桶的礫石都有」，亦可譯作「along the main roads where so much of the economy trades hands － from mangoes and piles of trousers to plastic pipes and buckets of pebbles」。由於椰子樹是棕櫚樹的一種，所以原文「椰子樹上掛著結實纍纍的椰子」，亦可直接譯作「the coconut palms hang heavy with fuzzy coconuts」。

5. 原文「沿著完美新月形的金黃色沙灘，幾間既小又簡陋的棚屋凝視著大海」，亦可譯作「along a perfect crescent of golden sand, there are little wooden shacks looking out out at the sea」。

Unit 38

38.1 中英筆譯互譯要點【英譯中】

Tips 英譯中要點提示

1. 專有名詞人名、公司機構名稱需查證固有的譯名，若沒有則以原文譯出即可。

2. 數字與百分比的寫法，直接以阿拉伯數用譯出，百分比以符號表示，50 percent 盡量不譯為「百分之五十」，以「50%」譯出即可。數字及數值的部分，務必精準正確譯出。

3. 英語的引號用於，引述人物言語。中文則以單引號表示引述的言語。

4. 翻譯時，為了流暢度並讓讀者充分了解文章要表達的意思，可在不更改原意的前提下，適時加入譯出文。

5. 英文人名的譯文要在姓氏與名字之間以音界號「・」分隔，且採直譯的方式。

6. 英文語法中，敘述人常放在敘述內容之後，但中文語法慣用先表明說話者。譯文依中文慣用語法表達，有利讀者理解。

7. 要注意 narrowly failed 是「失敗了」的意思，不是「險些失敗」的意思，不可誤譯。

Space Exploration Technologies（Space X） launched an unmanned rocket to the Internet Space Station on Sunday. While the cargo capsule was successfully delivered, the company reported that it narrowly failed in its groundbreaking attempt to land the rocket on an ocean platform.

"Rocket made it to drone spaceport ship, but landed hard. Close, but no cigar this time," Space X founder and chief executive Elon Musk announced on Twitter.

"The returning rocket ran out of hydraulic fluid to operate its steerable fins. Upcoming flight already has 50 percent more hydraulic fluid, so should have plenty of margin for landing attempt next time," Musk added later.

In an attempt to slash launch costs, Space X has been developing a rocket that it hopes can be easily refurbished and reflown many times.

＊launch 發射
＊International Space Station 國際太空站
＊unmanned 無人駕駛的
＊spaceport 太空塢
＊hydraulic [haɪˋdrɔlɪk] fluid 液壓液體

中文譯文對照
Chinese Translation

太空探索科技公司（Space Exploration Technologies）在星期日發射一艘無人駕駛火箭至國際太空站（International Space Station）。雖然成功遞送貨物艙，但是太空探索科技公司宣佈火箭在自行降落於海上平台的新考驗中失敗。

太空探索科技公司創立人暨首席執行長伊隆．馬斯克（Elon Musk）在 Twitter 發佈聲明，「無人駕駛的火箭成功抵達太空塢船艦，但是降落過於猛烈。雖驚險但是這次沒有產生煙塵。」

馬斯克稍後補充說，「返航的火箭為了操作可控安定翼（steerable fins）耗盡液壓液體（hydraulic fluid）。即將進行的飛行已經載有比原先多 50% 的液壓液體，所以下次企圖降落之際，液壓液體應該有充分的餘裕。」

Space X 嘗試大幅降低發射火箭的成本，已著手研發有希望能易於重新裝修且能多次重飛的火箭。

D 英譯中譯文討論
Discussions

1. 原　文「While the cargo capsule was successfully delivered, the company reported that it narrowly failed in its groundbreaking attempt to land the rocket on an ocean platform.」，其「the company」指的是「太空探索科技公司」，譯文需完整譯出是哪家公司，而不是照原文直譯為「該公司說」，會較有助讀者理解敘述人為何。

2. 新聞稿常出現專有名詞人名、公司機構名稱、職位頭銜，通常會出現許多沒有慣用中文譯名的專有名詞，僅需照原文譯出即可。原文「"Rocket made it to drone spaceport ship, but landed hard. Close, but no cigar this time," Space X founder and chief executive Elon Musk announced on Twitter.」，其「rocket」指的是前文提到的「an unmanned rocket」，應在譯文譯出。

3. 英文語法有被動語態，在譯出時必須符合中文語法，原文「can be easily refurbished and reflown many times」，不能直譯成「可以簡單的被重新裝修和重飛」，而是譯作「易於重新裝修且能多次重飛」才符合中文語法。

Unit 38

38.2 中英筆譯互譯要點【中譯英】

Tips 中譯英要點提示

1. 新聞中的數字、數值、日期皆必須精確無誤的譯出。
2. 專有名詞人名、公司機構名稱若為外國名，通常會在括號內附上原文，僅照原文譯出即可。
3. 英文語法中，敘述人常放在敘述內容之後，但中文語法慣用先表明說話者。譯文應依英文慣用語法表達，在敘述後再加入說話者。
4. 英語語法有時態，中翻英時必須看完整個句子、段落，了解其意思之後再譯出，每個句子皆需選擇文法與時態。
5. 中文的單引號用於引述人物言語，英語以引號「“ ”」表示引述的人物言語。

A 主題短文
Article

太空探索科技公司（Space Exploration Technologies）在星期日發射一艘無人駕駛火箭至國際太空站（International Space Station）。雖然成功遞送貨物艙，但是太空探索科技公司宣佈火箭在自行降落於海上平台的新考驗中失敗。

太空探索科技公司創立人暨首席執行長伊隆．馬斯克（Elon Musk）在 Twitter 發佈聲明，「無人駕駛的火箭成功抵達太空塢船艦，但是降落過於猛烈。雖驚險但是這次沒有產生煙塵。」

馬斯克稍後補充說，「返航的火箭為了操作可控安定翼（steerable fins）耗盡液壓液體（hydraulic fluid）。即將進行的飛行已經載有比原先多 50% 的液壓液體，所以下次企圖降落之際，液壓液體應該有充分的餘裕。」

Space X 嘗試大幅降低發射火箭的成本，已著手研發有希望能易於重新裝修且能多次重飛的火箭。

■ 請試著翻劃底線的部分。

E 英文譯文對照
English Translation

Space Exploration Technologies（Space X） launched an unmanned rocket to the Internet Space Station on Sunday. While the cargo capsule was successfully delivered, the company reported that it narrowly failed in its groundbreaking attempt to land the rocket on an ocean platform.（詳見下頁討論 2）

"Rocket made it to drone spaceport ship, but landed hard. Close, but no cigar this time," Space X founder and chief executive Elon Musk announced on Twitter.

"The returning rocket ran out of hydraulic fluid to operate its steerable fins. Upcoming flight already has 50 percent more hydraulic fluid, so should have plenty of margin for landing attempt next time,"（詳見下頁討論 3） Musk added later.

In an attempt to slash launch costs, Space X has been developing a rocket that it hopes can be easily refurbished and reflown many times.（詳見下頁討論 4）

D 中譯英譯文討論 Discussions

1. 報導的文章通常是已發生的事件，故結構主體通常以過去式文法為主。

2. 原文「太空探索科技公司（Space Exploration Technologies）在星期日發射一艘無人駕駛火箭至國際太空站（International Space Station）。雖然成功遞送貨物艙，但是太空探索科技公司宣佈火箭在自行降落於海上平台的新考驗中失敗。」，亦可譯作「On Sunday, Space Exploration Technologies launched an uncrewed rocket to deliver a cargo capsule to the International Space Station, but narrowly failed in a pioneering attempt to land it on a platform in the ocean, the company announced.」。

3. 原文「50%」譯作「50 percent」或「50%」皆可，比較常見的譯法是以阿拉伯數字加上百分比符號表示。原文「即將進行的飛行已經載有比原先多 50% 的液壓液體」，亦可譯作「The amount of hydraulic fluid will be increased by 50% for the next flight」。

4. 英文語法有被的語態，原文「易於重新裝修並重飛的火箭」即被動語態句型——**be 動詞 + 過去分詞**，不可直譯為「easy to refurbish and refly」，必須譯為「can be easily refurbished and reflown」。

Unit 39

39.1 中英筆譯互譯要點【英譯中】

Tips 英譯中要點提示

1. 翻譯時不可用直譯方式逐字翻譯，需看完整個句子、整個段落，了解意思後再譯出。為了譯文流暢度，可在不更改原意的前提下適時加入有助讀者理解的補充文字。
2. 專有名詞、國家名、組織名必須查證固有譯名，並附上原文。
3. 年分皆以阿拉伯數字譯出，西元年分的「西元」，可譯出亦可不譯，若文章是史料、研究文件、官方文件時，「西元」則需譯出。

A 主題短文 Article

2014 was not only a bad year for lots of countries, but it was also a terrible year for the very idea of countries. The pre-modern marauders of Islamic State（IS） rampaged between Iraq and Syria, and Russian forces dismembered Ukraine, as if borders were elastic lines rather than fixed frontiers.

Nigeria's sovereignty of its northern territories was threatened by Boko Haram while Al-Shabab spread insecurity to the Horn of Africa. Even the brand new country of South Sudan, only a mere three years old, imploded in civil war.

The Marshal Islands is one territory that has bravely resisted the forces of disintegration. They may be sinking, but by championing the struggle against climate change, they are at least going down with a fight.

---

* very idea（of something） 一想到（某事）
* Islamic State（IS）是「博科聖地」（以奈及利亞為大本營的伊斯蘭極端組織），組織譯名需以引號加註。「青年黨」（Al-Shabab, 一個伊斯蘭極端組織）。
* Iraq 伊拉克
* Syria 敘利亞
* Ukraine 烏克蘭
* sovereignty [ˋsaavrɪntɪ] 統治權；主權
* Boko Haram 博科聖地
* South Sudan 南蘇丹
* Marshal Islands 馬紹爾群島
* going down with a fight 明知道勝算不大，但仍不放棄

C 中文譯文對照 Chinese Translation

2014 年不只對很多國家來説是不好的一年，但是一想到國家，它真是十足糟糕的一年。現代時期前到處搶劫的伊斯蘭國（Islamic State, IS）組織，在伊拉克（Iraq）和敘利亞（Syria）之間暴走，還有俄羅斯的武力瓜分烏克蘭（Ukraine），彷彿國界線是有彈性的，而不是條固定的邊界線。

奈及利亞（Nigeria）在北部領土的統治權受到「博科聖地」（Boko Haram）的威脅，而「青年黨」（Al-Shabab）則是把非洲之角（Horn of Africa, 指索馬利亞半島）搞得動盪不安。甚至連三年前才誕生的新國家南蘇丹（South Sudan），也已爆發內戰。

馬紹爾群島（Marshall Islands）是一個勇敢抵抗國家瓦解的領土。他們也許正沉入海底，但靠著奮力對抗氣候變遷，至少他們不是沒有奮戰就放棄。

D 英譯中譯文討論
Discussions

1. 為了譯文流暢度，在不更改原意的前提下適時加入有助讀者理解的補充文字。

2. 原文「2014 was not only a bad year for lots of countries, but it was also a terrible year for the very idea of countries.」，亦可譯作「2014年對很多國家來說是不好的一年，一想到國家，它實在是非常糟糕的一年。」。

3. 原文「as if borders were elastic lines」，亦可譯作「彷彿國界線是條可伸縮的界線」。

4. 原文「Even the brand new country of South Sudan, only a mere three years old, imploded in civil war.」，其「imploded in civil war」若直譯為「內部爆發內戰」，就會有贅述的譯文出現，「內戰」一詞即是「內部爆發的戰爭」之意，故譯文直接譯作「甚至連三年前才誕生的新國家南蘇丹（South Sudan），也已爆發內戰。」。

5. 原文「They may be sinking, but by championing the struggle against climate change, they are at least going down with a fight.」，其「going down」在這裡有兩種解釋，分別是「沉入海底」與「衰落」，亦可譯作「他們也許正沉入海底，但靠著奮力對抗氣候變遷，至少他們不是就這麼沉入海底而沒有奮戰。」、「他們也許正沉入海底，但靠著奮力對抗氣候變遷，至少他們不是沒有經過一番奮戰就衰落。」或是「他們也許正在下沉，但至少他們會奮戰到最後，持續對抗氣候變遷。」。

Unit 39

39.2 中英筆譯互譯要點【中譯英】

Tips 中譯英要點提示

1. 本身為英文名的專有名詞直接譯回原文，不需再附上中文譯文。

2. 英語語法有時態，中翻英時必須看完整個句子、段落，了解其意思之後再譯出，每個句子皆需選擇文法與時態。

3. 譯文前後的連貫性與流暢度需符合英語語法，主詞在隨後接續的敘述中盡量皆以代名詞／指示代名詞／其他名詞表示，不要一直重複名詞主詞。

4. 其它：

   a 一想到（某事）是「the very idea（of something）；the very thought（of something）；the very concept（of something）」。

   b 到處搶劫的是「marauding」。

   c 暴走；橫衝直撞；狂暴行為是「rampage」。

   d 有彈性的是「elastic」。

A 主題短文 Article

2014 年不只對很多國家來說是不好的一年，但是一想到國家，它真是十足糟糕的一年。現代時期前到處搶劫的伊斯蘭國（Islamic State, IS）組織，在伊拉克（Iraq）和敘利亞（Syria）之間暴走，還有俄羅斯的武力瓜分烏克蘭（Ukraine），彷彿國界線是有彈性的，而不是條固定的邊界線。

奈及利亞（Nigeria）在北部領土的統治權受到「博科聖地」（Boko Haram）的威脅，而「青年黨」（Al-Shabab）則是把非洲之角（Horn of Africa, 指索馬利亞半島）搞得動盪不安。甚至連三年前才誕生的新國家南蘇丹（South Sudan），也已爆發內戰。

馬紹爾群島（Marshall Islands）是一個勇敢抵抗國家瓦解的領土。他們也許正沉入海底，但靠著奮力對抗氣候變遷，至少他們不是沒有奮戰就放棄。

■ 請試著翻劃底線的部分。

英文譯文對照 English Translation

2014 was not only a bad year for lots of countries, but it was also a terrible year for the very idea of countries.（詳見下頁討論 2）The pre-modern marauders of Islamic State（IS）rampaged between Iraq and Syria, and Russian forces dismembered Ukraine, as if borders were elastic lines rather than fixed frontiers.（詳見下頁討論 3）

Nigeria's sovereignty of its northern territories was threatened by Boko Haram while Al-Shabab spread insecurity to the Horn of Africa. Even the brand new country of South Sudan, only a mere three years old, imploded in civil war.（詳見下頁討論 4）

The Marshal Islands is one territory that has bravely resisted the forces of disintegration. They may be sinking, but by championing the struggle against climate change, they are at least going down with a fight.（詳見下頁討論 5）

D 中譯英譯文討論
Discussions

1. 整篇文章敘述的是過去發生的事，時態以過去式、現在完成式為主。

2. 原文「2014 年不只對很多國家來說是不好的一年，但是一想到國家，它真是十足糟糕的一年。」，亦可譯作「2014 was not only a bad year for many countries, but it was also a terrible year **for the very concept of nations.**」。

3. 原文「彷彿國界線是有彈性的，而不是條固定的邊界線。」，亦可譯作「as if borders **were elastic instead of fixed boundaries.**」。

4. 原文「爆發內戰」，因「內戰」是國家內部爆發的戰爭，故用「implode」一字。原文「甚至連三年前才誕生的新國家南蘇丹（South Sudan），也已爆發內戰。」，以過去式被動語態和現在完成式表示，亦可譯作「South Sudan, a brand new country which was only created three years ago, has disintegrated into civil war.」。

5. 原文「他們也許正沉入海底，但靠著奮力對抗氣候變遷，至少他們不是沒有奮戰就放棄。」，亦可譯作「They may be sinking, but by championing the struggle against climate change, at least they won't go down without a fight.」。

附錄 1

英譯中（English to Chinese）必備翻譯技巧

1. 中文譯文標點符號使用說明：

- 書名號「《》」—— 用於一般著作、報章雜誌、長詩（集）、論文研究、電影名稱。
- 章名號「〈〉」—— 用於期刊論文、歌曲名稱、短詩、章節名稱…等。
- 單引號「「」」—— 用於引述人物言語、強調內容。
- 雙引號「『』」—— 用於在單引號內所包含的文字，通常是間接引述或強調內容。
- 音界號「·」—— 用於區隔外國人名的姓氏與名字。
- 刪節號「…」—— 省略後續敘述。
- 圓括弧「（）」—— 用於引註原文、修飾詞句。
- 方括弧「〔〕」—— 在圓括弧的文句外引註原文。

2. 譯文以白話文為主，以正常速度唸文章時，該停頓換氣時，原則上就是需要下逗號的位置，但仍視原文而定。

3. 英語常用代名詞／指示代名詞／名詞連貫敘述，需適時在不容易了解該代名詞指向何者時，在譯文中把「你（的）／我／他（她）／其／那些／這／那」…等代名詞／其他名詞換成主詞名詞。翻譯時要留意譯文前後的連貫性與流暢度，一些主詞／代名詞／指示代名詞可在隨後接續的譯文中省略。

4. 英語語法與中文語法不同，不可用直譯方式逐字翻譯，需看完整個句子、整個段落，了解意思後再譯出。不要執著在每個英語單字的意思，在不同內容下，會有不同的詮釋方式，要譯其意。不可省略或誤譯重點文字、數值，更不可更改原意。

5. 翻譯時，為了流暢度並讓讀者充分了解文章要表達的意思，可在不更改原意的前提下，適時加入譯出文。避免錯字、異體字。

6. 年代、數字、日期譯文皆以阿拉伯數字表示，1984 譯為（西元）1984 年…等。文章來源為史料、研究文件、官方文件時，「西元」則需譯出。

7. 百分比以符號代替即可，如 10%譯為 10%。金額以阿拉伯數字合併金額單位表示，如 4 million 譯為 400 萬、forty thousand / 40,000 譯為 4 萬。

8. 計量的次數、成語，請勿以阿拉伯數字譯出，如 three times 譯為三次、to kill two birds with one stone 譯為一石二鳥，不可以阿拉伯數字譯為 1 石 2 鳥。

9. 各國貨幣符號盡量譯出譯名，不要只用符號表示，若是常用且辨識率高的貨幣，只以符號譯出亦可。、£10.99 譯為 10.99 英鎊、500 rubles 譯為 500 盧布。

10. 譯文為中文時，時間的表示以阿拉伯數字與中文字的組合表示，如 It’s twelve minutes to ten. 譯為「現在是 9 時（點）48 分」。

11. 專有名詞國家名、人名、城市名、著作名、公司組織名，以及專有名詞若有固定譯名皆需譯出，若是十分普遍常見的譯名，可不需再加註原文，否則第一次出現於文中時需以圓括號引註原文，其後則以譯名表示即可。在無固有譯名的情況下，直接以原文譯出。

12. 英語人名的譯文要在姓氏與名字之間以音界號「・」分隔，且採直譯的方式，不可將姓氏與名字的順序調換，英語人名的寫法為名字在前，姓氏在後。約定俗成之人名可以不附名字，逕以姓氏代表即可，如 Thomas Edison 僅譯為「愛迪生」。

13. 要特別留意英語語法中的時態、被動語態、倒裝句，譯文需符合中文語法，不可直譯。

14. 在英語原文中有以引號「“ ”」標註的文字，在譯文加上單引號強調譯文，再以圓括弧加註原文。如 “resilience” 要譯為「適應力」（resilience）。

15. 英語語法中，敘述人常放在敘述內容之後，但中文語法慣用先表明說話者為何。如 “I want to play with you,” said Blake. 譯為「Blake 說，「我想跟你玩。」」較有助讀者了解。

16. 專業術語 / 名詞之字詞譯名需查證，同樣的字詞在不同專業領域表達的意涵不同。

附錄 2

中譯英（Chinese to English）- 必備翻譯技巧

1. 英語文法 14 種標點符號的使用規則 ——

①句號「.」—— 用於陳述句的結尾，表示完成敘述。如「We are going to go to England.」。也用於縮寫形式字尾。如，「Mr.」。

②驚嘆號「！」—— 用於表達突然間的驚訝 / 吶喊 / 抗議情緒。如在文學作品中的對話體「 "Holy cow!" screamed Margaret.」也用於強調某事的語氣中。如「His rants make me furious!」。

③逗號「,」—— 在句子結構中區隔不同元素或概念（句子）。如「Ashley wants a big, bright, warm study.」，以及「Matthew went to play snooker, and Wendy went to the SPA.」。也用於信函開頭稱呼語和結尾辭之後。如「Dear Uncle Rob ,」。

④分號「;」—— 用於連接獨立的子句。比起句號更能顯示出兩個子句之間的相關性。如「Graham is happy; he knows we will all be going to his 80th birthday party.」。

⑤冒號「:」—— 有兩個主要用法，第一種用於引語、解釋、範例，以及系列之後。如「Our location: Trumpington, Cambridge」。第二種用於表示時間，區隔時和分。如「21:00 p.m.」。

⑥破折號「-」—— 用於介紹某種說法，加入強調語氣、定義，或是解釋。也用於隔開兩個子句。如「We weren't planning on buying a house so soon - but we met our dream house.」。

⑦連字號「-」── 符號相同於破折號，但用法有些差異性。連字號用於複合字、名字，以及單字音節之間，常用於文章結尾的下一行，以連字號區隔文章。如「Mrs. Sullivan – Gladys」，「face-to-face」。

⑧圓括號「（ ）」── 標註插入語或修飾評論。多數情況下可用逗號（,）取代而不更改原意。如「Max and Sophie（who are brother and sister）are both quick at learning.」。

⑨大括號「{}」── 用於包含同一單元內，兩句（含）以上的內文或列出的項目。不常在一般寫作中用到，較常在電腦程式類的領域中出現。

⑩中括號「[ ]」── 用於標註專門的解釋。在英語字典裡用來釋義並說明該單字的起源。

⑪撇號「'」── 用於象徵省略的字母或從單字中省略的字或表示所有格。如「can't、Joe's、cats'」

⑫引號「" "」── 主要用於標註章節的開始與結束，引述人物言語，強調內容。也用於指明意涵和單字有不尋常含糊不清意涵的狀態。

⑬省略號「…」── 通常以三個句號呈現，偶爾會以三個星號（***）表示。在書寫和打字中用來表示省略的意思，特別是字母或單字。省略不需要的單而不會影響其原義。常用於學生撰寫研究報告，或是新聞引用部分演講稿。

⑭單引號「`」── 已在引號中的引述。

2. 譯文前後的連貫性與流暢度需符合英語語法，主詞在隨後接續的敘述中盡量皆以代名詞 / 指示代名詞 / 其他名詞表示，不要一直重複名詞主詞。

3. 常見且辨識率高的各國貨幣符號僅以符號表示。如 10.99 英鎊譯為「£10.99」。辨識率不高的貨幣則需譯出英語名稱，如俄羅斯貨幣單位「盧布」，譯為「ruble」；土庫曼的貨幣「新馬納特」，譯為「new manat」。

4. 年分、數字、數值僅以阿拉伯數字譯出即可，百分比可譯出或以符號表示皆可。

5. 譯文為英語時，則儘量避免以阿拉伯數字表示時間，以英語表示，如下午 3 時 15 分譯為「three-fifteen in the afternoon」或是「a quarter after three」。

6. 英語語法有時態、詞性變化，中翻英時必須看完整個句子、段落，了解其意思之後再譯出，每個句子皆需選擇文法與時態。特別留意中文不易在文字中看出英語語法的時態與被動語態、倒裝句（除了「場所副詞」放在句首，需使用倒裝句外；當強調動作 / 事情發生的時間、主詞的狀態或當句中的主詞帶有一長串的修飾語，也常常將「時間副詞」或「形容詞」放在句首，形成倒裝句），翻譯時需符合英語語法。

7. 本身為英文名的專有名詞直接譯回原文，不需再附上中文譯文。專有名詞的人名、公司構構名稱，需先查證固有譯名，若無固有譯名即以羅馬拼音將中文的音譯出，並在括號內附上原文。如，Samsung（三星）、中文人名譯為 Lien, Ai-Hsu（連艾詡），以中文姓名慣用的方式直譯，不需將姓氏移至名字的後面，並附上原文。

Leader 023

Open Your「中英互譯」邏輯腦：跟著 8 大翻譯要點，快速提升 80% Up 翻譯 + 寫作能力

作　　者　連緯晏 Wendy Lien、Matthew Gunton
封面構成　高鍾琪
內頁構成　華漢電腦排版有限公司

發 行 人　周瑞德
企劃編輯　饒美君
校　　對　陳欣慧、陳韋佑
印　　製　大亞彩色印刷製版股份有限公司
初　　版　2015 年 7 月
定　　價　新台幣 349 元
出　　版　力得文化
電　　話　(02) 2351-2007
傳　　真　(02) 2351-0887
地　　址　100 台北市中正區福州街 1 號 10 樓之 2
E-mail　best.books.service@gmail.com

港澳地區總經銷　泛華發行代理有限公司
地　　址　香港新界將軍澳工業邨駿昌街 7 號 2 樓
電　　話　(852) 2798-2323
傳　　真　(852) 2796-5471

國家圖書館出版品預行編目(CIP)資料

Open Your「中英互譯」邏輯腦：跟著 8 大翻譯要點，快速提升 80%Up 翻譯+寫作能力 / 連緯晏, Matthew Gunton 著. -- 初版. -- 臺北市：力得文化, 2015.07　面；公分. -- (Leader ; 23)
ISBN 978-986-91914-1-8(平裝)
1.翻譯
811.7　　104010446